ANOTHER SIDE OF SUNRISE

A Novel

by

Eve Shannon

ISBN: 978-0-692-43637-0

Publisher:
Seven Sharp Pencils
Jackson County, Missouri

For my Father, and my Irish Grandmothers, not only for supporting an active imagination, but also for teaching me that it's one of the best gifts you can possess. Thank you for all the wonderful people, both real and fictional, that came into being because of you.

ANOTHER SIDE OF SUNRISE

She felt the elation of certainty as she signed the one line document that rested on the stack of others she'd signed throughout the weeks. They'd made it easy, one final signature, one final release without which the others would have no validity.

Yes.

Or no.

She felt the needle slide into her arm though it didn't hurt, the technician was practiced.

She felt the brush of an angel's lips against her cheek. His face was the last thing she saw as the world slipped quickly, quietly away.

ONE

Cailín was fifteen. She was walking on a dirt road through the countryside, and there were no signs, no markers, nothing to overtly tell her, but, as you know things in dreams, she knew she was in Ireland. She approached a low stone wall and saw a young man sitting on it. His hands were palm down, arms straight, and he was leaning forward swinging his legs as though they were splashing in a pond.

She started to turn back, curious, but feeling as though she was intruding.

"Wait! Ohh, please wait," he pleaded. She hesitated and looked back at him. Tall, lean, and dressed in clothes from centuries past, wisps of blond hair escaped from the simple black ribbon tied at the back of his neck to frame the most beautiful face she'd ever seen.

She thought she had it figured out. She must have died and gone to heaven, after all Ireland was the equivalent to her. As final proof, there was an angel.

"What?" She looked down at the long cornflower blue skirt she wore, then cautiously back at him. "Why?"

He jumped easily down from the wall and startled her. "Noh, please," he held one hand out tentatively, "dun be afraid. I have a story to tell." His voice was warm and melodic, and incredibly seductive without effort.

"A story?" she repeated, "I don't think …"

"You came here to find me, so presume ya wanna hear it?"

"You presume a lot then. I came here to find *you*?" She wondered why she didn't just run into his arms. She was certain now that she was dead, and equally certain it didn't matter.

"Ah, lass. Haven't changed much, so ya haven't," a hint of delight played across his eyes.

"Changed?"

"I have a story to tell ya. 'Tis a long story, it is."

"A story? You keep saying that. What story? About what?"

"Good things, bad things, all in all wan that's very precious to me."

"And just why should it interest me?"

"'Tis about us."

*   *   *

Cailín spent most of Saturday in her room under the pretext of an overload of homework, and wrote down everything he had told her. His words had left her with more questions than answers, yet somehow she felt they were true.

That night she hoped he would continue, but no dream came.

The first year he was in her dreams she figured there was nothing really remarkable about that in itself. But *he* was remarkable, and he summoned her to another time and place. She would sit next to him while he told her stories about things that happened when he was a little boy, and eventually he started telling her more about his family and serious matters.

The dreams began to shift. The transition was nearly undetectable; it was slow and seemed natural. She found herself walking with him and riding with him, sometimes both on the same horse. They laughed a lot. She had gone from being a listener to his stories and a witness to his world to being an active part in it.

He seemed to be a year or two older than her, and as she got older, he did too. She wrote down everything she could remember about the dreams so she'd always have them. She kept the first draft so that when she became a best selling author she could look back and say – well, everybody starts somewhere. Above all she kept it to remind her how they were during those years in time past. As she became more active in the dreams his illustration of events became clearer, and the way she put it on paper did, too. He gradually stopped telling her things that happened as they both assumed roles as participants. By the end of the second year she was living another life with him, and had over three hundred hand written sheets documenting it.

"I guess," she wasn't sure what he was getting at. "Hopefully I get most of it."

"Oh. Most," he pondered, tilting his head to one side. "I see."

A shiver went through her. Something was different. She was awake.

"Are you kidding me?" Cailín put her hands on the countertop behind her. "Don't do this! Please don't do this now." She sucked in her lower lip, hoping to stop the tears that threatened. "Why are you doing this?" she accused, "why?" He looked so solid, and the jeans and t-shirt convinced her that he had infiltrated her waking reality; he was coming into her world.

"I have to go to school." She ran past him, grabbed her book bag, and shot out the door.

She didn't want him to do this, she told herself, yet she paused several times that day to look over her shoulder.

It was a week before he came into her dreams again.

The dreams became somewhat less frequent as he appeared more and more when she was awake, and it seemed at random times. Then she discovered that if she wanted or needed to talk to him, all she had to do was ask, and there he was. Shortly after he began appearing in her world he started doing things. Little things at first, but they were there. She would never forget the first one, she was in class taking a test and he threw a paper airplane at her. Thus started her collection.

Most of his actions were less obvious, at least to others in the material world. One spring morning she was leaving her second class and on the way to her third at the opposite end of the building, and upstairs. She was hurrying down the hall as fast as she could without really running. It was always a challenge to make it on time to that one.

She didn't get far and there he was, jogging backwards in front of her and holding his hands out, yelling in her face, "Stop! Turn around! Goh thuh other way!"

She actually said out loud, "No, I'll be late," she was more than a little annoyed.

He wasn't having it, he said, "Dun make me – look, just please turn around. The look on his face made her take him seriously, as by now she had learned to trust him implicitly. So she walked the opposite way that she needed to go, wondering. She didn't have to look; she could feel him following her.

There wasn't a lot of trouble in her school, but on that day a nasty fight had broken out. If she had kept going she would have been right in the middle of it, and three of the boys had knives. Who knows? She supposed she could have been hurt.

* * *

Saturday afternoon, and Cailín had escaped to her grandmother's house. It hadn't been difficult, Joyce Stevens was busy preparing for one of her charity events, no small part of that being her usual speech about all the wonderful charities she supported. Never mind that that support consisted of writing a small check once a year, and throwing a lot of parties. She dismissed the thought; she didn't really care about her mother's superficialities at the moment, she was delighted that she'd be able to call home in a couple of hours and get a quick, dismissive approval to spend the night. She'd thrown a few things in her duffle bag, but she'd cover that fact by advising her mother that granny had extra toothbrushes and stray nightgowns. She doubted that the conversation would go that far, but when it came to her mother Cailín liked to have her bases covered.

She loved her grandmother's house; it was full of handmade things and a mishmash of flowered patterns, checks, and stripes that somehow combined to make a pleasing, comfortable environment. Every room had a different color scheme, and of course she liked the guest room where she stayed much better than her room at home. She had bought some flowered toss pillows a couple of years ago and put them in her room, trying to make it cozier. The next day she came home from school and they were gone. She hadn't bothered to ask.

"Cailín, come on to dinner now," her granny was dishing out generous portions of homemade chicken and dumplings.

Cailín ran to the kitchen and filled glasses with fresh sun tea and ice. "Ooh, it smells so good. Teach me how to make it?"

"Of course, darling. Seems like the only time you eat is when you're here."

"Not really, it's just the only time I make a pig of myself." They both laughed. "Someday, when I have my own home, I'll cook all the time."

"Your future husband will be one lucky man."

"Oh, granny," she put her fork down, "he's done it again."

"I see. Something to protect you again?"

"There was a dance at school Friday night, I went with some friends. It was just the usual stuff, you know. This boy, Bobby, was being a jerk. He kept asking me to dance."

"You've spoken of Bobby before, a bit of a smart mouth, but not quite a bully?"

"That's him. Too bad, he's kinda cute, if he'd just be nice he would have had plenty of girls interested."

"Well darling, he must be terribly insecure and he's overcompensating. Was he drinking?"

"Yeah, out in the parking lot. Bobby can't hold it. He kept trying to make a scene when I said no. I was sitting at a table with some girls, and a couple of boys, we were just joking around and having fun. Then Bobby came over. He pulled my chair away from the table and then he leaned over me and started demanding that I dance with him.

"I just said, 'ewww, you're drunk, get away from me,' but he got right in my face, and I thought he was going to fall over on me. Then I saw Spéir behind him –"

"It's 'Spee-ihr', love, it sounds more like that than 'Spear'. According to the spelling you said he gave you, and the fada makes the 'e' long."

"Oh! Cool," Cailín repeated his name, following her grandmother's instruction, "by the way, granny, do you know what his name means? I've never seen it in a list of Irish names."

"I haven't either, but the word itself means 'sky', so it's very lovely."

"I like that! It seems to fit him."

"Sorry, darling, do go on."

"So I told Bobby, 'No, you don't understand, you *have* to get away from me, NOW'. Too late. Spéir grabbed him and threw him about six feet up in the air and backwards over his head, and a good twelve feet across the room."

"Ohh my!" her grandmother looked like she couldn't decide whether to laugh or cry.

"How do I explain that one? One second the guy is being a jerk and the next he's flying through the air. Spéir told me to just be calm; he said not that many people were watching. Uh huh, that's maybe a little bit hard to miss, doncha think? A kid flying up and across the room just like that? An everyday occurrence. Everybody was asking 'what happened?' So I just said, 'well he's very drunk, I think he tripped'."

"How badly was he hurt?"

"A concussion, a couple of broken ribs, a fractured arm, too many bruises to mention, and a split on his scalp. Seven stitches. Good thing he was already under anesthetic," now they both laughed.

"That's terrible; just the same, you can't help but laugh. Go on, dear, what happened then?"

"I stayed for a while, trying to shrug it off. Accidents happen, he was drunk. No big deal, after all I'm certifiably insane, him being drunk and having a little mishap doesn't even compare."

"And he'll never bother you again. But what about Spéir?"

"I had a long talk with Spéir when I got home, and of course he refused to back down or promise not to do it again. Oh, granny, why can't he just totally, you know, be solid in this world?"

"Who's to say that he won't? I'm certain that he wouldn't answer if you asked him, but … possibly it's something you should try to be prepared for." Marian Casey reached out and placed her hand over her granddaughter's hand, "How do you think I found your grandfather?"

Cailín paused, a forkful of dumplings in mid air, unable to blink.

* * *

Cailín awoke on a Wednesday morning in June of her seventeenth year in a state of overwhelming bliss, wonder, and exhaustion. In her dream that seemed to last for hours and play out in real time, minute by minute, she and Spéir were married in the storybook southern Ireland village that she had come to think of as her real home.

"Kaylin! Are you nearly ready?" Her mother had always insisted on pronouncing her name wrong, ignoring the Irish way, and unfortunately it had stuck. "Hurry up! You'll be late for your tennis lesson." Even her mother's grating demand failed to annoy her.

"Please stay," Spéir whispered.

"I can't go today, I don't feel well." If she could have seen the glowing blush on her cheeks, she would have been even more confident in her lie.

"Do you need to see the doctor?" Joyce Stevens rushed through her doorway in record time, one hand on her hip, "I have to be at the Arts Committee meeting in half an hour and Candace is off today." As usual, her own agenda was her paramount concern.

"Uh, no," Cailín sat up and tried to look dejected. "Just some Pamprin and the rice bag, I'll be fine. I can get them."

"I'll send Candace up with those if she hasn't left yet."

"Thanks, I'm sorry I have to miss. I love tennis." That much was true and she hoped that she'd added a genuine note to her ruse. She added a sigh to her frown for effect.

Joyce disappeared as quickly as she had materialized, and Cailín sank back and pulled the covers over her head. "Is it true? We married? Is it really true? Was – is – that what really happened in our life? What we did, oh, does that mean we'll have a baby?" She reached to touch him, wishing more than ever that he was solid in this world.

"Aye, lass. Not yet, but wan day," his voice caressed her, "and I still love you more than …"

"Miss Kaylin?" Candace tapped on the door.

It was funny, she thought, how Candace calling her 'miss' had always seemed like a term of endearment rather than some snide reference to her being the boss's daughter. A rather pretty woman, and seemingly well educated, Cailín had often wondered why she chose this line of work. She supposed the money was pretty good, and living rent free in a very nice suite of rooms at the back of the house should allow her to save for an early and comfortable retirement.

"Come on in."

She balanced the requested items, along with a glass of water, on a tray. "I'm sorry you don't feel well, I can arrange to stay if you need me."

"Oh, no, Candace, I'll be fine, honestly, I just don't feel like going out. Tennis would be a disaster today."

"Understandable, but I don't like leaving you all alone."

Alone? Really? Alone? Cailín nearly laughed.

"Don't worry, I could always call granny, but thank you. Go enjoy your day." She genuinely liked Candace, but at the moment she didn't need company. She held her breath until the door gently closed.

She dove back under the covers, "Spéir, I want to do it again! If I can go back to sleep, will you — can we?"

"Shh, here …"

"Will you help me sleep?"

"Thinkin'. Probly." He began to generate the warmth that always lulled her into sleep.

"Spéir? If I died, would we be together all the time? Would I go wherever you go?"

"'Tis not meant to be that way, wee lass. Not for a fair long time. You have things yet to do. I need you here, truly."

"I need you *here*. But if I could stay with you, in our world… stay with you forever."

"You are with me forever."

"I mean… you know what I mean, both of us in the same world…" he was enfolding her more snugly, she began to feel like she was floating, and she yawned.

"Patience, love. Noh. Not now. Time will come. Always does." His voice was slow and rhythmic, "Sleep now, sleep, let's go…"

"Oh Spéir… it was… you're so amazing, better than…" she perceived a gentle tug as he drifted back into their world, taking her with him.

* * *

At eighteen Cailín was just beginning to get into editing and starting to delve into books about writing technique because it had become her mission to do the story justice. The story had gotten more complicated, more intricate. Some of it was difficult to write because their life three hundred years ago wasn't always easy, but it was all there from the tragedies to the triumphs, the sorrows and the incredible joy.

He wanted her to remember, to share it with him, he said she needed to know. She'd been deeply in love with him from the instant he walked into her dreams, she couldn't deny him this, or anything, even if she had tried. Sometimes she had to put the writing aside because it was so intense. He was patient about that, and would turn the dreams to happier times to give her a breather. She felt he knew she would always pick it up again in a few days, and that she wasn't going to stop until it was done.

In February of that year, he wasn't so patient. He said he had a letter for her, and wanted her to write it down without delay because it would be important very soon and couldn't wait. He said she could type it, and how he wanted it to look. So she did.

For a long time she'd known everything about Spéir, except how exactly all this was happening, but she had no complaints. She knew how he looked, down to the last eyelash. She knew how he walked, the sound of his voice, how he gestured, the warmth of his touch, everything. There was only one thing she didn't know yet, and it would be one hell of an ass kicker.

* * *

Cailín reluctantly arrived at what was considered the most upscale salon in Minneapolis. In her opinion the only thing upscale about it was the price.

"It was very difficult to get an appointment on the day of the prom, but I called in some favors. If you can't appreciate that, at least don't make a fuss about it, it cost me extra," Joyce had warned. At that point it was just easier to go than to argue.

"Hi, Kaylin, I'm Allison, but you can call me Ali. Chloe is tied up with a last minute perm, so I'm stepping in for her if that's okay with you." She seemed nice and Cailín nodded.

"Good. We've got some work to do so I'll start with the cut. The color will go faster that way."

"What!" She nearly jumped out of the chair.

"Oh, well …" Ali wasn't quite sure what to say, "… um, your mother said to cut at least six inches off, and color it to take the red out, and —"

Cailín burst into tears. *How could she? How dare she? I'm eighteen. She can't do this to me.* She huddled down in the chair and drew her arms across her stomach under the cape.

"Oh gosh. Oh no. You didn't know, did you?"

Cailín couldn't answer, she shook her bent head.

"Okay, look," Ali turned the chair around and knelt down in front of Cailín, "listen," she whispered, "we can work this out. I have an idea. We can't afford to lose your mother's business, or her friends, they drop a lot of money here."

She looked up, and Ali handed her a fist full of tissues.

"Here's what I can do," Ali offered, still in hushed tones, "we'll say there was a misunderstanding, since I took over for Chloe. I'm going to cut your hair, but only an inch or so, to even it up and take off the split ends. That kind of needs to be done anyway."

Cailín nodded. "But —"

"Our marching orders are to give you an updo anyway. The length won't be noticeable right away, so we're temporarily out of the woods there. Can you live with that?"

"Thanks, yes," she blew her nose, "thank you."

"Now for the color, we're supposed to dye it with an ash brown."

She began to cry again.

"No, no. Wait. I'm not going to do permanent color, instead I'll just use a rinse to drab it. It'll wash out, I promise. I don't think I could bring myself to do any different. Your hair is such a pretty dark auburn, and it's not too red at all. You don't have to do any of this, but I have a feeling that it'll be less hassle for both of us if we go ahead."

"Gosh, Ali, thank you." Cailín was now able to sit up straight and breathe. "Thank you for understanding. One night of being a sucky mess I can handle, my dress is so ugly that the hair won't matter anyway. But having a lot cut off and permanent blah color is too much to deal with."

"I do understand. I need a favor from you, though. When she notices the length would you just say something like we couldn't cut off more and have enough hair left to look right put up?"

"Sure, absolutely. And I'll say that the temporary color was just a misunderstanding. I'll call you, too, if it seems like she's going to make a big deal of it."

"I don't envy you, but it's only for one day."

"Yeah, but then there's tomorrow, and the next day."

* * *

Her designer gown might as well have been a clown suit. *All I need is some bright red blush on the tip of my nose.* She tugged at the shoulder of the one sleeve, her other arm bare. Lopsided was evidently en vogue, but to Cailín it just looked lopsided.

Her mother, of course, had prided herself on her good taste in selecting it. The simple cocktail dress with a white bodice and black skirt that she adored "wasn't nearly expensive enough" her mother had declared and that was that. *Someday I'll have a dress just like that, and I'll wear it somewhere I really want to go,* Cailín's promise to herself was all that got her through the endless afternoon of shopping with her mother.

The gold material was gaudy and the dyed to match shoes added the final insult to her injury. Her date was a nice enough boy and she vowed to be civil to him. After all, it wasn't his fault and maybe he was as unhappy as she was that their mothers had insisted on the pairing. The evening promised to be somewhat saved when, after the inevitable barrage of pictures, they finally crawled into the obligatory limo.

"You, uh, you look really, uh, nice." Jack had tried.

"And you look nearly as ridiculous as I do." She tugged at his matching gold tie and they both collapsed into much needed giggles.

"At least I have a nice black tux to kind of offset it."

"Yeah but don't count on that to save you. You'll have a bloody nose or worse before it's over, I just know it."

"I'm sure you'd run to help me, except I don't see how you can even move in that thing."

"I know, right? I think all we can do is pretend to be mega super movie stars, you know, trend setters."

Jack made a fist and held it in front of her face. "Miss Stevens! Miss Stevens! Over here! Who are you wearing?"

"It's from Mother's Checkbook, of course!"

Thus they survived the evening with running inside jokes, and even conspired to be an hour late getting home and made bets as to whether that would prompt the expected disconcertion. They shared a sweet goodnight kiss, and though Jack called a few times, she was friendly, but always 'busy'. After graduation two weeks later they never saw one another again.

* * *

"So." Spéir was leaning against the headboard, hands folded at his waist. He was dressed in his seventeenth century clothes, his long blond hair loose and somewhat rumpled. He looked infuriatingly handsome.

"You could at least take your boots off?" She attempted disapproval, and felt that she failed. All she wanted was to go to sleep so they could be together.

"Was it a good one?"

"What?" she stiffened.

"Kiss," his eyes were their darkest gray.

"You can't just spy on me any time you want!" She picked up a pillow and flung it through him.

"So was it?"

"It was – there. That's all. Just there." She threw the ugly gold gown on the floor.

"Is nice."

"Wha–" She realized she was standing in front on him in her strapless corset with tiny pink rosebuds on it, thigh high stockings and high heels.

"Oh. What the hell? It's not like you've never…" tears threatened.

"Beautiful, so it is."

Cailín kicked off her shoes, then threw them at him. "I hate you! I hate you! I wish you were solid so I could hit you!"

"Dun hafta be solid for ya to hurt me." He flicked the shoes off the bed.

"It was a kiss, alright?" she screamed. "It wasn't you. It was nothing like you, okay? It never will be. Never. Don't do this to me." She pointed her finger at him, "You do things. You do things in this world when you want to, when you feel like you have to. Why can't you…" tears blurred her eyes.

"Please come here," he said softly and switched off the lamp, "Please."

"Here? Where is 'here'? When? I don't even know what that means to you. I hate you." She pulled the covers around her and curled up as tightly as she could.

"I'll take ya to the other side of sunrise. Sleep, mo chuisle, shhh, sleep. Sleep and we'll be as we're supposed to be." She felt his essence circling around her, holding her fast. "Más é do thoil é, lass, dun say 'never'."

* * *

Cailín's parents were out for a rare evening together. Her brother, recently graduated from college, had gone straight to graduate school. Why he needed another degree in art, she had no idea; he could barely draw stick figures. He did have a good eye for it though, and he knew a lot about art history. Still, she suspected he was going to be a perennial student.

Richard had always been Joyce's favorite. He was so compliant, attending all the snob events anytime their mother asked. He would even take on the task of escorting her friend's daughters to school dances when requested, and thus gained a ton of social points for their mother to trade in. Joyce never liked it when someone called him Rick, so Cailín always did.

She was in the family room, her favorite place to study and spread books and papers out over the sofa. Spéir was quiet; he usually was when she was studying. After a while he asked her to turn the TV on, she said "Not for a while because I want to finish homework first". He asked again, she again said no, in an hour maybe. So he turned it on. She was a little annoyed, but the music caught her attention, and she started to watch.

A minute passed and then she caught the first glimpse, and another glimpse. Suddenly she felt hot and cold at the same time. She dropped to the floor, shivering uncontrollably, and crawled closer to the TV and screamed, "HOW DID YOU DO THAT?" She looked over her shoulder in panic, but Spéir was gone. She sat and sobbed and mumbled over and over, "How?" She sat mesmerized while he was singing, but five minutes later she was screaming again, this time "WHY ARE YOU DOING THIS? WHY?" It crossed her mind that she was probably having one of those dreams where you feel like it's really happening. She ran through the house, looking for him, screaming, "Come to me right NOW, explain this NOW."

She threatened, she begged. Spéir was nowhere to be found. She went back to the family room, and sat and watched and cried. She knew it must be a dream, but she grabbed a DVD, shoved it in the machine and hit the record button.

His hair was long, covering his collar, but three or four inches shorter than Spéir's, and of course his clothes were from the current time. Other than that, everything was – Exactly. The same. Everything. His smile, the sound of his voice, the way he walked, all were identical to Spéir.

Spéir didn't come back until the program was over. Her parents would be home any time now, and she didn't want to have to explain why she'd been crying her eyes out – because, well, she couldn't explain. She gathered up her books, and the DVD, and ran to her room. She threatened Spéir, "If you don't come with me – I'll... I'll make myself stop dreaming," and she cried.

She asked him again, and none too calmly, "Why?" He told her to read the letter he'd had her write for him just a couple of weeks before. Although she knew it by heart, she retrieved it from the hidden file in her computer and began to read. Her emotions swirled around the room like snowflakes; she couldn't speak. He said that it was something that they had to work through, and that they would make it. He talked softly while she cried, until she fell asleep in her clothes, shoes and all.

The next morning she was convinced that it had all been a dream; after all it wouldn't be the first one that seemed real. So she got ready and went to school and forced herself to ignore her discovery for a few days. Spéir was still much as usual, only quieter, which felt like a problem. Friday afternoon she came home from school, locked the door, put her headphones on, and put the DVD into her computer. The glorious young Irishman on the screen not only looked like Spéir, his eyes were the same ever changing mix of gray and green, he even gestured the same, and although she'd never heard Spéir sing, their voices had the same qualities.

Cailín was certain she was destined to spend the next few years in an institution eating with plastic spoons.

Spéir made a feeble attempt at a joke; he said his hair was naturally blond in the seventeenth century. She stood up and in rapid fire threw a book, a hairbrush, and a shoe at him.

* * *

"Mom!" Cailín bounded down the staircase. "Mom!" she stiffened at the parlor door. "Er, mother?" This was one of many times she wished she had a 'mom' instead of a mother.

"What is it, Kaylin?" Joyce Stevens sighed. She was always dressed as though ready to receive royalty.

"Um, well…" Cailín was competing with classical music and a very thick book. "I want to go to a concert."

"Don't mumble, and it's about time." Joyce carefully placed a leather bookmark. "But one more year and you're off to college, a short time indeed to acquire some culture."

"Not that kind, well not exactly, or I mean… it is, in a way. There's an Irish music group coming here in October."

"Good heavens, it's not that raucous group that call themselves some combination of a letter and a number is it? They're too old to be running around like teenagers. Besides, they're just – noisy."

"No. Not them. I, uh, mother please, may I use a credit card today, to get a good seat? I have babysitting money. I'll give it to you right now."

"And that's another thing, it's beneath you to care for other people's children, never mind the liability involved. And Irish? How cultured can that be?"

"I like kids. But mother, we have Irish ancestry, and you've always said that variety was good, well rounded. Please?"

"Oh, I think not. Surely something more worthwhile will present itself before October."

"Please, mother, please." Cailín knew she was whining but couldn't stop herself. "I'll go to any event you want me to between now and then."

"The matter is closed, Kaylin." Joyce Steven's dismissal was always irrevocable. There was no deal to be made with the devil today.

Cailín sat at her perfect desk, in her perfect room. Perfect, according to her mother's taste. Her homework finished, she began to search the internet and found a few hits, some with photographs. *Oh, he does, he really does have the face of an angel, even when he's being silly,* she thought. She covered her mouth and giggled with delight. There was a way to do this, there had to be a way. She would be in the same building with her future husband, and she couldn't fail.

Cailín awoke with the answer. She fidgeted in class, suffocated by every word every teacher spoke. Every second became a loud tick in her head. She grabbed a sandwich and carton of milk from the cafeteria, declined a couple of invitations, and found a shade tree on the outer edge of the grounds. She squinted her eyes. *Just let me be invisible!* For the next twenty minutes she was blissfully free to think of nothing but him.

She bolted to the parking lot after her last class. "Candace!" her voice shook to the rhythm of running "please let mother know there's a one hour study group. I'll be home right after."

Freedom. She plunged the key into the ignition and took a deep breath; there was no time for a traffic ticket.

"Oh! Thank you! Third row. I guessed it would be like row a hundred by now. This is awesome, I can't wait! Thank you!" All day she had worried that someone would somehow know that she had cash and she'd be robbed.

"Who's the lucky person accompanying you?" Cailín stopped herself just in time from looking over her shoulder, certain the woman behind the desk could see Spéir. The kind, concerned smile from this woman that was roughly her mother's age startled her and for a second she felt like she'd been caught.

"Oh, uh, I'm taking my grandmother! She'll be so happy we have the best seats. Thank you again."

* * *

Cailín changed clothes three times, even though he would never see her. Thank goodness she was staying at her Grandmother's house this weekend, otherwise she would never make it to the concert. It was bad enough just getting out of the house, her mother had questioned why she was taking so many clothes just for the weekend.

"Gran's going to show me how to do some mending," she'd answered.

"Just as long as you're not going to make your skirts any shorter," had been Joyce's response. Beyond that, she was sure it was of no interest to her mother.

Drums struck the first familiar notes and she was sure that her heart had leapt out of her chest. The very air seemed to crackle with an electromagnetic disturbance.

The first member of the ensemble led the march onto the stage, and the drums were nearly drowned out by the cheering crowd. Everyone was on their feet now. The second member was close behind, and the cheering grew louder still.

Here comes number three... Cailín held her breath.

His steps were cool and measured, his voice strong, clear, and determined. She could easily pick it out in all the group numbers, it was unmistakable to her. All the videos and TV appearances she'd watched had failed to prepare her for his actual presence. He was at once both solid and ethereal. She slapped her hand over her open mouth and hoped that her knees wouldn't give out.

She sank into her seat as everyone began to sit down, holding onto the sides because she felt like she was going to float away. The song ended, and she felt like dying when he exited the stage.

There were going to be two solo performances by others before his, and her mind drifted to the impressions of Skky that accumulated in her mind over the past few months.

At first he had seemed a walking mass of contradictions. He could change by the second, now every bit the smooth and confident world class performer, then a raucous pub singer leaving no doubt you'd lose to him in a fight. Serious, then silly. Smooth, then rough. He was all of that and everything in between, yet through it all he possessed a continuity of genuineness. His focus and concentration could only belong to someone that knew he was doing what he'd been born to do, yet he was consistently humble about it in interviews. One quality remained unchanged in her eyes throughout; he was an angel built for sin.

"Let's go outside for a minute, get some fresh air," her Gran nudged her. She followed in a daze.
"Your babies will be so beautiful."
"Don't we have to do something first – like *meet?*"
"You will, darling."
"How can you be sure?" Cailín stared, wide eyed.
"I believe that's part of Spéir's purpose."
"Yeah, but Spéir's …"
"Not real? Of course he is."
"Oh, gosh. How do you deal with loving a man like that?"
"You don't have any trouble relating to Spéir, do you?"
"Well, no, but –"
"But what? They're no different, you know, no different at all. Skky is flesh and blood, and being that, he wants the same things that you do. You'll meet him one day. I'd be getting used to the idea if I were you. For now, enjoy this night, it will be nice to look back someday and know you were part of this history."

* * *

On the last day of her senior year Cailín went to a local drugstore to pick up some things on her way home after school. She was leaving the parking lot, driving through a decently wide path between two rows of parked cars. A little black Corvette that she didn't see until she was right by it because it was parked on the other side of a truck squealed its tires backing out. Before she could react it was two feet from the driver's side of her car. She remembered thinking her parents were going to be upset because car insurance was probably about to go up.

It happened in a split second.

Her car slid quickly sideways twelve feet across the parking lot into two fortunately vacant spaces. She remembered thinking that she was all right, but that the car had to be ruined. Then she wondered why the air bags didn't pop. From the back seat she heard, "'S alright, just drive home, noh worries." He always went with her when she was in the car alone, and she had finally learned that it was no use to argue. When she got home and got out of the car, there wasn't a scratch on it.

* * *

Cailín slogged through a sea of molasses the summer after her senior year of high school. Endless lackluster concerts, boring plays, the usual garden club parties. There were saving graces though. "Of course, darling, but only if you order two." Her grandmother understood. The day the DVDs arrived they watched together. A song by one member of the group, though not her blond angel, featured one verse in Irish.

She searched the internet that evening, as she had so many others, and discovered that he, too, knew the Irish language. Three hours later, a bath towel draped over her head and the monitor so its light wouldn't betray her, she had printed out over one hundred pages to help her learn.

She rushed to her grandmother's house the next day with her discovery. "Why, that's wonderful! I know bits and pieces of the language. Your great grandmother spoke it occasionally." She laughed, "It always popped out when she was happy, or very angry, just a phrase or two. No one else could understand her! I do remember some of the sayings that she used most often, and quite a few words."

Cailín threw her arms around her grandmother and cried. "Then help me learn, please, can we study together?"

It would be important someday, she told herself. Very important.

* * *

By August time passed more quickly with college, and a relative form of freedom, in sight. Cailín's grandmother continued to be her co-conspirator, and mail delivery drop. She now proudly possessed the second DVD/CD set by the ensemble that her angel was part of, as well as her ticket to the Fall concert in Chicago. Her mother had wanted her to attend a prestigious university on the East Coast, but had quickly changed her mind when she discovered the superb reputation of a certain university in the Windy City.

"Their Liberal Arts and Sciences program is absolutely perfect!" she declared with the usual finality. "Just the things you need to know to not be an embarrassment to a husband in position to move up rapidly in the business world. A good general education."

She didn't care, she only wanted to get away. A school counselor had offered her the valuable tip that the first year of studies was general, and that often students didn't declare a major until late in their second year. That would give her plenty of time to discover what she wanted to do.

The only downside was that she was to be installed in a sorority directly associated to the one her mother had belonged to, and still referred to at length, "You'll make lifetime associations there, ones that will contribute to your social connections and standing. It will help you acquire a successful husband."

It could have been worse, she told herself, she had found ways around her mother's restrictions; these people would be a piece of cake in comparison. She didn't intend to 'acquire' anything other than a useful education.

* * *

Cailín's first two years of college had been like a parole from her mother's constant social climbing. The beginning of her third year was an acquittal. A fortunate acquaintance with a pre-law student led her to the Legal Aid department of the university, and paying only the cost to file a petition with the local Court she changed her surname to Casey, with her grandmother's blessing.

Now self-sufficient with a part time job, nicely paying babysitting jobs every weekend, and student loans that she had no qualms about being able to repay, she was no longer shackled by her father's fortune. She was on her own.

She'd been to a dozen of Skky's concerts when he was in town, or even within three hundred miles. She'd driven through the night more than once to get back in time for class the next day. More often than not she'd scored seats in the first five or six rows, although that became increasingly more difficult after his solo career got underway.

In the spring of 2010, she hit the mother lode. He was coming to a local TV station for a ninety minute special presentation of concert footage, promoting ticket sales for the summer concert. There would be breaks, of course, and he would be interviewed during those. Seeing a good money making opportunity, the station decided to sell tickets for admission to the studio audience. Skky had agreed to sign autographs and pose for pictures with the guests for an hour beforehand. Since the studio couldn't accommodate more than forty or so people the timing should work out, he was accustomed to keeping things moving while still being polite. The staff would be the bad guys; they'd give a mini lecture about keeping the line moving so everyone had an opportunity.

Cailín heard the announcement that'd he be in town for the airing over the car radio. She pulled over immediately and phoned the TV station on the outside chance, and discovered that tickets for the autograph session would go on sale the next day. She was at the front desk at 7:00 a.m.

* * *

Cailín twirled her pencil around and around. She glanced out the window for the thirtieth time, attempting to reassure herself that the clear blue sky she witnessed posed no threat to a safe landing. She had always made it a point to know what his tour schedule was, and what the weather forecast was for the city he was travelling to. *I don't stalk Skky, it's just that I have to know where he is at all times,* she thought, and laughed at herself.

She willed her impatience into determination. Two blocks down, eight left to go. If only she'd left earlier – but then how could she have known that there would be an unusually large number of traffic tie ups, let alone that her normally super dependable car would choose that time to quit.

Clunk, clunk, chunk. Fortunately she was in the right lane to be able to coast into a parking spot. The meter was going to run out before she would be able to get a tow truck, but what the hell? That was a responsibility that would have to be met later. Nothing was going to stop her from meeting Skky. Nothing.

The early September sun was relentless, pounding out ninety-eight degree heat that even the shady side of the street failed to abate. Her high heeled strappy sandals weren't made for walking long distances, and even her lightweight summer dress clung like a down comforter.

A bus stop! She hurriedly checked the schedule – of course not – the next one wasn't due for another thirty-five minutes. She kept going without hesitation, wishing she'd had a pair of sneakers in the car to change into.

A quick purchase of a bottle of water from a street vendor was the only diversion she allowed herself.

At last she stormed through the double doors of the television station, and gulped in the cool air. There was no one in the lobby, save for a single staffer behind the curved half wall that hid computers and telephones.

"Hello?" the woman behind the counter seemed oddly surprised to see anyone.

"I – I'm here for, uh, the signing and the taping." She plucked her ticket from her small handbag.

"Oh." The woman seemed almost annoyed. "Well, I'm afraid you're too late, the autograph session wrapped up several minutes ago, and the set is now closed in preparation for the broadcast."

"But, if it hasn't started yet –"

"The set is closed," the woman clipped firmly.

Cailín braced herself against the counter and hung her head, afraid that stress and exhaustion were finally going to take over.

A rush of hot air jarred her as the door flung open.

"Sorry, had to go get –" the voice was instantly recognizable.

A wave of cool air quickly replaced the heat as he ran past. Then he nearly screeched to a halt.

"Whawt?" He shot a brief glance at Cailín, then at the receptionist. That accent! Skky now stood in front of her and she fully understood what it meant to have rubber knees.

"I, well I came for the autographs and, of course, the taping, but…"

"The set is clo –" Cailín paid no more attention to the woman's voice than she would have a fly droning five miles away.

"… my car broke down a mile and a half from here and I had to walk, so I'm late."

"Mile and a half? Good lord! That's –" he held up a finger and looked at the ceiling for a second, "That's over two kilometers then!"

"Yes," she marveled at the instant comfort she felt, "it's nearly two and a half."

"So it is," his eyes were locked on hers.

"Apparently I'm too late?"

"Noh. Eh, well, at least the autograph can be fixed easy enough." For a split second he looked uncharacteristically shy, she thought. He glanced at the floor. "If you'd like, that is."

"I would! Yes, very much."

He smiled instantly, "It'd be my honor." He touched her arm briefly and pointed toward a doorway, "You need to sit down, here, come." The room was vacant, the rows of tables and chairs now empty. This must have been where they'd held the dinner for the ticket holders, she guessed.

He held out a chair for her and pulled one out for himself. "'Scuse me, just a second," he went to a cooler next to the wall and pulled out two bottles of water. "Thinkin' we could probly both use this," he said as he placed a bottle on a napkin in front of her. "Can't believe ya walked so far in this heat," his eyes took their time reaching her feet, "'specially in those. Which are very nice, so they are.

"See you brought programs, would you like…" he retrieved a pen from his suit pocket.

She still couldn't believe she was sitting next to him. "Oh! Yes, please, if you would sign one of these."

"Both if ya like, least I can do. Your name?"

"It's Kaylin," she said her name as everyone else said it.

"Kaylin," he repeated, "is it?"

"Yes, but it's spelled like 'Colleen' – the Irish spelling that is. My grandmother won on the spelling, but my mother insisted on the wrong pronunciation, which was too bad."

"All right, then, Cailín, spelled like Colleen in Irish," he laughed.

"Go raibh maith agus!" she blurted out her 'thank you' in Irish.

"You're very welcome. Uh. Seriously? Seriously!"

She laughed, "Yes, I do speak a little Irish."

"Uhmasin'. Well, don't run into tew many or any really, that is. Read and write, too, then?"

"Yes, a little."

"Am bettin' more than a little. Hmm, wonderin', 'cause, well, is unusual."

"My grandparents are Irish, mostly, probably ninety percent or more. I was born here, though, sorry to say. I began studying the language a few years ago, and I love it. I want to see it stay alive."

"A mission dear to my heart, am happy to hear," a genuine smile lit up his already incandescent face. *He really does have the most beautiful skin*, she thought. "But your name – ever think on insistin' that it be said right?"

"Oh, sure, but after years, that is – I was ten or eleven before I realized that it was an Irish name and that my mother had changed the pronunciation. At that point it was pretty much fixed, plus a child doesn't have much leverage, really."

"Mm, guess not," light seemed to dance in his eyes, "but it suits you, Cailín does."

"Thank you," she was amazed that she was still able to speak.

"'Scuse me, but," he became very still for a moment, his expression intent, "have we met before? At a show or somethin'?"

Time itself seemed to stand still as she began, "This is the first chance I've had to –"

"Mr. O'Keeffe, five minutes to air!" the receptionist had invaded their sanctuary.

"Ah. Thanks, noh worry," he dismissed without taking his eyes off Cailín.

37

"Oh, I should get going and let you…" she rose and started for the door.

"Wait! Em, hawareya gettin' home then?"

"I called a friend, she should be here soon."

"Ah, good then?" He stepped between her and the door. Before she realized what was happening, his arms were around her, "Poor wee lass, so glad I got to meet ya." He released her before she had a chance to sink in, but she caught his faint scent and it was identical to Spéir's. For a split second she wondered which world she was in.

"Thanks for takin' the trouble, an' I'm sorry about not bein' able to get in the studio, and not meetin' Colin."

"It's alright," Cailín was surprised that she could speak, but was fairly certain that she was grinning like an idiot, and about to burst into tears, "In all honesty, it's you I came here for."

"Sláinte," with the Irish 'goodbye' he was down the hall and taking the stairs three at a time. She was on autopilot toward the exit, clutching the programs he had signed, but turned around in time to see him stop and wave.

One last look at the man she loved, who had paused five seconds past coincidence, and she wondered what was stopping her from running after him.

She was relieved to see Caroline's car through the large glass windows. She had to stop and give the receptionist a glance to get the button pushed to allow her to leave.

His brief touch seemed to have penetrated every cell of her body. She sat back and closed her eyes, willing his essence to not leave her.

"Wow! You must be exhausted, all that walking in this heat," she dearly loved Caroline but was wishing she'd shut up, "I hope it was worth it".

"He's so awesome," Cailín sighed. "Oh, Caroline, you should see him up close, his skin is gorgeous …"

"Yeah. That must be an Irish thing, you're lucky," Caroline interrupted.

"… his eyes are amazing, his smile. I wish he'd had a short sleeved shirt on, I love his arms."

"Geez, why didn't you just rip his clothes off and have your way with him?"

"It's not like it didn't cross my mind," Cailín laughed. "How sweet he is, kind and considerate."

"Ah ha! So he was thinking of ripping *your* clothes off, too."

"I should be so lucky. Oh! And I got two autographs, two!" She opened the first program to the page with his picture and stared at his writing.

Cailín álainn súil agam muid le chéile arís

It was in Irish, and meant "Beautiful girl, I hope we meet again". She swallowed the lump in her throat, and opened the second.

ní dhéanfaidh mé dearmad ort, le grá, Skky

Also Irish, it said "I will never forget you. With love, Skky. " She closed the program quickly, before the first teardrop landed on it. He had broken protocol, she knew from years of photographs taken with fans – an arm around the shoulder for the picture, but for the band's protection if nothing else, no full on hugs like the one he'd given her were allowed. It was all part of the standard public relations template.

She wanted to go to sleep, right then, right there. She wanted to sleep so Spéir could hold her.

"Tomorrow after class we can get my car and pick yours up if it's ready," Caroline had offered.

"Thanks, see you tomorrow."

She climbed the half flight of stairs to her campus studio apartment, grateful that it wasn't more, and flicked the small window air conditioner up to full speed.

Cailín muffled a scream as she tried to remove her shoes from now swollen feet, the straps seemed permanently imbedded in her heels. She gave a small tug and suppressed another scream as her skin came away with the strap. The deep sting was the worst pain she'd felt in her life.

Thirty minutes and a few dozen Irish curses later she carefully placed gauze over the antibiotic ointment she'd forced herself to apply. The whir and click of her old VCR caught her attention, signaling the end of the promo she should have been at. She jumped up without thinking and nearly went to her knees, but switched on the small TV and hit rewind on the VCR.

She fast forwarded through the pre-recorded songs, she knew them all by heart. Skky was his usual charming yet unassuming self, answering questions politely and popping off a few funny one liners. It seemed surreal that only a little over an hour ago she'd been in his arms for a full five seconds.

I'm going to do it, she told herself, *if I don't do it now, I never will.* She carefully wrote his name and the P.O. Box number that his fan mail was sent to on the envelope. *He won't read it for months, if ever, so here goes.* She took a deep breath.

Dear Skky,

I was fifteen when I began having dreams about a young Irishman in the seventeenth century. He showed me our life together in that time and I wrote the story down. It became a book.

I was eighteen when I saw a young Irishman on television who looked exactly like the man in my dreams, down to the last eyelash. Your hair was a bit shorter, and of course you were dressed differently, but there could be no mistake.

Now I'm twenty, and I met you today. I'll never forget your sweetness and kindness to me. I'll never forget you. Your existence is an unfathomable joy to me, and I wish for you every joy it's possible to have in this life.

I've loved you for centuries.

Cailín

That's it, that's all. He'll never know.

She carefully folded the pale blue paper and slid it into the small matching envelope, and cried herself to sleep.

* * *

Exactly who would you have to be? Who? Or what would you have to look like? What kind of position would you have to be in, what connections or leverage would you have to have to get close to a man like that?   What would be *the* one thing he couldn't resist?   Was it partly a matter of catching him at the right time, the right stage of his life? What kind of magic would it take to make all of this come together?

Her answer came seven months after she'd met Skky in person. The story, though unconfirmed, spread quickly through internet circles. Lila Hanover, an already well known verging-on-super-status model had made the move. According to the rumors they had met briefly at a television station in upstate New York when Skky did a brief promo spot, and she recorded a statewide commercial. The next day, as the story went, her manager had phoned his producer and – viola! A dinner date was made for that evening.

The six thirty celebrity news show confirmed that the rumors had been true. A zealous fan had snapped a distant but unmistakable photo of the two sharing a goodbye kiss at LaGuardia after a week long New Year's tryst, and it went viral. The day after Valentine's Day they wed.

What was his reason for marrying the super model? He wasn't superficial, she told herself, though that thought was no comfort. He was only twenty-six and had all the opportunities he cared to consider, so he married for love, he must have, family was important to him. As usually had happened in his charmed existence, his impulsiveness hadn't slowed interest in his career. He was still in demand.

Lila wasn't a match for him; she seemed cold and distant in spite of her frequent posed smiles. It seemed that he was the very definition of 'arm candy' to her. She paraded him around in front of her friends much like Cailín's mother had paraded her in front of her friends. A status thing, that was all, though she couldn't imagine anyone not truly loving a man like Skky.

At least I can still see him in concerts, on TV, know something about his life through the media, and he'll record more CD's. She tried desperately to console herself as she clasped her hands together in an effort to stop them from trembling. *If only I'd had the nerve to give him my phone number, I wonder if he would have called? No, why should he? I can't compete with a super model – but he didn't know her then. But I didn't, I didn't do it and now I'll never know what could have been. I'll never have any more of him than I have right now.*

She turned off the TV, threw a half eaten hamburger in the trash, and closed her books and said, "Screw you. Just screw you, bitch! He's mine."

She crawled into bed with a wad of tissues in her hands, and begged Spéir to come help her sleep.

* * *

Spring, finals, and graduation came in rapid fire succession, and Cailín found herself free – and unemployed. She'd written to a dozen large financial institutions and scored interviews at three, but had turned down the two offers she'd gotten because the pay was too low and the benefits were non-existent. She had school loans to repay, and she wanted to save for a down payment on a condo in the city.

Between babysitting jobs and a temp agency she would manage to stay afloat, but there wouldn't be much left for savings. Concert tickets were the one thing she wouldn't give up, that was one piece of Skky that she could still get next to.

Late in June the temp agency called, and she sighed. They'd only been able to give her work three days a week, four at best. She wondered where they were sending her now, and how long it would take to figure out the parking situation. She hoped it wasn't another receptionist fill-in. Memorizing the names of all the top brass and trying to figure out who would take calls and who wouldn't at any given time was frustrating.

"… and they would like to interview you for a permanent position." Now the job coordinator had her attention. "You'll need to be there tomorrow at 10:00 a.m."

"Oh. Thank you, I'll be there."

* * *

"Hey! Watch where … oh."

"Sorry, uh, you were the one doing that turn around walking backwards thing though."

She got a good look at the cut of his suit and the expensive looking material. "Oh, great! I've just yelled at one the partners. And on my first day, too." On second consideration he looked too young, and the bed head didn't fit. Then again, you never know. He could be the junior Berman in Berman Meiner Berman.

"Hardly, but thank you … I think. You must be Kaylin."

"Yes, Mr. Robertson's new assistant analyst."

"Hi, I'm Brandon. And surprised."

"Surprised?"

"Yeah, I mean, after the great hoopla surrounding your arrival."

"Oh? Tell me more … and who says 'hoopla' anyway?"

"You're implying I'm a throwback?"

"Um, it does sound a bit dated."

"Guess I'm an old fashioned guy, or maybe just a fuddy duddy." He pressed his lips together and tried to appear serious. The result was a mutual good natured laugh.

"Hungry?"

"It's only 11:30."

"They're not super strict about that, as long as you get things done. There's a great bagel place just a couple blocks from here, let me show you."

He was pleasant, and Cailín had reason to believe she could get some good information about how things went at BMB, "That does sound good."

"Good, let's go. I'm starving."

"Just let me grab my bag."

"No, this one's on me. I just got my first paycheck. Your treat next time."

The two story interior brick wall lent a spacious feel to the long, somewhat narrow café. Cailín was beginning to sink in and enjoy the atmosphere. During her years at university she seldom had the time or money to spend downtown, every spare second and cent went to feed a more pressing passion.

"This way," Brandon nudged her arm, "view's great." He was leading her to the narrow stairs that led to the upper landing.

"No, uh, no… here," she shied away from the chair he held for her and grasped one closer to the wall.

"Aw, I'm very sorry – you don't like heights, do you?"

"Elevators either, but I guess I need to get used to it." She glanced toward the long windows across the span of the room below.

"Look, let's go back down. I don't want you to be uncomfortable." He started to get up, "I'll walk in front of you, er, you can put your hand on my shoulder if that helps."

Spéir – better late than never – appeared in the chair next to her, between her and the see through railing. She took a deep breath. "No, I'm good. Better sitting down."

"If you're sure…"

"Sure." She grinned, "You know, I think I may just like working full time. Evenings and weekends free, no homework."

"I should warn you, they'll have you working ten hour days if you're not careful."

She shrugged, "Might not be bad two or three days a week, I want to buy a condo soon. My grandmother is loaning me a down payment and I'll want to pay her back as quickly as possible."

"Good investment."

"Exactly."

"It's not a bad place to work at all. They're not really micro managers. As long as you get the work done, they don't fuss. It's a good philosophy, really, hire the best and let them have at it."

"Oh," she laughed, "a little out of character for stockbrokers, and – are we the best?"

"I think it's a safe bet. You do want to watch out for Doug, Randy, and Justin. Third floor," he said between bites, "think they're God's gift and all that."

"They won't bother me."

"They'll try."

"Not interested."

"Steady guy?"

"Not exactly."

"Oh. Oh, I see."

"No, not that either, but very progressive for you to assume so. I am committed though."

"Lucky guy. He lives here, in the city?"

"No. He – it's complicated. He travels a lot."

"I see."

"It's really not what you think. We, uh, sort of talk often, that's all." She understood that he didn't know what to say, so she changed the subject. "So, I really don't know what I'm supposed to be doing yet, that's the hard part. Personnel just sort of pointed me to my desk."

"You're supposed to be analyzing client portfolios, checking recommendations, possibly making new ones?"

"Well, yes, that's what Mr. Berman senior told me. But I can't really do that until I've attended the suitability training session, and there's not another one until Monday."

"Of course. That doesn't mean you can't filter through and take notes. Client intake will show their risk tolerance, and I somehow suspect that you already have a good handle on what 'suitability' means. I'll show you how to access the files assigned to you and set up your password."

"That's nice of you, but I'd feel bad about taking up your time."

"Hey, it'll take five minutes. Not a problem."

"Thanks."

"And I'll show you where to find stock research, although I'm guessing you'll want to do your own very soon. Just knowing where to locate a few programs and so forth will open up the playground and you'll be off."

"You like it, don't you? Figuring out the puzzle, the odds, the patterns, even the associated risks?"

"Busted. And if you want, we can fly some ideas back and forth."

"Speakin' of flying, say ya haven't forgot that ya can? A bit anyway." Spéir added his two cents. She couldn't very well smack punch his arm in public.

"I won't say no to that. Do most of the analysts share ideas?"

"Are you kidding? They play it close to the vest, don't want to share the glory."

"I think it could be an advantage."

"Agreed. Let's put our heads together and show them how it's done."

She accepted Brandon's earlier offer, placing her hand on his shoulder on the way down the stairs, although Spéir was right behind her, holding her arms. It was comfortable; she had a friend, one that was forthright without being pushy. And Spéir showed no signs of objecting.

* * *

Two weeks later Cailín spotted what she thought could be their first big venture. She grabbed her cell and punched the number. The ten seconds that passed before he answered seemed like five hours. "Bran," she half whispered, looking over her shoulder, "I think I've got something ... no, not here. Lunch? No, I'll meet you there ... yes, 11:45."

She hurried to a table at the back of the burger place.

"All right, Miss Cloak and Dagger, where's the treasure map?" Brandon's clear blue eyes were twinkling just a little too much and she felt her cheeks warm. "Do tell. Was it the butler in the library with a candlestick?"

"Geez, who says that? Fine. I guess I do feel a little silly, but I'll explain."

"Okay, spill. By the way, I ordered the usual for us."

"Great, thanks! Now, look." She produced three sheets of folded paper from her handbag. "Go ahead, just scan it."

"Mm," his expression sobered, "well, kind of hard to miss since you've highlighted... but yeah, yeah, definitely a pattern."

"See? Every three to four weeks this stock goes from somewhere in the four dollar a share range to over twelve dollars, all within a few hours. Next day it's back to four."

"Good catch. And yes, someone is driving it, no doubt. But why the secrecy?"

"It's not us is it?"

"Oh. I don't think so, never heard of it, never seen it in a portfolio. Tell you what though. I'll search it, cross reference just to be sure."

"If it comes up clean, then − do you see what I'm getting at?"

"Well… how long has this been going on?"

"Six months, at least."

"Then I would expect the pattern to change, or cease all together, any day now. Whoever's doing it has been half smart up 'til now. Even so, they've got to know it can't go on forever."

"Other than that, um pass the ketchup please? Other than that, risk verses gain – it doesn't fluctuate much at all."

"You're saying likely very little risk of loss, break even is the worst case scenario verses a possible three X gain."

"Exactly."

"We'd have to be very careful, document projected long term gain. If it looks good, it'd be justified. Then – bingo – would you look at that? Let's sell for a highly profitable short term gain instead."

"It could give a nice pump to a few smaller, struggling portfolios."

"Yeah, I've got a couple of those. Could also promote client retention to some larger ones. I agree on the low risk of loss."

"I'll print out the entire six month history for you; you check for our activity. How long can we hold it?"

"Based on what's here, no longer than four and a half weeks. If it doesn't happen by then… problem is, if we sell that soon it could look like churning."

"Absent a profit."

"Yes."

"Bran, look again. If the pattern holds it's due to go back up by the end of this week."

"Are you authorized to issue buy/sell yet?"

"Berman senior signed off for it to go straight to the broker, yeah. Only up to ten percent of the portfolio without consulting Berman, but no more than twenty thousand."

"We don't want to do more than that anyway. We'd have to do our homework quick, you ready for about three hours tonight?"

"I have a casserole ready to pop in the oven. We need to place our buys first thing in the morning, providing we can't come up with a reason not to."

"Then I should pick up a couple of salads, a bottle of wine, and I'll be at your place by 6:00?"

* * *

"I think we've got this right," Brandon declared after nearly three hours of pouring over client portfolios, carefully choosing amounts, and writing up thirty five buy orders between the two of them. "If this happens —"

"*When* this happens," Cailín interrupted, gazing at her coffee-table-turned-desk.

"—we'll gain roughly a million dollars total."

"Not exactly setting the world on fire, but a decent bump, and it'll help our performance review for the month."

"That's us, nickel and dime our way to the top. And, no fault on us or the firm."

Their friendship had hit a new level of trust and understanding, Cailín in her sweat pants and t-shirt, Brandon long ago sans tie and suit coat. His shoes were somewhere in the living room.

Glorious Spéir, lying on the sofa, appeared to be asleep.

Brandon stretched. "My parents are coming for the weekend. One day, really. Saturday afternoon to Sunday afternoon."

"Oh, that's good," she responded lazily, staring at Spéir's rumpled hair and unable to suppress a yawn, "do they visit often?"

"Nah, a couple of times a year. Of course I go home nearly every holiday, and we talk every week."

"That's nice. You're close with them?"

"Couldn't ask for better, really. Dad runs the local co-op, Mom stays home except to help at inventory time. She's involved in lots though, book club, community events. They've always been supportive, and, you know, guiding. Not pushy though. Not about career choices anyway."

Cailín laughed, "That's a fine art."

"So what about yours?"

"Just the usual, mother's an emotionally unavailable social climbing bitch. Dad's a field rep for a pharmaceutical company, travels a lot, bangs the maid when he's around. Stuff you do when you're filthy rich."

Brandon sat up straight, "Oh, God, Kay, I'm so sorry, it … sounds horrible."

"I learned to skirt around it, mostly", she shrugged. "I have granny. My granny is great. She's always been my rock, my 'go to' person. She's the best. One of two people that says my name right.

"I've never been close with my brother, he's five years older."

"What does he do?"

"Mainly complies with mother's every request. He's an art major and she set him up with his own art gallery in New York after graduate school. It flopped, so of course she set him up again, this time in Minneapolis. Of course she called in all the favors and her friends got him started. That won't last though, so who knows.

"But, given that, I did accept a check from dad for graduation. So my school loans are paid off. I'm still not sure how I feel about that, I guess its okay. Granny said it was okay, mom's thrown more than that away on Rick's 'career'. And I'm sure dad has Candace set up nicely."

"I guess that's life. It doesn't sound like your thing at all though. I can understand why you wanted out from under."

"And I made it. In all fairness though, looking back I can see that the way mother is helped him tremendously in his career," she grimaced. "They both wanted money, and they got it."

"Nothing wrong with money."

"Unless it's the ultimate goal." Cailín paused, put her hand to her mouth and laughed, "But look at what we're doing!"

Brandon caught the irony. "We're good," he quipped, "this is other people's money."

They placed their buys early. Shortly before noon saw their pet stock soar to nearly thirteen dollars a share and they punched in the sell orders. At one thirty Cailín ran through the elevator door that Brandon held for her.

"I was sure that you got the call, too," he straightened his tie.

"We're either in a ton of trouble, or we're golden," Cailín smoothed her skirt and ran her hands down the sides of her hair.

"Think positive!"

They started to step out onto the ninth floor, stopped, and while staring straight ahead said in unison, "Breathe."

"Good afternoon, Miss Casey, Mr. Sykes," The senior Berman in BMB didn't rise, but gestured toward the chairs opposite his massive desk, "please."

"Mr. Berman," Brandon offered with a nod.

"Good afternoon, sir," Cailín added.

"I see there's been a flurry of activity the past few hours."

"Yes," Brandon kept it short.

She was mentally on the edge of her seat in spite of being physically lost in the expanse of the chair.

"Mm hmm," Berman glanced at the open folder before him, then removed his glasses and fixed them both in his gaze. "A nice profit across the board, and all from the same stock. I take it this was a collaborative effort?"

Before either of them could find their voices he continued, "Well done. I'm going to increase your limits to fifteen percent and a maximum of twenty-five thousand per order. A five percent raise will reflect on your next paycheck." He closed the folder.

Brandon stood up first, "Thank you, Mr. Berman,"
Cailín followed suit, "Thank you, sir."

As Brandon opened the door for Cailín, Berman stood up. "Some other points."

This time she answered, "Yes?"

"I'd like for you to continue working together whenever practical. In fact, I'm going to give you a dozen or so struggling portfolios to work in tandem. Allison will be certain that you get them in the next few days. Now take the rest of the day off, paid of course."

They both smiled and nodded, and once inside the elevator they hugged briefly.

"Buy you a drink?"

"Of course," she laughed, "you can afford it now."

Brandon opened the door to the tiny bar just around the corner for her.

"Oh, now we're just another couple of high rollers, drinking with the big boys?" Cailín laughed. "Think he knows we made sure BMB wasn't in on it before we moved?" her brows knitted slightly.

"Had to. Not his first rodeo."

"You were right."

"About?"

"He hires the best, then gives them room to do the job. Think he'll give us the most pathetic portfolios ever?"

"Count on it", Brandon smirked. "Wonder if we can run the same stock again. How about a couple of Irish coffees to celebrate?"

"Perfect! Maybe. Maybe on a smaller scale. Basically, we should move on."

"Are you thinking front runners are doing it?"

"No, the scale is too small. However – whoever's driving this – a million is barely a blip on their radar, I'd bet. We should check more history, the volume."

"Sure, but it might be wise to wait and see, maybe skip a cycle. That'd put us up to roughly three months before we can do it again. Kay?"

"Hmm?"

"I need a favor. I was going to bring it up last night, but, well, we were under enough pressure."

"Sounds ominous, spill it."

"My parents are coming to town Saturday."

"You mentioned. You said things were good with them, is there a problem?"

"Sort of. Some things could be more comfortable."

"Oh, I'm sorry, Bran. What is it? What can I do?"

"It's not life threatening. Silly I guess."

"But apparently it's important to you."

"They, well mostly mom, keep asking, wondering why I don't have a girlfriend. Somehow the concept of 'just haven't found the right one' doesn't register. Maybe it's just me, but, damn, it gets pretty irritating."

"Do I ever understand that. What time should I come over on Saturday? Hey! I'll cook dinner, how about that? Oh, I need to see your place so I know where to find stuff in the kitchen."

"Damn, Kay, you're making this too easy," he laughed with relief.

"Told you, I understand. So? What? We've just had a couple of dates but it's tentatively promising? We'll be a little cute, you know, just friendly enough, try to keep the convo mostly on work."

"Wasn't that supposed to be harder? Awkward even?"

"Yes, it was. But there's a catch. I need the same thing at work to discourage the come-on's. Basically just a little whispering in the hallways, a touch on the arm, stuff like that should catch fire. Then, just a lack of denying the inevitable rumors."

"I get it, just make them wonder. Matter of fact, that'd actually help me, too. And the bonus is it's a cover for us being seen together more. If people get a clue it'll create more than a little resentment about Berman playing favorites. Could make our life hell."

"Wow! I hadn't thought about that. We can't afford that, it would slow us down."

"Worst case, maybe even some sabotage thrown our way. But avoiding some stress both personally and professionally? Win-win."

"Let's go have a look at your kitchen. Oh, and I'll make you a shopping list.

Thus began a friendly partnership that played to their mutual advantage over the next few months.

* * *

The twinkling lights of the boutiques across the street we no longer visible, and Cailín could barely make out the shape of the building that held them. A white out blizzard wasn't so bad when you had no where you needed to be, she decided. She was grateful that her Gran had insisted that she come another time.

She wondered what Skky was doing. In Ireland it would officially be Christmas Eve in another two or three hours, and she tried to picture his family gathered around the fireplace, singing of course. She thought about opening the bedroom drapes and crawling back under the comforter and how cozy it would feel with Speír there. She picked up her cell and started to click it off when it rang. "Bran? Oh, you're not stranded halfway between here and Des Moines are you?"

"No, dad called before I got twenty minutes out of town, said it was awful there, so I turned back."

"Thank goodness, it's gotten bad so fast."

"Yes and no. My car just got stuck. I did manage to slide it over to the curb though. No hope of getting a tow or anything at this rate."

"Where are you?"

"About a block and a half east of you, as far as I can tell."

"Get over here! Can you make it?"

"Think so, I've got a ski mask."

"Be careful. I'll come to the lobby in a minute."

Cailín started a fresh pot of coffee and didn't bother to change out of her sweats.

Nearly twenty minutes passed, and she was starting to worry when a snowy figure half stumbled through the door. "I had to-to stuh-stay close to the buh-buildings, read the num-bers to be sure I wuh-was going the ruh-right way."

"Take off that wet coat and stuff." She hoped the elevator wouldn't get stuck halfway up. "Got dry socks?"

He pulled off his muffler and patted his duffel bag. "Everything ruh-right here." He hesitated at the door to her condo.

"Don't worry about it. I'll hang your wet stuff in the shower. I've got food, movies, and a comfy sofa. Hey! We could string popcorn and watch Home Alone later! It'll be just a like a real Christmas. So get comfortable, you're going to be here a while. Help yourself to coffee, it's fresh."

"Thanks, Kay." He glanced at her Christmas tree. It was small, but it was a real one, and decorated with handmade items. "That actually sounds wonderful. I never would have made it to my place. Even if it was next door," he laughed.

"Warming up now?"

He sighed, "Yeah, thanks."

She fished his cell out of his parka, "Hey, call your parents."

"You probably were looking forward to a quiet day, sorry to interrupt."

"Hm. Shut up. Kind of glad for the company, although I would have taken you in anyway. Can't lose my partner in crime," she teased.

"Sorry you couldn't make it to your grandmother's."

"I can't imagine being stuck at the airport, or worse – not being able to land. So I was thinking soup and sandwiches for lunch, unless you're hungry now?"

He shook his head, "Had breakfast. If I hadn't taken time for that, I would have been farther out of town and might not have made it back. Coffee's a lifesaver though."

"Most important meal of the day, thank heaven you did. Lasagna for dinner."

"Damn, I have *the* worst luck," he laughed again. "I can't think of a better place to be stranded. Unless you tell me the bathroom's out of order."

It was her turn to laugh, "Actually, it is. Broken handle or whatever in the half, and I won't fault the Super for being busy with other things. Go through the bedroom to the master."

Brandon exited the master bath, decorated all in pink from towels to hand soap. Flower prints and ruffles entered his field of vision and he chuckled softly to himself. Kaylin, although always impeccably and conservatively dressed at work was definitely a very feminine girl. He was happy that she could express her tastes at home. Though he had helped her move in less than two months ago, the place was already put together nicely. These thoughts crossed his mind in a split second as he turned toward the living room.

He stopped dead still. Covering the wall parallel to the bed were dozens of pictures, a few of which were of landscapes that he knew must be in Ireland. Most of the pictures were of a young blond man, covering apparently several years of his life and capturing a range of emotions. Brandon recognized him, and remembered what Kaylin had said when they first met, "It's complicated." She was right about that, and he was worried.

He sat at the small table near the kitchen and stared at the white out that obscured any view past the patio doors. He had no idea where, or how, to start. "Kay?"

She was adding fresh coffee to her cup, "Warm yours up, too?"

He didn't respond, he barely blinked.

"Here," she filled his cup, and tried to decipher his mood, "cat got your tongue?"

"Who says that?" he responded automatically.

"Oh," she sat down beside him. "Oh. Skky."

He looked up at her, "When did you meet him?"

"Over three years ago. August."

"But he —"

"Married. Yes, nearly a year ago now. It's not what you think," she rested her chin in her palm briefly, "in fact it's not what anyone would think. It *is* complicated, and not in a normal way. If you like, I'll give you the Cliff's Notes version. But, you're stuck here in a blizzard with a crazy woman, so you can stop me at any time and we'll watch a movie, or play cards, whatever. We'll just write it off as a silly obsessive crush that's gone on far too long."

"You love him? He's the guy you're in love with?"

"Yes."

He touched her arm, "Tell me."

"Nine years ago I started writing a book because…"

Fifteen minutes later she concluded with, "You can read it if you like, well, maybe part of it, it's gotten fairly long. But a few pages should give you some idea."

"You sure? I … it sounds very personal."

"It is, but after what I've just told you it might help you understand a little. Not that I completely understand myself."

He nodded.

She disappeared into the bedroom and returned with a thick sheaf of paper. "I'm going to put the lasagna together now, then I'll make lunch. By then, you'll probably have had enough."

Brandon read nonstop for the better part of an hour. The ethereal whiteness outside made him feel like he was in an airplane, flying through a cloud bank, not to any particular physical destination, but backward through time.

"Enough? Soup's ready."

"Enough to know that it feels real," he said somberly. "Kay, it really is very good... interesting... makes me want to read all of it."

"I've done some polishing along the way. The story hasn't changed though."

He stood up and stretched, "Let me help with that," he carried the hot soup to the table, "I'm a lazy enough bum, so I'll clean up after we're done."

"Bran?" she turned to face him.

"Kaylin – sure, why not? Stranger things have probably happened. Even Hawking is likely a rank amateur when it comes to how the universe really works, the nature of what we call reality. All that stuff. No, I don't think you're crazy. In fact, I can't help but envy a love that's strong enough to cross the barriers. On the other hand, it must be horribly frustrating at times, and hurtful."

"I guess it's what you'd call a mixed blessing."

"Where do you think it's going?"

"I – " her voice tightened, " – I don't know." She broke into sobs.

It made Brandon wish that he could give her what, or rather who, she really wanted for Christmas.

* * *

"Hey! The New Year's Eve party should be a blast. I'm not usually crazy about company parties, but we can have some fun with this one, huh?" Brandon was doing his best.

She didn't bother to look up from her work. "Oh. Yeah, sure. Maybe we will."

"Aw, come on, Kay, we'll make a game of it, get to know some more people, and really cement the idea that we're a couple. It's made my life much easier around here. I hope it has for you."

"Of course, it really has, thanks Bran, I don't think I could bear…"

"Know what? You should take off early, I'll cover. Go check out the after Christmas sales. How about that dress you were drooling over in Morgan's window? I bet you could get a great deal on it now. Treat yourself, you deserve it."

That suggestion brought a tiny smile, "Maybe. I really do like it a lot."

"Alll-righty then!" his enthusiasm was starting to be a bit contagious, as well as a bit annoying. "Besides, it'll be Brownie points. I hear the brass like to be appreciated for throwing a bash."

She sighed, "I suppose so – but who says 'Brownie points'? and 'bash' in the same sentence even. Sometimes I think you should have been born fifty years earlier. I know I should have been born three hundred years plus earlier."

"I think it'll be fun, I promise to be as absolutely loony as possible."

"Who says… never mind."

"We're going then? It's not like either of us has … sorry. Let's just make the best of it. Bring a huge handbag. We'll have food for a week!"

That finally got a laugh out of her, to Brandon's delight, "Okay, okay, I will go check out that dress. Cover for me?"

"If necessary, of course. It's Friday, it won't be a problem, Kay, just go."

Huge piles of pure, white snow now covered in dirt were everywhere. Frozen and filthy suited her view of the world just fine. Even the dim lighting and cold concrete was an improvement as she pulled into the underground garage.

Cailín located her prize on the third floor and went to the dressing room to try it on. The seventy percent off sale price brought another small smile to her face, but once the dress was on she felt almost euphoric. It fit her like a glove, like it was made for her, and was very similar to the cocktail dress she'd begged her mother for to wear to the Senior Prom – only much better! But she wasn't thinking about the Prom, she was thinking exactly what she thought on the day she tried on the other dress five years before. This would be the dress that she would wear on her first formal date with Skky! It was something tangible, a piece of the puzzle. She changed hurriedly and nearly ran to the register. She'd go straight home, put it on, and indulge herself in the dream.

She did stop to grab a bagel sandwich on the way home. This was not a night to cook. She recalled not long ago when she'd heard one of those self-help gurus on a talk show saying that you should act as though you'd already achieved your goal, and that would help bring it into reality. That was exactly what she was going to do. Maybe she'd even talk Spéir into dressing the part.

Her new dress was carefully hung on the door frame for the moment. She set the table for two and pulled a small flower vase out of the cupboard. She flipped on the

T.V. and switched the channel to the evening version of the celebrity news magazine. Skky had been silent for several days, as she'd expected over Christmas. He had every right to celebrate in peace, hopefully with his family in Ireland if he had talked the ice queen into going. There might be some news by now; surely he had some plan for New Year's Eve.

A table cloth! That and two wine glasses would embellish the scene perfectly. Now to change into her new dress and don her sexiest black high heels, and coerce Spéir into materializing a tuxedo. It was a year from now, and Skky's marriage had come to its inevitable end. This time she'd slipped him her phone number at an autograph session six months ago, and they were on their way to happily ever after.

"... some rather distressing news this holiday season..." began the female reporter in a somber voice, "...apparently no one has heard from Skky O'Keeffe in over a week. Our reporters have been in contact with family members in Ireland, all of whom refused to comment when asked if he had spent the Christmas holiday at home. We suppose that much is natural, celebrities are entitled to some down time, but our level of concern was raised when we received the same 'no comment' from his agent. We then sought out his wife, super model Delilah Hanover, at the couple's New York apartment, who told our reporters, 'I don't know, and I don't care'.

"While we could possibly understand the silence if the marriage is breaking up, it's highly uncharacteristic of Skky to leave his fans hanging in the balance. We will continue to investigate and keep you informed, however at this moment, for all intents and purposes, it is feared that Skky O'Keeffe is – missing."

Cailín sat on the sofa, staring at the screen with her mouth open and her hand on her stomach. It couldn't be, someone as well known as Skky couldn't just 'disappear'.

Still, his silence, and the facts, seemed to lend some credibility to the story.

Her mood brightened temporarily – if he'd heard the story, or heard of it, as he must have, he'd be on Twitter, he loved to instantaneously blow any outrageous story about him out of the water. You'd think they'd know better by now.

She ran into the bedroom and turned on her laptop and began to search. Nothing. She half stumbled to the kitchen, pulled her cell phone out of her purse, and placed the call.

"Granny?" she began to cry.

* * *

Days crawled into weeks, and weeks into months and the only news of Skky's whereabouts was increasingly outrageous speculation from reporters. Dead air was filled with existing clips, photos, and commentary on his career.

Skky's already promising career had skyrocketed when he was twenty, took a quantum leap when he was twenty four, and by twenty six he'd reached dizzying heights of success. Somehow through it all he hadn't changed, he remained close to family and old friends and had never lost his sense of gratitude toward those who'd helped to put him where he was. He was still the same unaffected and charming boyo that'd he always been and his marriage to super model Lila Hanover hadn't changed the fact that he knew where his roots were.

They'd been photographed constantly since the engagement was announced and the wedding had been the usual dodge-and-misdirect-the-media circus common to those in the spotlight of public adoration. He kept his habit of tweeting once or twice a day about sometimes ordinary, sometimes newsworthy events in his life although he became increasingly guarded about giving away where he was at any particular time. It had all stopped. Just like that. No tweets. No more intermittent earthy and enthusiastic blogs. Even the ever so savvy and opportunistic paparazzi failed to snap a glimpse. After a couple of weeks serious questions began to be raised. His close friends and family still refused comment.

None of it was news to Cailín, yet she still watched and listened, hoping for some small clue to surface.

Brandon watched her with increasing concern, and found himself depressed as well as his attempts to distract her became less successful. At first it hadn't been difficult to coerce her into going to a movie, but he soon discovered that he had to be careful about the content or she would burst into tears. It wasn't long before any subject matter was a loaded gun.

He knew Kaylin functioned well enough at work, in fact those hours seemed to provide relief. One evening each week Brandon requested that they meet to go over portfolios in detail. More and more he noticed that she seemed more focused, even more relaxed, when they met at his place, so he began to request that frequently. If she knew why he was doing it, she didn't let on.

She didn't seem to be lacking sleep, and he assumed that Spéir could be thanked for that. Apparently Spéir hadn't, or couldn't, yield any information about Skky. Brandon felt certain that she would have shared that knowledge with him had there been any. He was relieved that her interest in cooking hadn't waned. She'd often tell him at the end of the work day not to make any plans for lunch as she would be bringing leftovers for both of them. Once in a while she'd show up with a new blouse or a pair of shoes, so he knew she'd been shopping and her love of hitting the sales for good quality items hadn't vanished.

She would mention something her grandmother had said now and then, leading him to believe that their weekly phone calls hadn't been interrupted. Mrs. Casey had come for weekend visits in March and again in May, and although he was always invited to visit and go places with them, he declined everything with the exception of a Saturday lunch. He knew those weekends were good for Kaylin, and even seemed to pick up her spirits for a few days following. Yet he felt somewhat ashamed that they also afforded him a needed break.

To someone that didn't know her as well as he did it would appear that nothing was wrong. He was relieved that she was taking care of the basics of life well enough, but he knew there were times when she broke down. He considered suggesting that she see a psychiatrist, but dismissed the idea quickly. Her reasons for not pursing professional help were the same as his – who was going to believe either of them, and what could they possibly do? Besides, he didn't think she was crazy although he was pretty sure he was by now.

Brandon was nearing the end of his rope early in July when he was approached by a total stranger with a plan that was so outrageous that it just might be the answer for both of them. He'd asked for, and was given, a month to decide.

* * *

By early July of 2014 even the ragged shards of hope Cailín possessed were disintegrating fast. Since Skky had disappeared six months ago the world had stopped the slow turn she'd felt since he married eighteen months ago. The first year had been rotten enough, although she'd tried to be happy for him. She told herself she *was* happy for him, she wanted everything for him. Now the constant yearning that had gripped her for the past nine years was threatening to suffocate her amidst the gnawing feeling that something was very, very wrong in his life.

Lila was cornered by a zealous reporter who'd used the almost never fail, if not marginally illegal, method of tracing her credit card. He'd stretched his expense account to the limit and boarded a plane to the Cayman Islands where he confronted an unenthusiastic, leggy young woman attempting to hide behind sunglasses and a huge straw hat.

"Lila!" he rushed her as she walked from the beach toward the luxury hotel. "Lila! Please? Ms. Hanover! Are you vacationing here with Skky?" Her answer was a snapped "none of your business", but her tone of voice and strained expression betrayed the fact that something was indeed wrong and she didn't know much more than the reporter himself.

The unproductive encounter had immediately escalated speculation in the media and Skky's father once again declined comment, heaping another layer of angst onto loyal fans.

It had been the last straw for her and the grief that she'd attempted to suppress for the past few months erupted in waves of anguish and despair. She cried herself to sleep that night with a silent Spéir wrapping his ethereal body around her.

Cailín awoke the next morning feeling like a bomb had exploded in her body. She stumbled into the bathroom and started the shower, but was shivering so hard she couldn't bring herself to take her pajamas off. She grabbed her sweatshirt and pants from the drawer, struggled to get them on over her pj's and crawled back into bed and pulled the covers around her. Spéir somehow generated enough heat to ease the shivering. She fumbled for her cell phone, "Gail, I have a bad cold, or flu, I won't be in today. I will, thanks."

It took what little energy she had to absorb what happened next. Spéir left, then reappeared instantly, and sat down on the edge of the bed, a glass of water in one hand, a bottle of ibuprofen in the other. "Here, lass, you need to drink this… and these," he shook the bottle, "I understand sometimes 'tis a help?"

"You amaze me," she said just before she sneezed. "Can you – can you open it for me?"

"Well, no surprise, ya know I can move stuff if I need to," he twisted the cap off and tapped two tablets into her shaking hand.

She gulped the tablets down, "I, yuh, yes, seem to recall."

He curled around her again, and in a minute or so she began to feel the warmth radiating from him.

"How do you do that? Make me warm?"

He chuckled softly, "Ya know, am nawt exactly sure, I just kinda think of it."

"Mm – huhh," she coughed. "Yeah, that explains it. Does it make you tired, drain your energy?"

"Noh, well, it used to, nawt so much anymore," she loved his voice, the full vowel sounds had always had a soothing effect on her. Besides, it was so Irish – and as she'd long ago learned, identical to Skky's voice.

"Spéir? Why is this happening?"

"Whawt?"

"Why can you come to me like this? And in the dreams?"

He was silent for a few seconds before replying, "'Why', 'tis easy, we belong to each other – I wawnted ya tew remember. 'How' – not so easy."

"Where do you go when you're not with me?"

"Dunno, to be honest. Can't remember much."

"Will you come for me when I die? Will it be you? Will you take me to Ireland forever?"

"Now, now lass," he gently scolded, "yer not gonna die, 'tis just a wee cold, be fine inna day or tew."

"I know – I just want to know if you'll come for me... I need to know." Half delirious with the fever, she wasn't really certain if they were having this conversation or not, or what it meant.

"Would do the same for me, wouldn't ya? I will, 'course I will."

"Of course I would, I promise – so you promise?"

"Promise," he whispered, and she fell asleep.

* * *

"Feeling better? I mean are you okay now? Seems like you had a rough couple of days." Brandon had insisted that they go out for lunch instead of staying in. He suspected the true cause of her illness hadn't been a cold, but he gave her the benefit of doubt. It didn't matter anyway, he just wanted to give her a chance to vent away from the ears of co-workers.

"I didn't ask for this, you know," she was close to tears, "any of it. I didn't ask – and I didn't make it up."

"I think it's more a matter of accepting."

"Accepting?"

"Yeah, accepting. I think tons of people have these, um, visions, ideas, whatever. But most people don't pay attention, or just dismiss it."

Cailín laughed a little too hard, "Dismiss? Dismiss? How is he even possible to dismiss?" she collapsed into a fit of giggles. "Like – like he could be dismissed. Or ignored. Or sent away, that's not even possible." She sobered and looked at Brandon as though he was crazy. "I don't think it's possible," she said flatly.

"Maybe not," he guessed he looked as guilty as he felt. "Dunno, Kay, maybe it's a combination of … you being open and accepting and he, uh, Spéir, or Skky, being so strong. Let's face it, he's stupid strong if he can appear when you're awake, and fling people and cars around. The car – who knows? I wish we could go back and get a security cam tape of the parking lot that day. But, throwing the guy across the room, I mean, people saw that. Anyway. I'm just trying to sort, to understand."

"It's not easy, harder I guess if you've never experienced it. Have you?"

"No, no I haven't. I have to say it again, though, I'm envious."

"Envious? Of an otherwise rational, logical person who just happens to have an imaginary playmate?"

"Thing is, Skky is very real. And yes, envious of something that strong, that – um – persistent."

"Bran, I do accept what's happened. I just can't accept the fact that I can't have him. He's in this world, and I can't reach him here. It's like being given a glimpse of heaven, then being told you can't stay. So what good is knowing?"

"Maybe more good than you know."

"Meaning?"

"Meaning there must be a reason for this. Or do you believe that the Universe just randomly taunts people?"

"Hope not." She tore at tiny pieces of the paper napkin in her lap. "Who knows? A reason?" she began to tear faster, more deliberately, then wadded it up in a ball. "It'd be nice."

"Kay, here's the thing," he propped his elbows on the table and laced his fingers as a resting place for his chin, "I might seriously be inclined to think you are nuts, except for one thing."

"Oh my God, what a relief!" She threw her hands up, "Pray tell, what *is* that one thing? I'm dying to know."

Brandon frowned, "Come on, you know what I mean."

She shrugged. "You know I can't stay mad at you, so go on, tell me."

"The fact that Spéir appeared first, and not least of all the letter that he dictated just before you saw Skky for the first time. You know, for me that's the kicker. What are the odds that this guy in your dreams is a dead ringer for someone you see later?"

Her chin quivered.

"Goddam. Sorry, very poor choice of words."

"Guess I should be used to it by now, and it's not your fault after all. Yeah, you have a point. If it had happened the other way around the explanation would be, well, relatively obvious. Easier to understand anyway."

74

"There has to be a solution, Kay, there just has to. Damned if I'm sure though. I'll think about it."

* * *

The day began with a quiet determination, much like any other day. Cailín allowed herself to savor the aroma of fresh coffee mingled with the shower steam.

Her carefully arranged closet held work clothes on the right. Black skirt, white blouse, black – no – red shoes today. She picked a red belt and scarf form the hooks on the back of the door. One last check that the coffee pot was unplugged and she grabbed her large thermos cup. Office coffee sucked.

She unplugged the coffee pot and like every other day, she walked back into her bedroom and stood in front of her favorite, a nearly life sized poster. Light gray eyes and blond hair filled her vision. She placed her fingers to her lips, then touched them to his.

"Come to me, Skky," she whispered, "please, Skky, please."

The July heat and humidity had already given rise to a primordial soup so thick that Cailín wondered if it was going to spontaneously spawn a version of Jurassic Park. She mouthed a silent 'thank you' to her little car for still having a working air conditioner. The oppressiveness was persistent though, and it amplified her undefined feeling that something was wrong. She was already dreading the short walk from her parking spot to the office building. She reached for the radio button, hoping for an upbeat song to distract her, but her fingers stopped just short. *Dammit, I know better than that…*

Ten minutes into the meeting the cogs slipped quietly, smoothly into place. No one else had spotted their most recent stock picks and she couldn't wait to tell Brandon. She hoped he had similar news. If he did, it was just a matter of timing and their next coup would be launched. She would determine how the latest fluctuations figured into the pattern they'd discovered and they'd plan the buy/sell cycle, then go through the motions the next couple of days trying to suppress the pins and needles and the anticipated rush of another win. By Friday they'd be golden.

"A couple more of these and we'll negotiate small offices – with doors!" Brandon whispered excitedly.

"Don't forget a raise. Maybe other perks, too," she returned.

1:00 p.m. came quickly enough. Cailín and Brandon exchanged just-shy-enough glances as she passed him in the lunchroom. Their ruse of calculated hints at a relationship that went beyond working together had successfully uncomplicated one aspect of the workplace.

She chose a seat near the TV and greeted the other girls who gathered to watch the celebrity news magazine.

"So what's it gonna be today," Cheri remarked, "another Beebs disaster, or who made the most politically incorrect tweet?"

"Probably both," Cailín laughed and pretended to be interested. It was the perfect cover, if there was any news whatsoever about Skky it would turn up on this show.

"… big sale at Morgan's Saturday, *but…*" Stacy paused for effect, "you can go Friday and ask them to hold things for you!"

"Oh yeah, I know," Tiffany was smug. "I do that all the time. See? I got these shoes last −"

The overly dramatic voice of the female host rose a few decibels, "… body on found the shore just this morning was feared to − " A stunning close up of Skky flashed onto the screen, "− missing music sensation Skky −".

The walls snapped sideways and the room went black. Brandon shot to her side and knelt down, "Kay! Kaylin, hey!" His arms were around her, pulling her to a sitting position. Stray words came into her awareness.

"Well, he should…"

"Pregnant, I bet."

"Shh! Don't jump to conclu –"

Brandon's voice next to her ear broke through the fray with an urgent whisper, "Not Skky, promise. They just said it's not."

"Open your eyes," he said out loud, "c'mon now, you're alright."

"Get me some juice, please," he said to one of the girls, "pretty sure it's her blood sugar. Probably skipped her mid morning snack, that would do it."

He held the glass for her, "that's it, you'll be better in a minute."

Cailín did as he said, realizing he was covering for her. She remembered his words and took a deep breath, "Oh, gosh – guys I'm sorry."

"Are you okay now?" Stacy seemed genuinely concerned, "Is the sugar working?"

"Definitely," she took another swallow of the juice, "much better."

"All the same, I'm going to see that she gets home. Jackie, if you'd let Ross know? I'll be back in an hour or so."

"I'm fine now," she smoothed her skirt and smiled into Brandon's glare, "but I'll take the afternoon off and go home."

"Right," he helped her to her feet, "let's go."

"What the goddam hell?" Brandon growled as he slid behind the wheel of her car. "Media whores."

"I'm so sorry, thanks for smoothing that over. I just – thanks. I can drive, really," Cailín babbled, "I'm okay, you don't have to … I thought, I thought it looked like they were saying…" She broke into sobs.

"I know," he rested his hand on her knee as he drove off, "I know."

"There's casserole in the fridge."

"Sounds good, thanks," Brandon busied himself with the microwave.

"What? Uh." She reluctantly took the plate from him.

"Kay, you need to eat. We don't want you passing out for…"

"For real? Right."

"This has to stop. It's taking over your life."

"Taking over? 'It' took over a long, long time ago, and he *is* my life, Skky is, and if he's gone, then…"

"You've got to refocus, you can't let −"

"What? I do fine at work, don't I? Of course I do. I do fine. And if I'm not mistaken, I've helped you a little bit. I've helped. We do fine."

"Look, don't be upset, I'm just, I'm worried, that's all. I don't really want to leave you alone. Can you – will you call your granny, or something? That might be good. Will you?"

"I might. Maybe later. She'll think something's wrong if I call when I'm normally at work. So tonight."

"I'm gonna stop by after work."

"You don't need to."

"I'll see you about six. Besides, I need your car to get back to work. If you want we'll discuss those stocks, make plans."

"Just leave the dishes. I'm gonna take a nap."

"Kay…"

"I'm fine. Yes, of course he's here. It'll help. Use your key."

"Well, probably do you good."

Brandon stopped just outside the door, looked down, and sighed. He was being pushed from both directions, although in different manners. He had a huge

79

decision to make, and he had to make it soon.   He was afraid he knew what it had to be.

* * *

Friday afternoon was a near carbon copy of many others, everyone marginally making a pretense of working. Cailín wasn't even trying when Brandon rounded the corner and jarred her from her reverie.

"Aw my god. Bran!" she withdrew her hand from the small picture of Skky in her desk drawer.

"Kay, honestly, what're you doing?"

"Honestly, I'm doing nothing, as you can see."

"Not exactly true, but what do I know?" he slumped into the chair at the side of her desk and glanced at Skky's picture. "Most girls would have a pic of their fiancé, boyfriend at least." He regretted that remark before he'd even completed it. This absolutely, positively, could not go on.

"Pfft," she winced, "I don't have either, so I'm using the 'love of my life' theory."

Brandon leaned forward, and lowered his voice, "I need to talk."

"Oh, honey, of course, what is it?"

"No, not about me, well sort of about me, but we need to talk. Not here. Definitely not here. Let's seriously ditch."

She had never seen that degree of urgency in her friend's eyes before. "Sure."

"Too funny. Like, way too funny," Brandon chortled from the back booth of a trendy Chicago bagel shop not a block from the towering glass office building.

"I know, right?" her mood had lightened with the relief of skipping out. "Let's have chicken salad on wheat. Early, early dinner, I'm hungry."

"Fun to just run out and do something you want to do. Ever wonder what it'd be like on a grander scale?"

She sobered a bit, "What do you mean?"

"You really love him, don't you?"

The dam broke. "I didn't ask for this, I know I've said that before, but" Cailín choked back a sob, "none of it. Or maybe I did. Wait... I think I did. Okay, so I did."

"Kay... what?"

"But I didn't make it up out of the clear blue. It just happened." She picked up a napkin and methodically began tearing it into little chunks, "In living, breathing color. Boom. Like that."

"You know the thing – here's the thing about you. I think everyone has access to information like that. You paid attention though. You accepted it, embraced it."

She laughed without mirth, "Yeah, like I could ignore it."

"You could have. You could have and it – he – would have gone away," he rested his chin in his palm, "but you didn't."

"No, I didn't. But that's how we do it, Bran. Every lifetime, that's how we do it. The dreams. They're how we begin to find each other, how we know, or remember. Oddly enough, it's taken me a while to realize that."

"Yes, I remember why you started the book, it all started with the dreams."

"Uh huh, except in the 1600's they didn't have television. I think that's an unfair advantage."

She leafed through the latest tabloid, acquired on the way to the bagel shop despite Brandon's protests. "It's too long, it's been too long."

Brandon Sykes looked nothing less than distressed himself as he viewed the downcast young woman sitting next to him. "Kay, honestly. Stop reading those rags." He snapped the tabloid from her hand. "You know it's just fabrication sprinkled with speculation. Just to sell copies, that's all. Bet his family knows, from what you've said about him he wouldn't leave them in the dark, they know where he is." He hoped that thought would cheer her a little.

"Yes. I would think they would. But – *what* is it that they know? Do they know that he went boating and never came back? Are they waiting until his body is found? Do they know…"

"Stop!" Brandon held up a manicured hand. "Don't do this, Kay. If he was dead, why would his family postpone any announcement? They would want to stop the speculation, closure at the very least. If they don't know anything, wouldn't they have everybody in the world out looking for him?"

"How do you know they don't?"

"He probably just wanted – needed – to disappear for a while."

"But why? He has everything going for him. If he wanted some time off, he could have just taken it. He was in a position to write his own ticket, he could have just…"

"Yes. Disappeared. It seems that's what he chose to do."

"But – was it really his choice? He must be in horrible pain to do this." She drew in a ragged breath. "He's not dead. I can't believe that, he's not, he can't be. Right now, just disappearing sounds good."

"Kay." Brandon said a bit too gently, "Kay, I'm going to need for you to listen closely. Let's talk about what we can do, but not here. Privately."

"Does it involve ladders or kidnappings?"

"No, that'd be too easy."

* * *

"No, no actually she chose me."

"I don't understand," Cailín retrieved the jar of sun tea from her four foot wide French balcony. She didn't use it much, but it was cool to have it there. For a third story the view wasn't bad, overlooking a strip of boutique shops.

At night it was interesting. The strings of teeny Christmas lights, all white, that lit up the shop windows at night year round, as well as the small trees that lined the parkway, were clichéd but the effect was cheerful. The shop windows were crammed with brightly colored offbeat articles of clothing common to boutiques. Baubles of turquoise, ruby, silver, and leather that were near throwbacks to the hippie generation were scattered with determination on the mannequins, on the floor, and on other props. Skky would like it, she thought.

The scene reminded her of the Medieval Festival. Maybe that's what her life had become – a series of bright and shiny dreams punctuated with trinkets that didn't exist in the real world. It was a carnival constructed of false fronts and illusions that were fleeting, unsubstantial.

"Could almost be offended, lass. If I believed that was how ya really felt, that is." She came close to answering Spéir out loud, but remembered Brandon's presence.

"Let me back up," Brandon rubbed his chin. "I think I got ahead of myself. We met at a party about a year ago, talked a lot, got on great really. Long story short, we got separated for a while and somehow she left and I didn't know until it was too late. I wish I had gotten her number, or at least offered her mine."

"So you were pretty smitten with her then?"

"Smitten?" Brandon laughed, "Who says that?"

"My granny does, so shut up."

"Gotcha. But yeah, she stayed on my mind."

"No! What's a thing like that like? But go on, go on."

"You should know. I did think about her a lot, wanted to kick myself. Anyway, a few weeks ago I get this strange phone call."

"Oh! So she found you?" Cailín picked up a blue flowered toss pillow, wrapped her arms around it, and settled in, prepared to be genuinely happy for her best friend.

"Not exactly. Sort of. It was this guy named Smithson on the phone. Said he had a sort of business deal, a proposal for me. Said it would require very little from me other than my permission."

"And a paid first class flight with a briefcase full of dope?"

"Huh. Exactly what crossed my mind. Turned out to be something stranger."

"Bran! Get to it! Dying here."

"For some reason the guy sounded, well, not like a crook or a nut case."

"Sure, the latter would be you."

"Hear me out?"

"I'm trying, I'm trying. Go."

"I agree to meet him for coffee. Public place, what could it hurt? She was with him. Talk about blown away."

She burrowed back into the sofa. "Wow, I guess."

"He, this Smithson guy, he says he knows I must be confused, have a million questions. Then he says he's come to ask for my help. I agree to come to his office with them, to talk in private."

"Bran, you're giving me chills. What the hell?"

"She, Sara, has advanced cancer. Seventy five years from now there will be a cure. Sara tells me that she wants to be there, to get the cure, but she doesn't want to be all alone."

"Wait – what?"

"They're going to send her to the future, Kay, where there is a cure."

"Um?"

"Sara tells me that she thinks we're very compatible, that she's seriously attracted to me, and is certain that she could be happy with me. And – they can 'regenerate' people from DNA. At this point I feel like I've swallowed that briefcase full of dope. Head's ready to explode."

"I'm not so sure it didn't."

"And at this point, Smithson says he needs a confidentiality agreement signed before he can tell me any more."

"You're kidding me. Bran, are you alright? Did something happen? Tell me, I'll help you somehow. A couple of good friends from university are out of law school now. And the rest – we'll work through it."

"Kay, I'm not crazy. I haven't lost my mind – I don't think."

"What? Bran? What did they want from you? This happened? This really happened?"

"Yes, it did, Kay. We agreed it would be good for us, Sara and me, to spend some time together. I took it was mainly to be sure that I was what she truly wanted. Kay, I've fallen in love with her."

"So... so what are you going to do? I don't understand. They're going to take her DNA and clone her seventy five years in the future so there will be a cure when she develops the same disease?"

"They wanted my DNA so they can regenerate me in the future. Meanwhile I – me now – I stay right where I am."

"So there's two of you running around? One seventy-five years from now? Ha. I guess if you live long enough, you could go to your own damned funeral? What?"

"Two hundred years at the least, seventy-five is too short, they think there's a small chance that someone might recognize us and they can't take that chance."

"Oh. Two hundred years? Fine. Now it all makes sense."

"They're not going to regenerate her from DNA. That'd mean she still dies here. Not only can they send DNA into the future, they can send people. They'll send her."

"What the fuck?" She slammed the glass of tea down on the coffee table and ignored the spill. "Okay, Bran, I don't think you're crazy, I think you're messing with me. What's the point here?"

"I didn't give them my DNA."

"Of course not, because you're not totally cray-cray."

"Who says 'cray-cray'?"

"Ellen."

"Kay, I'm going with her. I'm not shipping off my DNA, not even for a few hundred grand."

She stood and walked slowly toward the kitchen area, then turned toward him. She spoke slowly, "This has gone far enough. I don't think you're nuts, not entirely anyway, but I don't… I don't know why you're doing this to me."

"I'm sorry, I know, I know this sounds outrageous, but I swear I'm convinced. I'm in love with her, and I can't stay here knowing she's two hundred years in the future, and she's well, she's cured, but she's still alone. She's even said – what's the point of that? And me. I'm without her forever.

"Forgive me, please, I had to talk to someone. I couldn't think of anyone else that might understand, maybe even support me."

"So you're saying that you're going to just take off?"

"Something like that. I'll put in notice at work, say I'm moving to Alaska, I don't know. I have a little time to formulate that."

"You're good, Bran. You're good. You make the whole thing almost sound like it could have happened."

"But it did, it is."

"Uh-uh, no you don't. This is the part where I bust your story wide open. You said you signed their agreement, so if you tell anyone it's over."

"That's right."

"Well then you can't possibly go now. Because you just told *me*. Game over."

"That would be true, except – "

"No!" She threw her arms in the air and pointed upward, "Huge 'game over' sign. Flashing. See?"

"The reason I'm telling you –"

"Stop! Stop it, Bran. This is crazy and I need you to leave."

"They're offering to talk to you."

"Get out!" She took a couple of steps backward. "I mean it. Why should I listen to this?"

"Because they can give you Skky."

* * *

There was no time for errands and chores; those would have to be caught up during the week. Cailín strolled aimlessly from one quaint shop to another. The small burg was more of a stopover than a stay over, but the cabin court with half a dozen single units had appealed to her and left no reason to drive beyond the two hours she'd spent on the offbeat two lane.

She sat in the small café, 'Maybelle Lee's', and suddenly found her appetite when the homemade chicken salad and steaming potato soup appeared.

"You just passin' through town, honey, or come here to do some annteekin'?" Maybelle was a classic, somewhere between a Norman Rockwell and American Gothic.

"Oh, I, well I was passing through, but decided to stay the night and look around. It's so peaceful here. And yes, I will have fun looking through all the shops."

"Jist a little getaway, a little thinkin' time."

She smiled, the woman was pleasant but she didn't really feel like talking. "Something like that."

"Mmm hmm, boy trouble. Your young man actin' up is he? More 'n likely jist can't kuh-wy-tuh move off the mark?"

"Not exactly." Cailín was a little annoyed in spite of herself; the woman meant no harm.

"Now don't you worry, honey, before you know it that boy will be down on one knee, and you can take that to the bank! Your aunt Maybelle knows these things, just ask anybody 'round here. Aunt Maybelle knows things."

She allowed herself to get caught up in the fantasy. "You think so?" she smiled.

"Ohh yes, I get these feelin's you know. I'm mostly right, mostly always right. You ever jist git a feelin' 'bout somethin'? 'Sides, purty little thing like you? Some lucky fella gotta be jist waitin' on pins and needles. When you go to him, you'll see," she waved an authoritative finger. "You'll see."

"What?"

"Trust aunt Maybelle, young 'un, she knows. Sure she does." Amidst a soft, self-satisfied laugh the jolly matron strolled off, seemingly lost in her own thoughts.

She wondered if aunt Maybelle would give up the secret to her potato soup, it was superb.

Mrs. Stone reached into the pocket of her crisp white apron and unlocked the door. "No phone hookups anymore. You carry a cell phone like most folks?"

"Oh yes, I'll be fine," Cailín assured.

"Anything you need then, honey? Feels like rain comin' in, might turn cool. Matches right here in this drawer." She gestured toward the small gas heater.

"Thank you, I'll probably be under the covers before long anyway."

She fished around in her duffel bag and arranged things for a quick morning shower. Rain began to plink softly on the roof. The flowered coverlet and overabundance of pillows on the daybed beckoned. She wondered how long she would be alone.

She clicked on the small old fashioned radio and turned the lamp off. Pale light from the courtyard lamp reflected sapphire rivulets inching down the window screen. Perfect weather for sleeping, as her grandmother would say. She wondered if it was raining in Ireland, and if he was there to see it, or if he was – anywhere at all.

His honey voice was right on que. She wondered if she turned the radio off if the song would continue. Of course it would, if he wanted it to.

In the distance his guitar sang in tune with him, evoking a melancholy plea that was somehow undefeated, and tentatively held onto a hope: This is how it used to be, this is how it could be again.

The disembodied wail of a distant train whistle interrupted the song for a moment. *Why does it sound so lonely? Is it because it makes you think of someone leaving? Someone moving on without you... And how does he do that? The timing is impeccable.*

His voice was in stereo now, coming from the radio and... She turned away from the window.

"Room for me, is there then?" He was transparent in every sense.

She stared at Spéir and pulled back the coverlet and patted the mattress beside her.

He complied and used his energy to replace it, although his apparition was still completely visible in spite of it. A shimmer of pale light surrounded him.

"Comin' for me are ye then, lass?" he whispered. This was the first time he'd mentioned anything even remotely connected to the possibility.

She felt warmth from his body, though she still thought it was physically impossible. He curled around her and Cailín fell asleep quickly. In her dreams she felt him, in her dreams he was solid.

* * *

She couldn't resist. Early Sunday afternoon Cailín returned to Maybelle's.

"Well, now, stoppin' by for some fortification before your drive? You come to the right place, I got a passel of fried chicken just hot off the stove. Mashed taters, too. Best gravy you ever had. I'll go fix a plate."

"No, wait. I mean – that sounds wonderful, but I really want some more of your potato soup! If there's any?" Upon second consideration, she hoped she could decipher the subtle ingredients.

"You kiddin' me? It's a staple 'round here. Comin' right up, honey."

She ate slowly, thoughtfully, trying to figure it out. "Aunt Maybelle?" might as well try... "Aunt Maybelle, I know this is a lot to ask, but, well, my young man is extremely fond of potato soup. There's something in your soup that I can't quite place. I was wondering..."

"Honey," her tone was hushed, conspiratorial, as she put her hand on Cailín's arm, glancing around at the dozen or so other diners, "not a man alive can resist my recipe. I'll write it out for you, neat as you please." Maybelle leaned closer, spoke more quietly still, "Now you got to realize, this is top secret. Once you get home I want you to memorize it and tear the paper up in teeny pieces. I don't give this to many."

"I will, I'll do that." She beamed and placed her own hand over her mentor's. "Thank you! Thank you so much."

Ten minutes later, Maybelle wove past her other customers and with a wink placed a neatly printed ticket on the table.

```
Soup    3.30
Iced tea  .85
Tax      .21
Total   4.36
```

Thank you!
COME AGAIN

Underneath the ticket was a neatly folded square of paper. Cailín found herself looking around to see if anyone was watching and quickly slid the square into a pocket of her jacket. She placed a twenty dollar bill on the table and exchanged a knowing smile with Maybelle as she left.

"Kay, hi. I'm just about to leave. Racquetball with Mac and Tony, hopefully pick up a fourth." Brandon sounded normal.

"I just wanted to touch base."

"Meaning you want to know if I'm wearing an aluminum foil hat," he laughed, "or sitting on top of the Sears Tower with an assault weapon. Well, come to think of it, that wouldn't be practical, but all the same "

"I'm sorry, really sorry, Bran, its crazy, but I don't think you're crazy. It's just a lot to absorb, you know?"

"Believe me, I do know. Boy, do I know. But I love her, Kay, and that's the main thing. I'm happy. I just wanted to share it – give you the chance, maybe."

"So, your telling me, that's not going to throw you out, is it?"

"No. They're pretty sure you're not going to tell anyone. I think I convinced them well enough, or they wouldn't have given me permission."

"Hmm, well… I'll miss you. Oh hell."

"It wouldn't hurt to talk to them. Just talk, Kay. No obligation except for signing the confidentiality agreement if you want to hear them out. You can walk out at any time, they'll tell you."

"Seventy-two hours?"

"Less now, a little over twenty-four. It would be 4:00 p.m. Monday. You can call any time, day or night, until then."

"And after that?"

"The number will be deactivated without a trace, as I understand."

"That's a little cloak and dagger, don't you think? Night time TV FBI soap opera written all over it. I mean, does nothing about this raise big flaming red flags to you, Bran? Honestly?"

"Not so much, oddly enough. The technology really isn't such a stretch. Fantastic to us, yeah, but think how far things have come just in our lifetime. And what would they have to gain? I'm not rich, not even close in terms of the risk to them. And this isn't something that's ready – if it ever would be – to be mainstreamed. Can you imagine? It was to be on a limited case by case basis. They have to feel like there's a good reason, a real need, and an excellent chance of success. Like, I don't know, a sincerity."

"And you convinced them I had that?"

"Not quite that simple. Just like you they can back out, they can call it quits. But they are open to talk to you, so I guess I did okay."

"By 4:00 p.m. Monday?"

"Nothing to lose by just talking."

"Except my mind. Which is a done deal anyway." With no warning she began to sob. "Bran, you're not – you wouldn't do this to me, let me think there was some way –"

"Think about this, it's not just for you, it's for him, too. Look, enjoy your weekend. Relax. Then if it feels right, just talk to them."

* * *

It was one of those times, one of those places. It's that place that we've all been, whether recognized or not. The air was still, but not stifling. A five degree rise of the mercury and it could have been called a warm day. Five degrees less and you might perceive a chill. So delicate was the balance that a butterfly wing could change everything. Cailín recognized it that afternoon in the middle of rural Illinois.

"They're simply wonderful, aren't they? Spoil them rotten, fill them with sugar, and send them home to their parents."

"Grandchildren are such a joy!" The second woman answered the tidy, homespun woman behind the counter of the small five and dime. She became suddenly aware that her life was a world apart from theirs though they stood separated by a few short yards. *Someday*, she thought, *someday I'll overhear my children's grandmother having a similar conversation.*

The slanted rays of the sun blended, floating effortlessly through the windows. The generously stocked shelves were lined with trinkets and necessities, in no particular order. The pattern on a silver box that held toothpaste sat next to a box of playing cards and broke shards of light into tiny glittering prisms.

Filtered gold washed the room in a monochrome, freezing the moment in time. Her world had halted in soft focus and she felt that it need not ever move again if Skky was not in it. Cailín felt she could stand here forever, never reaching the point in life that the two older women shared. She would be all right, she would be fine. But that was all.

"You know," the first woman's voice came into her awareness again, her words coming from a world away, "just the other day, my Billy…" her voice trailed off into the ether.

She scanned the objects on the shelves for an answer, for a clue to bridge the gap. A gaudy but oddly endearing porcelain leprechaun winked as he stood next to a pot of gold. A rainbow perched above his head. She plucked the trinket from the shelf and walked with determination to the front counter. Tiny primitive lettering scrawled across the base of the figurine, "Make Your Own Luck," the words advised.

Deep within her mind she pushed a gate open and ran through it. Her decision was made, and the world shifted on its axis and began to move again.

* * *

TWO

"No, no. Thanks. I'll be fine, it's just a virus or something." Cailín shifted from one foot to the other, took a deep breath, shrugged, and snapped her cell phone shut.

Eleven thirty-five a.m. She slapped her palm over her watch and willed it to turn back. She was five minutes late, and it could change her life. She tugged at her skirt, then smoothed it. Her hand went to the back of her neck. She bit her lip. Somehow it felt right though, somehow it was going to be right.

FUTURE CONNECT

A Personal Development Organization

No Admittance Without Appointment

Thank You

The cold steel of the doorknob was solid, expected. The heavy door swung open easily.

"Uh. Hi. I'm Kaylin…"

The pretty blond with just enough strawberry lipstick stood and smiled. "Kaylin Casey. Please, come in. I'm Gina. This way."

She nodded and followed Gina to a large, plain wooden door, the only other in the sparsely furnished room. She drew in her breath sharply, the six foot square room held the only thing she hated more than small enclosed rooms – one that moved. The doors were open, beckoning them away from the nondescript wallpaper and utilitarian carpet.

"I don't really care for them either," Gina offered, "but they *are* efficient, sometimes necessary. You won't mind, will you? It'll only be seconds."

Cailín wondered how small she could make herself. "No – er, well not normally, not that much I guess." She was grateful for the mirrored wall that made the elevator seem larger. The seven story trip she took several times a day at work had become routine, almost bearable. There were usually five or six other people along for the ride. It was the only time she welcomed idle chatter and now and then someone would remark how they hated 'these things' confirming that she wasn't the only one.

"Nearly there!" Gina's voiced dragged her back into the moment. Cailín glanced at the panel as the light blinked '2' on the way from 5 to 1. She tried to swallow and couldn't – they were travelling downward. She had taken two flights of stairs up to find the suite number, now they must be three levels underground! Mercifully the doors parted to reveal a pleasantly large space. The room was flanked with two glass enclosed offices at each end. Carved double doors lay straight ahead.

"I'll introduce you to our director who will assist you along the way. Would you like anything? Water?"

She shook her head.

"Right over here." Gina walked elegantly in her high heels; Cailín hoped she didn't fall off hers. Another richly carved door, one of several at the beginning of a hallway, bore a gold nameplate:

Alexander Smithson
Director

His impeccable tweed jacket and vest gave the impression that he should be rotund, though he wasn't. He was barely her height.

"Please, do come in, Miss Casey," he said with all the aplomb of an English butler without the detachment. "I've been looking forward to our meeting. Please choose a seat, won't you?"

I'm trapped underground with complete strangers and if they're going to do something horrible to me, I have no one but myself to blame. Her thoughts threatened to run away with her, but she saved herself by remembering that Brandon had been here and was apparently unharmed.

"Allow me to tell you a bit of what to expect." Smithson could have been a mature thirty-five, or a well kept fifty-five. His steady voice offered no clue. "Firstly, if at any time you wish to leave, Gina will be along quickly to escort you. I must say that if you so choose, the process is irrevocably terminated. Fair enough?"

She glanced around the room, her eyes resting on an eight by ten frame that held needlepoint letters, but was otherwise unembellished. Still, it seemed incongruous in the otherwise tailored surroundings, until she read it:

> What was changed yesterday
> Has already changed tomorrow
> Such is the nature of reality

"Yes. I... yes, Mr. Smithson."

"Very well then. I'd prefer you call me Alec, and I'd like to address you as 'Kaylin', if I may?" His lighthearted warmth was reassuring.

"All right."

"I would like to chat with you a bit if I may, then there will be some preliminary paperwork, initially not burdensome at all, I assure you. Then, we shall join others for one of my favorite activities – a delightful lunch.

"Kaylin," he leaned forward a bit, "Please understand that I – all of us – do realize that this process is not an everyday occurrence. You're no doubt wondering what you've gotten yourself into."

Cailín remained poised on the edge of the chair.

"I'm sure you must have many, many questions. If you will grace us with a little patience we should be able to further your understanding. And get you out of here by four o'clock, four thirty at the latest. Beating rush hour, always a bonus." Smithson glanced down at the notebook on his desk.

She sank back into the oversized chair and took a breath.

"Of course, you must realize, due to the nature of the, em, process, there will be a myriad of questions put to you as well. Most of those will come from our psychologist, Dr. Logan. There are the rights of others to protect, not the least of which concern the well being of your Chosen. For you, and for him, to have the best possibility of future happiness – well, now that's why we're here after all, isn't it?"

"Will he ... will he be the same?"

"There are few, if any, guarantees in life, but I can promise you that your Chosen will be exactly, precisely himself."

Alec Smithson sat his tray down on the oval table and stepped gingerly behind Cailín to secure her chair. Realist paintings of outdoor scenes carefully placed around the dining room nearly made her forget that she was underground. Soft music, a piece that she didn't recognize, added to her relaxation. *Yes*, she thought, *these people are engineers. Of something.*

"Let me take that for you." Gina snapped up the empty tray, "I know where to stash it. I've been to this joint a time or two."

"Kaylin, I'd like you to meet Nick Logan. Dr. Logan is our resident psychologist."

Logan was tall, his dark hair and clear blue eyes were handsomely in contrast. "A pleasure. How are you, Kay? We'll be meeting privately after lunch, that is if you should decide to stay."

They certainly offered enough openings to jump ship. Cailín supposed the reassurance was planned, nevertheless it served to steel her resolve to stay.

"So sorry to bother you with this at mealtime, but as you have come thus far, it is necessary." Smithson produced a single sheet of paper and a pen.

The computer document consisted of a few sentences that simply elicited her promise to never speak of Future Connect with anyone not directly associated with the organization. She signed immediately. Who would ever believe her anyway?

"We're all just like you. Most people want the same thing, deep down." Gina's hand rested for a brief second on Cailín's. "Try to think of us as friends – or at least as people who also have hopes and dreams and so have some understanding of yours. The only thing unusual about us is that we have a way to increase the odds of making those dreams come true."

"Well spoken, Gina," Smithson dabbed the corner of his mouth with the linen napkin. His gaze shifted to a tall, older man in a white lab coat bursting through the door.

"Apologies for being late... research. I'm Dr. Benson," he extended a steady hand, "one of two medical doctors on staff, the other being employed only on the off chance that someone requests a second opinion." A slight twinkle in his brown eyes was counter to his serious tone. A sprinkle of friendly laughter echoed briefly around the table.

"I was wondering when the men in white coats were going to show." She instantly regretted the remark and feared they might terminate her chances right then and there. Instead, the laughter redoubled and she drew a sigh of relief.

"There, you see," Smithson chimed in, "we do take our work seriously, I assure you. Not so much ourselves."

Logan leaned slightly in her direction, "Something I believe it might help to know, one of us has been through this process personally".

"Happily so!" Smithson added.

"And I'm going in two months! I can *not* wait!" Gina was effusive, nearly jumping out of her chair.

"Indeed, yes. We're very happy for her," Smithson beamed in Gina's direction.

"I have no need, though if I did I wouldn't hesitate." Dr. Benson was matter of fact.

Smithson added, "You see, Gina was very correct when she indicated that we are much like you."

"Yep," Logan eased back in his chair. "Been there, done that," with a grin he added, "remind me again why we don't get to wear the t-shirt?" This time Cailín joined the laughter as a co-conspirator.

"Shall we proceed?" Smithson was the very definition of 'chipper'. "There are several appointments scheduled for this afternoon with various department heads. Should answer many of your questions to sufficient satisfaction, for the time being at least."

"Yes, well... could I have a few minutes with you first?"

"Of course, my dear, of course." His cheer dampened instantly. She felt that he was fond of keeping things on that schedule of his. As he was obviously the mastermind and director of the operation, he seemed the logical choice to answer her concerns.

He closed the door behind them.

"What about money? How much does this all cost?"

"I see I've been remiss in discussing finances. There will be paperwork to list your assets. However, might you give me an overview?"

"The short version is – I doubt I can afford this."

"Now, now. Give me some idea."

"I have my condominium.. It's been a good investment given that I bought it less than a year ago. There's an outstanding mortgage, of course, but I got it at a great price and have at least a twenty thousand dollar equity in it already. I'm very happy about that, but I can't see it being enough to finance an operation as – extensive – as this."

"What else, go on please?" His countenance had returned to its usual pleasantness, he didn't register concern, nor did he write anything down.

"Mmm, there's my car, paid for, hopefully still worth five thousand. Thirty five hundred in savings, not impressive, but I've been working on it. Two thousand in my retirement fund. The company doesn't kick in anything extra the first two years. The rest is negligible, furniture, TV, computer, clothes. I don't think those things would liquidate for any significant amount. So, my net worth is thirty thousand at the most."

"Not shabby at all, for someone your age."

"No, I suppose not, but –"

"Well, let's see, definitely twenty thousand at a minimum, anything over that – all to the good."

"I can't count on selling the condo quickly, not for the right price anyway."

"No matter, there's time for that."

"There is?"

"Nearly all the time in the world. Allow me to explain. You'll need to begin to think of things in much different terms from now on. There will be documents for you to sign prior to leaving; those will transfer all of your assets to our organization. Our crackerjack legal department will handle that and explain it to you. It's rather complicated, the assets are transferred to a holding company, a dummy corporation if you will. It's all rather circuitous, all designed not to leave a paper trail that would draw undue attention."

"All right, I can understand that. I still don't see how you could accomplish all this with a mere twenty to thirty thousand dollars. It's not making sense. This space alone, not to mention salaries of your staff, and the…"

"You *will* need to begin to think in different terms, and now would be a good time to start. You are employed by a large investment company, I'm certain you're familiar with compound interest as well as the benefits of fortunate investments."

"Yes, but…"

"Consider one aspect alone, compound interest over three hundred years!"

"Oh, uh, oh my!" Cailín suddenly felt incredibly wealthy. "There's inflation to consider though."

"That's where the 'fortunate investments' come in."

"Oh gosh! For an organization with knowledge from the future!" She began to laugh. "Forgive me, but no wonder the paperwork is 'circuitous'. There must also be a way for you to transfer knowledge and assets, from 'there' back to – now."

"One would have to assume such, wouldn't they? Although one would not speak of it." Smithson sat back in his chair, laced fingers resting at his waist, and appeared very self-satisfied. The young lady was smart, and willing. With very little prompting, she had written the script for him.

* * *

"Seems too good to be true, doesn't it?" Nick Logan, PhD. gestured toward an oversized chair and sprawled his six foot frame into one at a right angle to it. "Please, be comfortable, kick off your shoes, whatever." His easy smile allowed her to take a deep breath. Logan could be a model for one of those magazines filled with ads for pricey attire, his looks were a little edgy, intense like that.

"It does. Honestly." She took his offer and slid her shoes off, curled her legs up and scooted to the back of the too wide chair. "It does, except for, well, whatever has happened to Skky here and now." Her gaze rested on him a little too long, for the first time she became aware of the gold band on his left hand. "You, uh you said you've been through the process?"

"I have, and am extremely happy. More than that, I'm sorry, I can't give details. I'd do it again in a heartbeat." He straightened and leaned forward slightly. "I also know that there are questions and concerns on both sides. What are yours?"

"What if it doesn't work out?"

"Out of four hundred eighty four instances, ninety seven percent have been successful. Due in large part, I'd say, to our tedious screening process. And no, we've never lost a body."

"But what happens to the others? I mean, there you are and…"

"Reassignment is possible, and thus far has also been successful."

"I can't imagine. But if it isn't?"

"In an extreme case, yes, it would possible to reintegrate a traveler into his or her previous circumstances. Details as precise as the other processes involved have been given immense consideration. It hasn't happened as yet, and we don't actually foresee a necessity. But, bases are covered."

"Oh."

"Don't over think the possibility of failure," Logan advised. "Attitude is everything. Doubts are understandable. Frankly we'd be worried if you had none." He gazed at the ceiling for a few seconds, as though searching for the right metaphor. "Consider this, once you're there, once you've arrived, and especially after you've met your Chosen – that in itself is so fantastic that it tends to suspend, if not obliterate, any other concerns."

Cailín laughed, "Yeah, I imagine at that point you'd believe anything was possible."

"Exactly. The final phase, the actual move, is so incredibly short. And of course you'll be asleep, so it will seem to have happened instantaneously. The weeks leading up to it tend to seem like forever to most people, but we're here to help you through that time in every way possible. I'll give you a number that you can call at anytime."

"That's... good."

"There's a lot of ground to cover." Logan sat back and laced his fingers. "Tell me why – what's so special, out of all the men on earth, about Skky O'Keeffe?"

If it had been strictly up to Nick Logan, the interview would have ended right then and there. Her eyes softened and the smile that she couldn't suppress at the mere mention of his name said it all.

Cailín sat up straighter. "He's fourteen one minute, and forty the next. He always seemed happy, and that was contagious. It's hard to imagine you could be in a room with him and not feel it. He's talented, obviously, well, obvious to me and I guess a few hundred thousand other people. His voice is rich, but the accent! The greatest thing! Just the greatest – he doesn't lose the accent when he sings! Gosh the Irish accent – he sounds like home. How could he not sound like home to a girl with Irish blood? He's capable of incredible focus, it seems to me anyway, yes, it'd have to be focus. He's always completely *present* in the moment, whatever he's doing.

"You know how when the Beatles sang, there wasn't really much of the British accent there? Sorry, are you familiar with the Beatles? I mean, I'm sure you've heard their songs, but if you've heard them in interviews…"

"Yes," Logan smiled, it certainly was no challenge to get her to open up about her feelings for Skky, "I can't say I'd ever really thought about that, but yes, for the most part, if you'd only heard them sing it might not be completely obvious that they were British."

"Exactly! But hearing Skky sing, you know, there's no mistaking it. I think the Irish blood must be thicker than English," she laughed. "And that's only a part of his genuineness. He stayed grounded; he even credits his family for that. They're such an important part of his life, grandmothers, aunts, cousins, and all. Old friends, too. It's like, you know, he's always connected to where he came from, he never lost that. He's so kind. He just has this – beautiful, bright spirit. How am I doing so far?"

Logan laughed, "Fine, fine. Remember, there are no wrong answers. I do find it interesting that you are talking about the, uh, his essence. Meaning your description isn't superficial."

"Oh? Am I supposed to say that he's gorgeous and he's rich? He is. He's gorgeous. Maybe he's not to absolutely everyone, quite a few though, I know. But, yeah, to me he's gorgeous. He's not perfect, I'm aware of that, but even his imperfections are perfect, you know? It's like he was made for my eyes.

"He doesn't always have the best taste in clothes. It's a guy thing maybe, to an extent. I mean, you can always tell when he's wearing what's been picked out for him, and when he's just grabbed something out of his closet or suitcase. It's funny; he looks good in anything, in his own way. It's his face, his smile. Maybe it's a good thing, because when he's dressed in things that truly suit him, that really bring out the best, it's completely killer. Unfair even. I think maybe the world just couldn't handle him being dressed at his absolute best all the time. It'd be overload. Sheesh, it is anyway."

"Describe him in one word."

"Only one? " Cailín didn't hesitate, "Exquisite."

* * *

This should be interesting. Cailín wondered if the meeting would be a waste of time. After all, what could he really tell her? She was going to go 'poof' and wake up in 2314. End of explanation. Anything beyond that was classified.

Is it coincidence that all of the men involved in this project are attractive? What's the probability of that in math or scientific terms? Varen Whitaker was better suited to the pages of GQ than he was to a lab coat.

"I apologize for keeping you waiting." His smile was genuine as he eased into the leather chair. He leaned forward and folded his hands together on the desktop. "I'm sure you have questions."

"It's only been a minute or two, no apology necessary."

"I've been looking forward to our meeting, I've –"

"Heard a lot about me?" She laughed. "It's alright, I understand. The next lovelorn wannabe traveler enters the equation."

He sat back. "Actually I'm intrigued by your reported interests in quantum mechanics and physics."

"Superficial compared to your knowledge, I'm sure."

"Maybe not." He measured his response. "Maybe not at all. Concepts are concepts. Long mathematical formulas can support or disprove theories, but more often than not they raise more questions. A proven result is the only thing that is empirical."

"The proof of the pudding, seeing is believing, can't argue with success, and any other cliché that can be named."

"Basically, yes," he registered amusement. "So let's start with what you know."

"About time travel? Nothing, other than it makes a good read on the beach."

"Let's start with concepts that you've read about, ones that interest you. Maybe we'll happen onto something."

"Talk about not knowing where to begin. Time travel?"

"By that you mean the nature and mechanics of time."

This guy is good, she thought. "If that earns a passing grade, then yes. But yeah, those aspects can't be separated, can they?"

"You want to know what I can tell you."

"I guess. Although I'm not sure it even matters. All that matters is that it works."

"Results."

"Yes."

"Of course. Surely you must have questions, a curiosity."

"Oh. I get it. Without a question there can be no answer."

"I might be tempted to say that was a philosophical statement, but when it comes to quantum theory the lines blur," Whitaker stated evenly.

"They do, don't they?" Cailín was enjoying this.

"But in a cohesive universe concepts interrelate. What purpose is there to consciousness unless there's something to be conscious of? Would consciousness even be able to exist?" He was beginning to sound like 'Professor Whittaker' now.

"I'd have to say it wouldn't, but because of its duplicitous nature maybe it could by observing itself?" she offered.

"Meaning nonexistence absent counter, or co-observation, yet viable if consciousness relates back to itself."

"I see what you're saying, since the act of observation influences quantum or sub-atomic particles."

"I believe that might answer a potential question."

"Mm, I almost wish I could be awake during the process. And really, why is that not possible? Would I change the outcome by observing?"

"Essentially, yes. We believe it would alter circumstances a great deal. In fact we believe that so strongly we feel it would be an irresponsible risk."

"I don't quite see why. As an observer I'd be pulling for a positive outcome."

"You would be bombarded with such an overabundance of information there would be no time for your physical brain to process it and react."

"You've got me there. I've spent hours staring at the wall over the Heisenberg Uncertainty Principle and what it implies, not to mention the duplicity of waves and particles."

"Then it must follow, philosophically at least, that you would fail miserably as a stand-in for Schroedinger's cat?"

"Maybe not, I firmly believe not only that the cat knew what would happen all along, but influenced a positive outcome."

* * *

"Hossah!" The players of Ye New Medieval Theatre were out in full force and regalia. Cailín remembered the dust up reported on the local news last Fall, Ye Olde Medieval Theatre Players had a "falling out regarding creative differences" with their elected officers that had resulted in all the players, sans four officers, regrouping and subsequently renaming themselves. She thought she might have recognized the buxom middle aged woman that flounced towards them as being one of the more vocal in the group shot, standing directly behind the unflappable local reporter, shaking her fists and yelling.

Now the woman snatched Brandon's arm, nearly putting him off balance. "Wellll, well deary, aren't ye a fine one?" Brandon blushed, but not as mightily as the perfectly round painted circles of bright pink on the woman's face. She gathered up a handful of her full skirts as she yanked him down the entry path. "Aye! I fear I must be stealin' ye from the young lady. Younger ladies are not wise in the ways of the world, you see." She flashed a theatrical wink at him, her long, wildly tumbled hair exhibiting a life of its own.

Cailín laughed hysterically as he stammered, "Well, uh, just here with my friend…"

"What! You'll be away with me, spendin' a gold coin, for – hmm, I'd be thinkin' two or three minutes of my time would do it?" The woman's eyes grew round as she tilted her head in mock seriousness.

She was doubled over now, of no help whatsoever. Brandon rallied and offered a grin, "I brought me own wench, and heaven help me," he made a grand sweeping gesture with his free arm, "she's made away with all me gold already!"

"Oh fie! 'Tis true, a fool and his money, and such a skinny waif at that!" The woman whirled and skipped away, having her next prey already firmly in sight.

Brandon and Cailín linked arms and half staggered down the sawdust path further into the park. After a few steps he found his voice, "Do you suppose they just pick the ones they think will go along with it?"

"Years of practice sizing people up. But what do you suppose they do the rest of the year?"

Swirls of color surrounded them. Adult players in jewel toned royal costumes strutted and strolled and gave an occasional condescending wave to their subjects. Young men sporting tights and tunics, most with long hair tied back, cavorted in the thoroughfares entreating guests to attend jousting events or visit merchants. They ran into one another, pushing and shoving, followed by a mock fight complete with gymnastics to be broken up by one of the buxom women.

"Mm my gosh, doesn't everything taste better outdoors?" She took another bite of the turkey leg, eyeing the ear of corn sitting precariously on her knee.

"Not sure, I somehow think that brussel sprouts..." Brandon's remark was drowned out by the laughter of half a dozen grade school aged girls with ribbons in their hair and flowers painted on their faces as they ran past. Wings fashioned of net in every shade of pastel graced their small shoulders, and more of it circled their waists. A wandering minstrel paused his strumming and humming long enough to find a wooden bench and began a more structured tune. The tiny fairies flew toward him, skipping and jumping more or less in time with the music.

"Where did you go?"

"Whuhh...? Oh, somewhere in Ireland three or four hundred years ago, give or take." Cailín glanced around at the brightly painted 'buildings', some painted at the base to resemble stones, others with a second story façade, all transparently incomplete structures when viewed from any angle but straight on.

"Funny how the illusion is so easy to get lost in, how easy to block the chunks of reality that don't fit it," Brandon sighed. "Scary."

"Is that what we're doing, Bran? Are we seeing only what we want to see because we want so desperately for it to be real? What're we overlooking?"

"I'm not sure. The science involved, technology, whatever... that honestly is, well, logically believable. It's like, you know, the government doesn't tell us everything either." He laughed, "Like Area Fifty-One, call me Muldar, whatever, I want to believe."

"This isn't the government, though – didn't you say you believe it's confined to the private sector, a very small tight knit group? So I have to wonder – aren't they taking a terrible risk, letting us in on the knowledge, then letting us walk out the door until the time comes?"

"You'd think," Brandon shrugged, "hmm, but if they do have the technology... then who's to say they don't have the technology to wipe any association out of our brains? Remotely, even. Just zap us with a laser, whatever, bam! That part of our memory is toast."

"Yeah. I think it's more like I first thought... and by the way, meanwhile they pick up and leave the suite of offices without a trace. But like I first thought..."

"What's that?"

"Most people thought Muldar was just nuts. Even his colleagues. Even Scully mostly. Potential to come off like a major nutcase, if nothing else, would probably keep us from going to the news media."

"Might as well get a toy flying saucer and make a video?"

"We'd probably get farther with that. I'm almost surprised we haven't tried it. They've got us there. They know if we want to back out that we wouldn't do anything to unravel our lives here and now. But in the final analysis, maybe it's the money that makes it real, believable."

"Oh. Yeah, 'cause they couldn't pull off the technology, and everything else involved, without financial backing."

"Right, and since all they ask is that we sign over everything which, let's face it, isn't anywhere near enough, then the growth over a couple hundred years, and the ability to transfer funds, well, backwards, has to be real. It has to."

Oh, boyo. Spéir was lounging on a tree limb nearly fifty feet away, but it was unmistakably him, one leg dangling, and the other bent at his knee bracing him as he leaned back against the trunk.   Dressed in his three-hundred-years-ago clothing he didn't look out of place at all in this setting, not that anyone else could see him, Cailín reminded herself.

"Bran?"

"Uh huh?"

"Do you think there's, um, such a thing as a multiverse?"

"You mean like parallel universes?"

"Sort of."

"Oh, no, this is one of those quantum mechanics type things, isn't it?"

"Hmm, I think I said that wrong, quantum mechanics says that all possibilities are real, meaning that every one of them exists. What I mean is do you think that all time exists simultaneously?"

"You mean, for instance, that what happened three hundred years ago really wasn't three hundred years ago as we know it? So, like, it's all happening at the same time?"

"Yeah, like a matter of perception, what you're focused on at any given moment is 'real'."

"Great. Ha. He's here, isn't he?"

"Well it's not like he's a ghost, or anything to be afraid of. He's yards away anyway."

"F.C. is gonna have a ball with you!"

"I don't plan to tell them about Spéir."

"Probably best. I guess, I mean they'd likely understand. Better than I do, for sure. But do you think you'll tell Skky someday?"

"Probably. Yes, I would at some point. At least I hope I have the chance." She looked away and blinked. "But about everything being simultaneous ... if they can do what they say they can do, then the future Skky already exists."

"Only if you decide."

"Oh, geez, probabilities and stuff," Cailín rubbed her forehead with her knuckles "That's not right, cause and effect, or... what the hell ever. Do I even want that kind of power?"

"I think you do, definitely," Brandon stated. "Honestly though? It doesn't seem to me that it's entirely up to you. Look at Spéir, wherever he is. From what you've told me about him, he has to be Skky, and vice versa. Wouldn't they – he – have to be in agreement?"

"I don't even know why I think of them separately. Somewhat anyway."

"Mmmkay, well, I can see why you would. You said that all possibilities are real, or that's what that one theory says. So, you've got past, present, and future Skky. Each one exists in a different, different from our perspective, set of circumstances. In terms of the 'time' they live in that is."

"There's just one thing wrong with that, I don't have Skky – now."

"But you met him a couple years ago, right?"

"Yes, but that's not the same as having him."

"Don't be so sure. On some level of consciousness, whatever, every version of him must be aware."

"Maybe so. I guess."

"The bottom line for me is the Ben Franklin list."

"Pros and cons, two columns?"

"Sure, say, what's the worst that could happen? Absent any problems with technology, which we've already mostly discounted, what's the worst outcome?"

"Uhh, that'd be the relationship not working out at all, no chemistry, whatever, but it fails."

"Exactly. The big goal, so failure of that happening, that'd be the worst. Okay. Now the best?"

"Almost unimaginable."

"Exactly."

"But an even bigger plus… Bran, I want him to have another chance, like you want Sara to have another chance. I want him to be alive and well, some *where*, some *time*. Too much time has passed here, he… he's been gone too long, I'm afraid…" she tried to stop the quivering of her chin by sucking in her lower lip "… I want him to have another chance."

More than ever, she seemed like a little girl that he wanted to protect, "Kaylin, it would be all right to just want it for yourself. That's reason enough."

"Ugh. It's complicated, I know. I think my brain is taxed to headache level. Funnel cakes?"

"I'll try any cure, let's go."

* * *

"What does money mean to you?" Logan was never slow cutting to the chase.

"In what respect?"

"Any respect, in general, specifically."

"Oh. You're asking if part of my attraction to Skky is based on his wealth."

"More or less, yes."

"That's a fair question. I can take care of myself. I have a good job, and a promotion due in six months, possibly sooner. Beyond that, I'll have enough experience in another year to change jobs if I don't get what I want. I'd do well if I stayed, probably even be reasonably wealthy in a few years with the right investments.

"I'm happy for Skky. He should get what he deserves. I don't get the impression that he does it for the money, but in relative terms money *is* the score card. I don't need him to take care of me though, well in that respect anyway."

"Define money, what it represents."

"That's easy enough, most people would say security. I hear the word 'security' all the time. I don't see it quite that way. To me, money equates to freedom. Now more than ever."

She considered Logan for a moment, almost convinced that she could see what he was thinking. He seemed to accept her answer, but she didn't wait for him to remark on it, she had a concern of her own. She stood up and started to pace.

"Is this right? Is any of this right? Is it okay to do, and if it is, why is it okay to do? I want something. I want it so terribly bad, I'd do anything, absolutely anything. Yet in relative terms, this has been easy. But is it right? What gives me the right? And – what gives *you* the right? All of you, what gives you the right!"

"Alright. That's – those are fair questions." Logan was calm, as usual.

"Are you not taking this seriously? Is this some kind of joke?" she accused.

"Quite the contrary. This is no joke. Exactly. This is not a joke. I'm just relieved this issue has come up, it's about time."

"Oh? Am I truly that predictable?"

"Hardly. But since I know you a little by now, I, well I'd like to think that I was anticipating these questions." Logan was smiling, but not smug. "I guess I'd be disappointed if you didn't pose them. Disappointed, and frankly, a little worried."

"Why?"

"For one, because it seems unlike you to just skip over this issue."

"Does everyone ask this?"

"Only the ones that make it through."

"I see." She sat down.

"So let's break this down, identify your concern, your questions in plain terms. Spell it out for me, please."

"You're making a copy of the man of my dreams for me. You're going to clone Skky, you –"

"We prefer to call it regeneration."

"Sure. Whatever. You're going to send me three hundred years into the future. Meanwhile, whatever 'meanwhile' means in relative terms, according to Dr. Whittaker, you're going to create this exact copy of Skky in the proper time frame, to be ready and waiting to be the right age when you transport me there."

"That's about the size of it."

"How can you … how can I let you, or direct you, or even allow you to go through with this? To create someone just because I want to travel forward and hopefully have him fall in love with me? How can that be right? Am I really that selfish? Or am I just as delusional as all of you?"

"Eh. Delusion, illusion, it's all the same. But you're overlooking the fact that it's already been done. To be exact, four hundred..."

"Four hundred forty eight times, yeah, yeah, I know. Just because it's been done doesn't make it right."

"I can't dispute the morality, or maybe even the logic of that statement."

"But really, just to cause someone to be created for no other reason than my own selfish pleasure? Oh! Oh no! Is it already too late? Is it too late to stop this?"

"Of course not. It's not too late until the second that you sign the final document, put on the suit, and leave. We can stop at any time prior to that."

"Are you sure?"

"Positive. If this is something you find you can't live with, of course it can be stopped before it's started. Remember the whole 'nature of time' conversation you had with Professor Whittaker? I know those concepts are difficult to grasp. Future Skky is a potentiality right now, um I'm not the best at this. Think of it like kinetic energy, possibly, if that makes sense? I think you might have an advantage though, as I recall you enjoy studying quantum mechanics and the like just for fun." He stopped and laughed, "Who does that? Anyway, even so, it's still a difficult concept. I don't want to frighten you, but we don't even understand it completely. We do know our methods work though."

"Sure. Results. So I've been told. You all are so very sure of yourselves. Maybe I just don't understand..."

"I believe you understand most of the process nearly as well as most of us do. Where we have a supreme advantage lies in the fact that we've seen it happen successfully so many times. Not to say that we take it for granted, it's a miracle each and every time.

"But back to your original concern, concisely put, you wonder why anyone has the right to cause another human being to be created for their own pleasure. Does that sum it up?"

"Pretty much."

"Good. Do you want children? Do you plan to have them if possible?"

"What the hell does that have to do with anything?"

"Bear with me, please. Do you?"

"Well, yes, I do want children in a year or two, or whatever time frame suits us, provided it's with the right man. That'd be Skky, of course."

"All right. Providing we go ahead, you'd want children with Skky."

"Yes, that's what I just said."

"Why would you want children?"

"Why would I not? Not only do I know that he loves children, but it would be an extension of *us*, a part of us that would go on. We could have a family that actually functioned, like his, not mine. The whole experience would be a great joy."

"Let me get this straight. You would, or the two of you would, create human beings for your own selfish pleasure?"

"Did… did you just throw my own words back at me?"

"I did. How is it so much different? Wait," Logan leaned forward, "I'll answer that with another question. What if you could create, uh, regenerate a human being with known advantages? A good family life, a reasonably happy childhood, talent, deserved success. But let's take it one step further. What if you could guarantee that child a chance, a very good shot, at finding the love of his or her life? Not everyone does, you know. What if you could guarantee a child of yours all of those advantages? Would you do it if it were in your power?"

"Of course. Of course I would, I …"

"Kaylin, this isn't a usual patient-counselor relationship. I couldn't do this in the mainstream system. I'd be asking you a few questions, mainly encouraging you to talk, but I couldn't offer my own thoughts, at least not to this extent. Here, my role is more to be a friend, a confidant to you. I like that, this job makes me happy. Point is, it's alright to be happy."

"Yeah. But this happy?"

"In spite of what you've heard, or been made to feel to the contrary."

* * *

She was lying beneath him, running her fingers down his back, competing with a jealous sun to claim him. His weight was comforting, reassuring, not confining. Solar plexus to solar plexus his breath rose and fell in unison with hers. Silky blond hair fell across her cheek, she reached to touch it. Though they were alone, he whispered next to her ear…

"Damn it! Oh! Damn it!" Cailín startled herself by saying it out loud. Why, oh why, does the dream always end too soon? Why is it that you can never go back to sleep and will them to continue?

She flung the covers back and stomped off to the shower. Was the universe trying to tell her that she wouldn't be able to go through with it? No, that couldn't be, everyone had the same frustrations with dreams that end earlier than they would have liked. Lots of friends had told her of similar occurrences through the years. It wasn't just her. It wasn't. And it didn't mean anything. Not anything bad anyway, it was merely a symptom of her growing impatience. The simplest explanations are usually the most correct, she'd heard that too. She could verify that with Logan, he'd confirm it.

She stopped and purposely bumped her head lightly against the apartment door three times before she left. *Please be all right, Skky, wherever you are, please be all right.*

* * *

"Do you think the soul chooses its circumstances? I've always thought that, that we're more responsible for where and who we are than maybe we'd care to admit. What do you think?"

"I think so, too... personally, that is," Logan said. "If you believe in free will, which I think is the obvious case, to most of us anyway, then yes. Do I already know where you're going with this, Kay?"

"Probably. Do you think Skky – Skky *now*, would choose the same circumstances all over again?"

"I don't know, can't answer that. That'd be up to him, wouldn't it? But are you asking if your future Skky will be the 'same'? Yes and no. Ideally, the soul evolves."

"The old 'you can never step into the same river twice'? Is that what you mean?"

"Somewhat. For instance, are you the same person you were two, three weeks ago? I think not."

"We can't really know, can we?"

"That? No."

"I'm not sure I'd want him to be, I don't know."

"Why would you say that?"

"Something's obviously gone wrong. He ..." Cailín tried to collect herself, "... he's still missing. Something went very wrong somehow, in some way. I wish I knew. I just wish I knew he was okay. It hurts my soul to think he's suffering. But something..." she was choking back tears now, "...went wrong. When people just disappear, it's seldom good. I wonder if it would happen again? What if future Skky has, I don't know, the same life path or something? Is he going to disappear again?"

"I don't have a specific answer to that, but I do know one thing. Something will be different, something that has the potential to make a positive difference in his life."

"Something?"

"Someone. You."

"Oh," she paused for several seconds. "Will I ever know, in the future, what happened to him, I mean to Skky – the Skky of here and now? If even he is here anymore. Will I be able to find out?"

"Absolutely. Not right away, definitely not in the first few days, maybe not for years, it all depends on a number of things."

"What things?"

"That's out of our control. It's more up to you and how things unfold in the future. It's up to when you need to know… or when he feels he needs to tell you."

"But I *need* to know now!"

"I understand, and I'm sorry, but it's all part of the equation. All things in due time." Another easy laugh from Logan, "We can't throw our future Skky a curve ball, not in that regard."

* * *

Cailín walked into the restaurant alone, something she normally felt uncomfortable doing. Today she would welcome the solitude; she would ask for an out of the way table. She scanned the dining room, hoping to find a spot to request of the hostess. She was a little surprised at what she saw.

Gina was sitting alone at a booth for two near the kitchen, one of the least coveted seats in any restaurant. Smiling and waving her over, Gina rose and started toward her. "Is this all right? I mean, can we…"

"Mmm," Gina took her arm briefly "yes, of course, well you know," she leaned closer to Cailín's ear, "provided we're not overheard to any extent, and take care not to be too specific."

"I understand," Cailín glanced over her shoulder, an uneasy feeling of guilt and self-consciousness gripped her. She wasn't altogether sure she was ready for her two worlds to collide. With Brandon, it was different.

"Are you excited?"

"I'm not sure, I guess, I'm almost afraid to believe it. I'm still processing it all. I don't even have all the questions yet, let alone the answers. There's so much at stake here."

"Oh, I know. It's overwhelming at first, to say the least. Once that calms down the excitement takes over, then it's really hard to wait. I'm happy for you! After you've waded through all the technicalities and homework," Gina laughed and leaned forward to speak more quietly, "think what's waiting for you! Skky is amazing! A real little hottie honey for certain. I went to one of his concerts two years ago, the group concert that is."

"You did?" Cailín beamed.

"Yes, it was kind of a happy accident. Some friends had tickets and at the last minute couldn't go, so my sister and I went. I wasn't exactly excited, I didn't know

126

anything about them, but I figured what the heck, you know? A new experience possibly wouldn't be all that bad. Oh man! Was I pleasantly surprised! The whole thing was great, but Skky, mmm he just shines doesn't he? So handsome and so talented."

"He is… just so beautiful in every way. Ah!" Cailín snapped into the realization, "Oh my gosh, I'm sorry, I forgot. You said you're going in two months. Oh wow, so you've already been through the −"

"The mill, er the process?" Yes," Gina smiled, "I have. But believe me, it's not that awful, these are wonderful people that I work with. Everything is designed to make it as right as it can be, it really is. And, they truly want you to be happy, but I think you understand."

"Of course. There's someone else directly involved. At least there potentially will be. Gosh, your co-workers must be even more nervous than I am. They have a huge responsibility to my − to Skky. Absolutely huge." Cailín shook her head and stared past Gina, "Of course they have to be sure of me, if I fail they've screwed up big time. I wouldn't even begin to know how they would fix that, and worse, how they could justify it in their own minds. I think I can assume that, I think they really do care."

"There has to be a lot of trust between everyone involved. The whole process is designed to cut the margin for error to as close to zero as humanly possible. Even Dr. Whittaker would have to admit, grudgingly of course, that absolute zero is absolutely impossible. Yet, the odds for success are definitely skewed in our favor."

"Can I − I mean is it ok? Can I ask who your Chosen is?"

Gina's eyes sparkled. "I'm going to turn the tables. I'm going to put my trust in you. Promise you won't tell, or ever mention it. But, I'm not at work right now, I'm just a private citizen."

"Okay."

Gina leaned across the table and Cailín did the same. Gina put her hand up to cover one side of her mouth and whispered a name.

"No way!" Cailín sat bolt upright and covered her mouth with her hand and immediately lowered her voice, "Oops – but honestly? No way!"

"It's awesome isn't it?"

"Oh." Cailín instantly sobered and felt sick, "Oh my God, Gina... I'm so sorry, I –"

"Yes, the car wreck..."

"It – it was about six weeks ago, wasn't it?"

"Six weeks, two days and twenty three hours." Gina blinked hard.

"I – I can't imagine, oh, I am so sorry, so very sorry."

"Kay, it would be unbearable if I wasn't – involved in this, if I wasn't going." She shifted in her chair, "I can sympathize with your situation, too, it must be terribly hard not knowing."

"Yeah, your imagination runs wild, and never to a good place."

"I understand. But we have to look ahead, not back."

She wondered if Gina knew something she wasn't telling her.

"You have to look ahead, it kind of makes it bearable," Gina continued. "See, I cling to the idea – the reality – that I'm giving him a second chance. It's going to be different somehow. How, I don't know, although I do a lot of daydreaming about it. I try to imagine how things would be different. Maybe I'm making lunch and running late, so he gets on the freeway, or the equivalent of whatever it will be in the future, ten minutes later than he would have, so it doesn't happen. Maybe we have to take the dog to the neighborhood vet, so he doesn't get on the freeway at all. Maybe I insist on thirty seconds more for a goodbye kiss, and that's just enough. Maybe... I don't know, I just go wild imagining. I can't anticipate those things, but what I do know is that in some way his life path will be altered just because I'm there. I'm there, and I'm giving him a chance."

"I... yeah, I see what you're saying. Even a small, seemingly inconsequential alteration could change everything. But it's like – you can't worry about what that might be. You just have to trust."

"Yes. And look ahead. Whatever has happened this time, you have to look ahead and trust that it will be different, better."

"And we'll be together. It really is amazing."

"It's a gift. Who doesn't want a second chance? And with a smokin' hot man at that?"

The two young women laughed with sheer joy as they clasped hands across the table, now complete co-conspirators.

Cailín didn't want the encounter to end, it was fascinating as well comforting. Gina must have felt the same, she offered as they left, "Could we do this again? If you'd like to. Say, next week? Same day, same time, same place?"

"If it's all right, sure, yes, I'd really like to."

"Great! Done! And I'll see you Saturday at the uh, you know."

Gina turned back to Cailín as they started to go their separate ways, and hurriedly walked back to her. "Kay?" she took her hand, "I do believe that the soul can be reborn. I do. He's out there, Kay, I believe that he's there, and he's waiting for you."

With that Gina turned and walked away. Cailín began walking back towards the building where she worked, blinking hard against tears of hope.

It felt like things had moved rapidly, and it felt like there were years left to go in the process. A very strange thing, time, and the perception of it.

* * *

Friday afternoon Cailín had to make up an excuse quickly.

"Mr. Smithson and Dr. Logan have requested a meeting. How soon can you be here?" Gina was all business.

"I'm coming in tomorrow morning as usual. Or I suppose I could come directly after work."

"It can't wait."

Cailín twisted a strand of hair around her finger. "Oh," she fought the lump in her throat, "give me an hour, possibly a little less?"

Her hands shook as she collected and fastened the sheaf of papers. *Thank goodness I'm always one step ahead.*

"Oh! I'm so sorry!"

"No harm." Reese from accounting looked at her quizzically.

"Good. Sorry again," she resumed her brisk walk down the corridor, trying to be more cautious.

"The analysis Mr. Browning requested."

"Thanks." Sandra smiled. "How −"

"Sorry, gotta run. Later," Cailín said with a quick wave.

* * *

She fidgeted with the collar of her blouse and smoothed her skirt three times. She flicked on fresh lipstick and willed herself to the elevator. No time for the stairs.

"What is it? Has he been found?" She rushed past Gina to the elevator.

"Kaylin…" Logan motioned her inside and pressed the "down" button.

"Is he alive? What happened? Is he hurt?"

"Slow down, slow down."

"It has to be something; you've never called me at work before. Is he alright?"

"Let's have a seat."

"Next you'll offer me a glass of water, then… oh, goddam! He's hurt, or dead, I…" Teardrops made dark circles on her navy blue skirt.

"Kay. There's nothing new in that regard. This isn't about Skky. Not directly anyway."

"Whuh?"

"There's no news. I'm sure you don't see that as positive. All the same – I do apologize. I really should have known you'd take it this way."

"Yes, you should have." She blinked and blotted her face with the tissue he offered.

"Now. Water seems like a good idea anyway. Again, I'm sorry. Take a minute."

She sighed deeply. Whatever it was, it couldn't be as bad as what she had allowed herself to imagine.

Logan stood gazing into the large mirror. "Better?"

"Oh, I'm just dandy. I'm used to wondering every goddamned minute of every goddamned day where he is, whether he's dead or alive, if I'll hear it on the news when I get home. Or, will Brandon come to me at work with that look on his face."

"I know it's distressing."

"No, you don't. You don't know. In fact, you cannot possibly imagine. I think he must be dead. Then I think – what I'm doing? There are still things that are hard to grasp. But deep down I think this – this may be the only chance he has. I want that chance for him, wherever, whenever. So I hold onto that. I don't care what I have to do, I don't care. I'll hold on.

"Why did you bring me here today? Get on with it."

Logan stood, his expression intent. "I don't believe I've truly let myself see what exactly this must be like for you. At the risk… well, I apologize again."

"No need. My choice. As we've talked about a million times, it's a choice."

"Of course. All right. So let's continue, move forward. I'm sure there's an explanation."

"For what?'

"You know we do our best to be thorough in every aspect, to protect you both."

"Yeah. And?"

"You were born Kaylin Marie Stevens. You've never married, so –"

"Son of a … You really did eff that up! If you'd gone a little further in public records you'd know that I legally took my grandmother's surname in my third year of college, after I realized that with the miracle of student loans I was free to break with my parents completely.

"I became good friends with a pre-law student. He even drafted the Petition and Order so it didn't cost anything but the filing fee. Six weeks later, ten minutes with a judge, and bingo."

"I understand. That explains it."

"Oh, no you don't."

"Hmm?"

"You're not finished yet. You say it's for his protection, I'm all for that. Finish it."

"It won't —"

"Yes, it will be necessary. Call the county courthouse before they close. It was four years ago, 2009. The Order was signed and filed on April 19th – no, the 9th, I filed my tax return with my new name that year. What a mess, I nearly got audited."

"Sure, let's put this to rest." He clicked the intercom button on his phone, "Gina —".

Cailín stood up and stretched and a shallow sigh of relief escaped her. *No news is good news. Well, maybe.* She blinked at her reflection in the mirror. *If only everything had such a concrete explanation.* She stepped to the side and looked at a different angle. For a few seconds her reflection seemed to float on its own, the room behind her had disappeared. She looked more closely.

"I'll be damned."

Logan was off in his own world of note making. "Hmm?"

"It's a double mirror, a two-way mirror I mean."

"Um."

"I never thought about it. It's so Smithson, and whoever, can watch." She smiled and wiggled her fingers at the mirror. "So you don't have to spend hours relating to others what I've said, how I acted."

Logan was on his feet now. "I did mention a while back that this wasn't the usual psychologist/patient relationship. But yes, you're correct on both counts."

Logan walked behind her, meeting her gaze in the mirror. "Would you like to see?"

"Sure, why not?"

He pushed a button under his desk. A slight whirring sound accompanied the mirror on its descent into the wall beneath. The room was small, containing only a table and three upholstered chairs. She saw the single door close a final three inches or so. Apparently one, or possibly two, of the occupants hadn't cared to remain. Probably

Varen Whittaker and Dr. Benson, she guessed. Dealing with anything other than straightforward medical and technical facts was not their forte. Smithson, of course, remained.

"Good afternoon, Kay. I see you've discovered our subterfuge. Sincere apologies if it distresses you."

"No. It's not a problem. Truly." He could see that she was bemused by the concept. "In fact, it's a good idea. Efficient. I actually don't mind at all. After all, I did sign a document that allows cross communication, so no, not a shock at all."

"Very well then. I must say your poise and understanding are to be admired."

She laughed. "Think back ten or fifteen minutes, and you might want to reconsider."

There was a soft knock, but Gina entered without hesitation. "They were nice enough to fax it." She handed the papers to Logan. With only a brief glance he said, "Excellent. Just file it, please."

Gina looked sheepish. "Kay…"

She held up her hand. "No, Gina, and I swear if one more person apologizes to me I may top my earlier hysterics." She smiled. "Okay?"

"Okay." Gina sighed audibly.

* * *

Gina was nearly skipping toward her as she waited outside the door of the restaurant. "Let's skip lunch!"

"Oh. Your schedule too tight? Time to grab a sandwich to go?"

"No, no. Unless you're starving."

"Not really, but –"

"We're going shopping!" Gina grabbed her hand, "Come on!"

"Wha –" Cailín came to a halt at the door of the lingerie shop.

"Ohh, yes. It's time. We can't be hanging around Their Royal Hotness without some unfair advantages. Think red, black, and hot pink. Trust me."

"Can I help you ladies with anything?" the attractive woman in her mid-thirties asked.

"Not just yet, thank you," Gina flew past her with Cailín in tow, "we have some looking and thinking to do first."

"Certainly, just let me know if you'd like to try anything on."

Gina tugged Cailín past white and pale blue pretty but practical bras and panties. "Oh! Here! Over here! This one, and this one, pick your size." Gina nixed the leopard print, "It's fun, but not serious, and it's too distracting. We're going for hardcore I-mean-business."

Ten minutes later they set up camp in the luxurious dressing rooms. "This is cool, I like these," Cailín had no problem getting in the spirit.

"Pretty good, huh? I think you're getting the picture. Oh, hey, try this." Gina tossed a red bra over the partition.

"I have one of these. This one is a size too small."

"Just try it on."

"Nope. It doesn't fit, I'm spilling out over the top."

"Exactly. Be grateful – then try to think like a man for a minute."

"Oh," Cailín said thoughtfully, "ohhh."

"Take them both," Gina laughed.

"Gina, if I buy everything I've tried on it's going to come to nearly five hundred dollars."

"Think of it as the best investment you ever made."

"I know, but what about – I listed my assets, uh, you know? This money is probably needed for the, for my, errr for the trip."

"Don't worry, it's me here, Kay, I've already cleared it. It's fine. Next week, shoes!"

* * *

"There's an aspect to your future relationship that we haven't covered as yet."

"Oh? I thought by now you'd be tired of hearing my soliloquies about the endless wonders of Skky O'Keeffe."

"He's not my type, but it's been interesting," Logan grinned.

"It's still fascinating to me, the way a woman thinks about a man. Your insights have been interesting, more in depth than I would have expected."

"I'm sure your wife would have plenty to say about you." Cailín's cheeks felt warm, but she recovered. "So what's the missing piece of the puzzle?"

"You've never mentioned wanting him physically. I assume since you want children that would have to enter the equation."

"Sex? You're kidding me! You mean I'd have to do *that* to have kids?" She decided it was time to give Logan a taste of his own humor. "Ugh. I was hoping for artificial insemination or something, maybe a surrogate? I just wanna sit around and look at his face, listen to his voice.

"But honestly, *are* you kidding me? He's gorgeous. He has straight, broad shoulders. His arms show that he's active, you know, just enough muscle, nicely shaped, but not all bulked up with bulging veins like body builders. I hate that, it's like if you touched an arm like that it might explode or something. Kinda creepy. But Skky's arms? Ohhh, they'd feel so good around me.

"He's got really nice legs, too. But – oh my god! He's got the cutest, tightest, just rounded enough, little butt. Like my granny would say, 'you could bounce a quarter off that thing!' I can't wait to get my hands on it. And I think… I'll bet he's got just the softest down on his inner thighs, I wanna rub my cheek against it… the thought alone nearly makes me pass out. Seriously. I get dizzy.

"There would be no need for him to shower ever again, I have a tongue. It all adds up to the fact that it would take next to no encouragement at *any* given moment for me to jump that fine boyo and ride him all the way to China.

"Does that clear up any doubts?"

All Logan could do was shake his head.

* * *

The days seemed to crawl to the end of the week. Friday had been her last day at work. There was no going back now.

"Never really discussed how your resignation went."

"He offered me a promotion, a raise, on the spot." She sank back on the sofa and admired her boots. "Said no, thanks, of course."

Boots are so substantial, they take you places, I love these boots... she thought, and nearly laughed out loud remembering Spéir's love of his boots.

"Told him I was moving to Oregon, to be near my favorite cousin. He asked if I'd found work there yet, if I'd sent resumes. Told him he wouldn't believe the paperwork I've done."

"That much was true." Logan's easy laugh was always reassuring.

"I miss Brandon," she sobered, "felt lost without him yesterday."

"Only a week now. How does it feel?"

"Great! I'm so ready! Well, except for packing."

"What will you do to pass the time, other than pack?"

She laughed. "You never seen a woman pack, have you? And with so little space to work with it's like a puzzle." She threw her hands up in the air. "Don't care, I'll love every minute – and you're forgetting my seven DVD collection. The week is gone!"

"I'll see you Tuesday and Thursday, and my cell number is good twenty-four/seven. Use it if you need."

"I should call you at three a.m. just to protest more blood tests."

"Can't say I'd blame you."

"I just, I wondered, do you have his DNA already? Have you…"

"You know I can't speak to that specifically. Everything will be in place for your arrival, rest assured."

"But – wait." Every muscle in her body twisted, Logan had seen that look before.

"Kay…"

"Hold on a sec. You –" her hand pressed her midsection. "By now you either have it or you don't. Somewhere along the way, the past few weeks, or days, either you've started the process or you haven't." She stood and clenched her fists.

Logan quickly sorted through his thoughts, his skills, but was too late.

"God damn you!" Cailín whirled on the heel of her boot and her eyes fired blazing arrows. "All of you! God damn you! You've known. All. This. Time." She turned again to face the mirror. "You miserable sons of bitches, you've known all along if he's alive or dead!" Her anger became more deliberate, "You know where he is, how he is. Tell me. Tell me now, God damn you!"

She turned to face Logan. Wracked with sobs she screamed, "You son of a bitch!" She threw her arm out behind her, finger pointing at the mirror, "You've known all along, damn you all!"

Logan went to her side, "Kay, please, let's –"

"Don't touch me!" She screamed her great grandmother's Irish curse, "Go hifreann leat! Go to hell!" She was inching backward away from Logan, her palm held up in front of her. "All of you! He's dead, isn't he? He's dead and you won't tell me! If he was alive we wouldn't be doing this. If you think I'm right for him – so many ways that would be simpler than flinging me three hundred years – you could, you could arrange for us to meet. There'd be no need… How stupid, how stupid I've been not to realize… I just, I just wanted to believe," she sobbed. "That's all, just believe." She pointed a shaking finger at the mirror, "All of you go straight to hell." She ran out the door.

Logan was immobile, staring after her.

His bosses' voice came over the intercom. "Nick! Stop her, get her now. Enough is enough. Go get her, or I will."

Logan ran to the elevator. Too late. He bounded up the stairs three at a time, pushing his lean body to the limit. He hit the correct button on his cell. "Gina!"

"She just ran out, what the −"

"Call Sam and Ronald, stop her. Hurry."

Cailín ran out onto the sidewalk. She hesitated to catch her breath. She should have taken the side door, her car was too far away. She looked around, wide-eyed, gasping, not noticing that people were stopping to stare and murmur.

She looked over her shoulder and ran to the corner of the building; from the other side she could find her car easily.

Two men in matching gray suits met her head on, grabbing her arms. "No!" she screamed.

"Miss, we're Dr. Logan's assistants, please come with us."

There was no escaping their grip.

"Help! Help me!"

A breathless Logan swung around the corner as a uniformed policeman ran up behind the two men who were struggling to keep a tiny Cailín in their grasp.

"Officer!" Logan held up a hand, fingers spread. "Officer, Dr. Nick Logan," he was trying not to act desperate himself, "my patient just received some very bad news and is suffering severe emotional trauma." Regaining some professional poise he plucked a business card from his pocket and thrust it at the young policeman.

"Yeah?" the officer looked as though he was trying to remember something. "Oh, I heard uh you from the

142

doorman. Couple months ago maybe? You're with that new outfit, Future somethin', isn't it?"

"That's correct, fairly new here." Logan was back in command. "Excuse me, please, just a second."

"It's alright, Miss, I'll get this straightened out, you're fine." The young officer tried his best.

Logan flipped open his cell and heard, "Whatever it takes, anything, just do it or I swear −"

"Yes, I believe she'll be fine." He snapped the cell shut.

He shot a look at Cailín, slumped and sobbing, she would have been on the sidewalk save for the two men bracing her as gently as possible.

The officer reached for his radio, "This young lady needs some medical attention. I'll radio for an ambulance."

"Please wait, officer," Logan was calm and collected, and believable − he hoped. "My patient has just learned that someone very close to her is missing. Family asked me to break it to her. As you see, she took it extremely hard."

Cailín straightened up and tried to shake her hair away from her face. "Gone?"

Logan felt his strength would fail.

"Nooo-oh." Her voice came from an abyss so deep, so far away, that he wondered if he could ever pull her back.

This time he caught her as her legs gave out and put his lips on her ear so no one else could hear. He whispered urgently, "You have to go to him. Give him that second chance. You're the only one that can, Kaylin," Logan spoke with certainty, "only you".

From behind glazed eyes she whispered a faint, "help me then".

"Miss," the young officer registered concern, "it seems that you need medical attention. Would you like for me to send for an ambulance, get you some help?"

She blinked. "He, they… can help me." She looked at Logan, "Fix this. Help me fix this. I'd like to go back in now, please."

"We will, Kaylin, it will be all right."

Gina appeared next to Logan. "Let's go talk about what we can do to help," she frowned. She linked her arm through Cailín's, "Can you walk?" She gestured toward the two men, "Ron and Sam will follow us. If you need more help, they'll call immediately."

"We have two medical doctors on staff, both presently in. If anything further is needed, we won't hesitate." Logan told the young officer, who seemed reassured with Gina's presence.

"She won't be left alone, I'll be with her for the next forty-eight hours straight, at least," Gina said as Logan took Cailín's other arm.

Logan added, "Right now I feel it best that she's with people she's comfortable with. We're familiar with her history."

"Okay. But a detective will need to follow up. Will you be at the number on your card?"

"Absolutely. And we'll all be right here, in my office, until we determine the best arrangements for the young lady."

"Someone will contact you in a couple hours, maybe less."

"Thank you very much, officer." Logan realized he would have to pass damage control to someone. Likely Smithson would be free in time.

Though she was silent in the elevator, Logan felt she was beginning to get back to herself. Even if he'd known about Spéir, he could have neither seen nor felt his presence let alone hear him whisper to Cailín, "We dun die, lass, you and I, we just move on."

Logan guided her to the sofa. "Here, put your feet up. Gina's gone to get something to eat."

Dr. Benson had swooped in, pricked her finger, and set the blood pressure cuff in motion. "Both somewhat low, nothing critical." She winced as he shone the pen light in her eyes. "Rest and eat and there's nothing to worry about."

"When you feel like it, we've got plans to discuss. No hurry." Logan was gratefully settling back into his casual demeanor.

"I'm going to move forward."

"Yes, you are." He was relieved at her more normal tone of voice. "Definitely."

"I think I knew it all along. Maybe? Maybe. I'm not sure."

Dr. Benson held out a capsule and a glass of water.

"I don't want tranquilizers." She shrank back and wiped a single tear from her cheek. "I need to feel this."

"It's only B vitamin complex, a little C thrown in, nothing more. Stress is physical, too, your body could use it."

"I guess. What next?"

"I think you'll like this," Logan looked happily relieved himself. "I've just spoken to Alec. Assuming you're up to it, you can leave in two or three days, not a week."

"Really?"

"Yes. Gina and I will go home with you later. Tomorrow I'll likely get out of your hair, and she'll help you start packing."

"Skky?"

"Kay, he'll arrive at the location we've chosen tomorrow. If you're feeling up to it, we'll send you as early as Monday."

Color instantly came back to her face, and so did the tears, "Skky. He's… Skky."

"Yes, Kay. We've had no doubts for a while now that you would move forward, so we set things in motion. I'm confirming that he exists, and I'm happy to say, is very much himself. All that's missing is you, but not for long.

"And I have something for you, just arrived, a rather long journey in a short amount of time. I wasn't going to give it to you for a couple of days, but… " Logan reached behind his desk and picked up a plastic bag, "… I think this might help."

She took the bag he offered, thrust her hand inside and pulled out the folded material. "It's Skky's! It's Skky's t-shirt," she was shaking, but smiling, "the one he always called his favorite." She held it up by the shoulders and stared, then looked at Logan, "oh, thank you, thank you!" She pressed the material to her face and drew in a deep breath. *It's his, it smells like the earth, like oak, rich and sweet, almost as if he'd just taken it off,* she thought. "It's his, it's really his!" She drew in another deep breath, "And – he's worn it recently – he's alive again."

She began to cry again, this time tears of joy.

In the room on the other side of the mirror its sole occupant folded his arms on the table, put his head down, and cried too.

* * *

146

"Are you fucking kidding me!" Cailín screamed from the living room.

"... interview that everyone's been waiting for, exclusively here on 'Speak Out'."

"Wha..." Gina ran. Cailín stood in the middle of the floor, fists clenched at her sides, eyes glued to the TV set.

"Does she know?" the female host asked provocatively.

"Or will she tell?" the male host drawled in conspiracy. "Stay tuned for the answers, only on 'Speak Out'."

"Oh my. His wife?" Gina put a protective arm around her. "Here. Let's sit."

Cailín sat on the edge of the sofa. "She doesn't know, does she? She doesn't know anything, why is she..."

"Publicity, no doubt." Gina went into practical mode. "Her career has slumped since −"

"Good evening! I'm Randa Kline, and you're watching 'Speak Out', America's premier celebrity news magazine. Tonight we have an exclusive interview with Delilah Hanover, wife of missing superstar Skky O'Keeffe."

"And I'm John Phoenix. First, let's take a look at the charmed and illustrious career of Skky O'Keeffe, who gained recognition and fame −"

Pictures and footage of Skky onstage at several large venues flashed across the screen, followed by footage of Skky and Lila during "happier days".

"Now the moment we've all been waiting for, over to you, Randa."

"Lie your ass off, bitch," Cailín snapped.

"I'm sure she will," Gina said thoughtfully, "you know, I think she had something to do with whatever went wrong."

Cameras switched to the interview section of the set, Lila and Randa seated in formal chairs at just the right angle. Lila wore a white two piece suit with a very short skirt, and was of course posing properly. "Lila, thank you for joining us this evening, I'm sure the past few months have been a very trying time for you."

"To say the least," she spoke in a clipped Scandinavian accent, "possibly for reasons other than you might imagine."

"Well, we know, the entire world knows, that Skky has been missing for over six months now, so on behalf of our viewers I have to ask. Do you know where he is? Have you heard from him?"

"No." Her tone was patronizing. "But he's not 'missing'."

"What do you mean? As far as we know no one has heard from him or seen him."

"He's not missing," she scoffed, "he's hiding. He's done it on purpose, I'm not completely sure why. He's selfish and self-centered, he always was."

"But why, at the height of his career…"

"Because he's a spoiled brat, his family, his entourage of buddies, they all bent to his every wish, his every demand. Naturally he expected me to do the same."

"Bitch!" Cailín yelled at the TV, "That's not true. That is SO not true. Oh my God, Gina, you're right!"

"You seemed so happy," Randa leaned forward sympathetically, "why would he leave you, one of the world's most gorgeous super models, to –"

"Seemed happy? That was all an act. I soon realized I was nothing more than a trophy to him, something to show off to his friends, another stepping stone to more success."

"More like the other way around," Cailín seethed.

"He sabotaged my career at every turn. He just wanted me to follow him around so he could do his own thing. He wanted me to give up everything." Lila was good at posing indignant and wounded.

"It must have been very difficult, you both being stars in your own right, to keep up with schedules." Randa felt the interview slipping away from her. Was this really going to make good press? Something was missing; she needed an ass kicker statement.

"Difficult? It was impossible for me, being told to give up everything I'd worked for."

"Now you two had a fairy tale wedding in the Irish countryside, and to the world seemed so happy." Randa tried.

"Fairy tale? Well, certainly not one of the good ones. A hundred people at the wedding because *he* wanted only family and close friends.   I should have known by then, it was always going to be all about him."

"Lila," Randa's thought was clear on her face. *When the hell did I become Barbara Walters? Or worse, Dr. Phil.* Randa concentrated on what the head producer had told her from day one: *"If the situation warrants it, then you must ask the hard questions. An opportunity lost cannot be made up later."*

"Lila," she said again after a deep breath. The clock was ticking. "It sounds like you were miserable in your marriage. Were you ever abused?"

"Not physically, if that's what you mean.   Other things are just as bad."

Well damn, Randa thought, *might as well wrap this and move on.*

"Thank you for taking time out of your busy schedule to join us tonight. We –"

"Look," Lila never had been shy about grabbing the spotlight, "all I want is for the selfish bastard to stop playing games and come out of hiding so divorce papers can be served."

The money shot. Randa couldn't repress a hint of a smile.

"We want to wish you the very best in your career. I'm sure we'll be seeing a lot of you."

"Thank you." Lila put on her best 'poor little me' smile.

"She did, Gina, she did." Cailín fell back against the cushions, "It was something she did, I know it."

* * *

"You'd love it here!" Cailín wrote with a flourish on the back of the oversized postcard with a photo of a grand German castle, signed her name and addressed it to her mother and father.

"Hamburg at Night" read the caption on the next, the first one that would be mailed to her cousins in Oregon at the appropriate time.

The next one would be mailed to them a week or so later, "I ran into Jess and Suzanne in Hamburg on their way to Sweden – imagine! – couldn't resist joining them! You really have to see this part of the world someday soon!" The front of the card bore a photo of breathtaking scenery near Denmark. A duplicate would be sent to Brandon at the office, although he wouldn't be there it would surely be passed around and further the scheme to forestall any missing persons report.

"There!" She beamed at Smithson, "what a brilliant idea".

"All aimed to forestall any unwanted concerns, for a time that is."

Damn, Cailín thought, *if they're planning to do away with me, I've just helped them cover their tracks...*

"And...after 'a time'?"

"Let the chips fall, can't be helped." She purposely neglected to tell him of the long letter she'd posted to her grandmother.

Smithson registered an uncharacteristic concern, "What is your feeling in that regard?"

"Can't be helped. That's all." *Skky is not dead, he's waiting for me... somewhere in the future. So what do I care? This way, maybe both of us have a chance. Nothing else matters, nothing at all.*

"Very well then, if you're comfortable with..."

"Yes," she was too quick to jump in, but determined "yes, let's proceed."

151

She felt the elation of certainty as she signed the one line document that rested on the stack of others she'd signed throughout the weeks …

* * *

- THREE -

Cailín awoke. Her left hand inched to the lightweight silver mesh on her right arm, thinking it should be cold. It wasn't. She struggled to remember. What was it? Three hundred years? Funny, it didn't seem that any time had passed at all. They had said it wouldn't.

The silvery fabric that covered her entire body seeped slowly into her awareness. It was like a cat suit straight out of some bad sci-fi movie. She laughed out loud at the thought, but her laughter was muffled by the clear bubble that encased her head. An invisible barrier prevented her from sitting up. Her heart raced and heat blasted her face.

The invisible shield had somehow retreated and her second attempt to sit upright succeeded. Masculine hands came toward her face and mercifully plucked the clear bubble from her head. She screamed, as much from anger as from terror. She had told them! She had told them in no uncertain terms that she was claustrophobic, how was this allowed to happen? They'd promised…

The two hands lengthened into arms that quickly wrapped around her. "Hey, sleeping beauty, it's all right, it's all right." His voice was warm and reassuring with a measured amount of concern. "You woke up a good ten minutes before you were supposed to," now a hint of mirth crept into his speech, "you must *really* be anxious to get on with it."

"Whuh… what?" She began to sob, and against what would have been better judgment under more ordinary circumstances, she threw her arms around him and buried her face in his chest.

"Hey, sorry for the nasty scare, but really – I mean, seriously, you weren't due to wake up so soon. The test run…" His voice was truly comforting, but even as she relaxed more tears came. "Another five minutes and we would have had you out of there before you woke up, and Smithson would have already been here and…"

Her tears slowed, then stopped as she became more and more aware of his presence. He was incredibly handsome – and incredibly familiar.

"That's better," he nearly cooed, "I take it you must be remembering why you came here."

Amazingly, she hadn't until he spoke the words. She gasped and straightened from his embrace. She looked at him. A good, long look. Yes, it was him, she would have recognized him anywhere. He was the last person on earth she had ever expected to find here.

"Oh my! Awake already are we?" Alexander Smithson burst into the sterile room as though being chased by the devil himself. Indeed, maybe he was!

What was he *doing here! How did he get here? Oh dear lord, he must be…*

The question was written across her face as clearly as if with a magic marker. "Yes, dear girl, it is I, my once and future self, with full knowledge and permission. A bit of a revolving door for me, so to speak. Allows me to recommend confidently, you see."

"Son of a –" She turned to her rescuer, who shrugged with an "I know nothing" look. Of course. He had to be as well. She found comedy in the situation and began to laugh.

"There we are!" Smithson looked extremely relieved. "I do apologize for your disconcertion upon awakening. You took us quite by surprise." He studied her for a moment before continuing. "I trust that now we can focus on your purpose and set about achieving it? As you were previously advised, there will be a twenty-four hour period of acclimation and orientation and of course some rest. Rain will assist you with anything and everything you need, including most questions." He smiled and seemed satisfied that she wasn't going to disintegrate before his very eyes. "Have you any questions for me before I get on about my duties?"

She'd been "here" a mere five or six minutes and realizations were floating in slow motion. Now, the only thing that mattered crashed into her awareness. Her hands flew to her face and she gasped once again for an entirely different reason. "He's here! He's really here? He's *here*?" She wrapped her arms around her waist and doubled over.

Rain put a strong and steadying arm around her. "Yes." He spoke deliberately. "Yes, Kaylin, he's *really* here. Promise."

* * *

"You'll find the clothes you wore this morning in here." Rain gestured toward the open door of the small bathroom. "You okay? I'll be right outside. Oh, and there are a couple of ladies nearby if you need −"

"This morning?" she began to laugh. "And, what? Do people usually faint or something?"

"Just want to be sure you're comfortable, that's all. Well, that and you haven't eaten for what? About five hours?" Don't take too long, I tend to be a worrier."

"Nice. Now let's get you fed." Rain insisted as he guided her up a flight of stairs and through an unmarked door.

"I'm not really hungry."

"Oh, you've heard about the food here?"

"You're, uh, you're −"

"Look just like him, don't I?"

"I loved his, um, your work, there was nothing like it, it was great."

"Glad you think so, and more than that I can't say." He pulled out a chair for her and gestured to the menu. "Now, tell me what sounds good."

"Uh, I don't know, really."

"Trust me. Just be a sec." She watched him walk through a door at the back of the room and felt a twinge of panic. He returned within seconds, much to her relief.

"Gosh, didn't realize I was so hungry, this is perfect." She stabbed a large forkful of the chef salad and reached for the warm bread.

"Pretty much the specialty of the house, and not bad at all." He studied her for a second. "Headache? Anything? Kinda depressing, no windows. Don't worry, we'll fix that, I'll take you to your accommodations soon as we finish."

"Yeah I'm fine, I think, I mean I feel normal I guess."

156

"That's good. There will be, well, the types of things you're used to. It's not like you travelled to the moon or whatever. Promise."

They didn't leave the building as she'd hoped; instead they climbed two flights of stairs. There was a '9' on the door that he slid the small plastic tag into. "Does this mean that there are at least eight others here?"

He smiled. "Maybe. Not necessarily. Take it as arbitrary if I were you."

The suite was tiny, and she rushed to the double windows. "Oh, it looks like an ordinary small town."

"Probably because it is. And this," he gestured, "is only for the first twenty four hours. Tomorrow we'll have a look at two or three more homey places."

"Oh, I get it." She remained at the windows. "They're going to monitor me closely, make sure I don't sprout a third arm or something."

"Or something. No one expects any problem. They will bother you with blood pressure cuffs, and so on a few times."

On que, there was a soft knock at the door.

"Hi, Kaylin, I'm Margie." The petite woman's open smile was reassuring. "I'm going to take your blood pressure and just a tiny blood sample." She was efficient, practiced. "There. Now, do you have any questions or any complaints? Are you feeling normal?"

"I think I'm fine, honestly."

"You seem so to me, so I'll leave and let Rain help you get settled. I will be back in about three or four hours, just to check in." She stopped at the doorway. "I need to let you know, though we don't foresee problems, but for your peace of mind —" She pointed to a small orange square. "There's another just like it, in a similar position, by the bathroom door. If you feel you need anything at all, if you feel out of sorts in any way, please feel free to use it.

Someone will be here immediately. No concern is too small."

"I understand, and thank you."

"Thanks Margie." He closed the door behind her. "Now, let me show you around." In the adequate bathroom there was a small closet. "Margie picked out just a few things that she figured you might need tonight, or in the morning. If there's anything else, I'll send someone to get it. Your stuff is in storage until you decide amongst what's available tomorrow, then they'll bring your belongings over in record time."

"Oh." Cailín stood by a small window on the other side of the building that offered a different view of the town.

"You're looking for him."

"I – yeah, I suppose I am. Yeah."

"Must be hard to know he's close by, yet you can't see him 'til tomorrow."

"It is, it −" she began to cry.

"Hey now, it won't be long. Give yourself a chance to get used to being here."

"Yeah, after all it's been seven years, what's another day? But I just – it's hard to believe. It's going to be a long night alone."

"Not exactly."

"Huh?"

"Did you think I was going to leave you here alone? I'll be right here."

She stepped back out into the main room with a small kitchenette and table at one end, a sofa and TV at the other. She laughed. "I don't know, that sofa doesn't look like it would be too comfortable, you're rather tall."

"Oh. It pull outs. One of those sleeper bed things. It'll be fine."

"Where's the bedroom?"

"What bedroom?"

She looked around the room; there were no doors other than the entry and bathroom doors.

"We can watch movies, got a few of those to choose from. Of course there's no live feed TV, guess you were told about that, no current papers and such. Or, we can play cards. Got a few books, too. Then there's always good old fashioned talking."

"Is he really here? In this town? In this time? Is he really here?"

"Guaranteed. I've met him. He's here."

"Prove it."

"Hm. Yeah, okay. I'm ready for that one."

"You are? How?"

Rain opened the double doors on the small stand that held the TV. "This look familiar?"

"Are you kidding me? My digital camera! I didn't pack it, I didn't think…"

"No worse for the, uh, wear. Are we good, or what? Here's what we do. You check it, I think it has a new memory card, it should be blank. Check the date. Of course you can't put it too far ahead, best to leave it at 2014."

The card was indeed blank. She left the date as it was.

"Cool. Now take my picture."

"Not sure, I don't want to seem like some creepy stalker or something."

"A little late for that, isn't it? Remember, we know you well."

She laughed. "Fair enough. Say cheese."

"Crackers. Now, I take one of you. Uh, smile at least. One more, and just one more, a long shot." He stepped back and clicked the camera a third time. "Insurance. Good. Now look at them, memorize them, four pics in this camera, nothing else, date set, right?"

"Right. But —"

"Now we get you set up." He bent down and pulled a plastic box from the back of the cabinet.

She gasped. "My DVDs!"

"Or exact replicas. You know you can't let him see this, or know it's here? Probably won't be able to place it in your more permanent residence, so enjoy."

"I understand."

"Here's the remote," he pushed a button on the TV "volume here, just press 'play'." He took the DVD and slid in it the tray. "There. I'll be back in no more than thirty minutes, okay?"

"Uh huh. Oh! You're going to −"

"Exactly. I'm a sneaky devil, I'll get the goods. Soda and snacks in the fridge. Oh, and button by the door, don't feel silly if you want to use it."

"I'll be fine, don't worry. And, thank you."

He pulled out his cell phone, pushed a few buttons, and was gone.

* * *

"Joe sent me." Rain, the perennial jokester.

"I broke up with Joe eons ago. Do come in."

Her eyes immediately fastened on the camera.

"Yup, I have something for you." He grinned mischievously, holding the camera above his head as she sprung to her feet. "Uh, not so fast."

"Hey!"

"Hold on, hold on." He reached into the cabinet and pulled out a cord and attached one end to the TV.

"What…?" She was half jumping.

"Watch." The TV screen was solid blue. "Hocus pocus, nothin' up my sleeve…"

She drew a sharp breath and dropped to the floor in front of the screen. Skky, in jeans and a t-shirt, beamed back at her in living color. He sprawled on the park bench as though he owned the world, his typical alpha male pose. His just above shoulder length hair was delightfully ruffled every which way. Finally, it was his eyes that held her attention.

"Look at the date?" Rain flipped backward to the four pictures they'd taken earlier. "See?"

She waved her hand to the right twice and Rain forwarded to Skky's picture again.

"So, I did good?"

Without taking her eyes off the screen, she answered, "Better than Christmas morning at your granny's house when you're five years old. Better than anything ever."

"Two more, ready?"

"You, you saw him! You were right there with him!"

"Uh, yeah, that's kind of how I was able to get the pics. Said I needed to check my camera for light exposure, whatever."

"Is he really alright? I mean −"

"As you see. Met him yesterday, think I told you that. Accidently on purpose, you know, to be sure he was, well, normal. Really nice kid. Couldn't understand him too well sometimes, the accent."

"Kid?" she giggled. "Honey, that's a *man*. And I have no trouble understanding him at all."

"Willing to bet that's true."

"Oh," she covered her mouth with her hand, "he's alive, he's alright…" and she broke into sobs.

* * *

"What's it to be? Movie? DVD? No matter really to me. Checked. Our dinner has been planned, looks like we'll be eating here."

"Oh. Thanks."

"Last chance, if you like anything in particular."

"No matter." Cailín was still sitting in front of the TV, clicking back and forth between the pictures.

"Or, you could just do that all night. Or me."

"Great opening, but I'm not taking it."

"All right." His dejected tone was nearly convincing.

"I'd really like to get out for a while. Is that possible?"

"I'll make it possible. An hour or so until dinner, we can walk around some if you want."

"Thanks, that's great."

"Gimme a minute." Rain flipped open the cell phone.

This time he spoke to the person on the other end, no codes, no texting. "Yeah, she's feeling fine, wants to get outside for a while." He winked at Cailín, "Uh huh, just around here close, was thinkin' the park, maybe peek in a shop or two. Right, just some fresh air. Yup, big hit." He laughed, "Five minutes. All right."

"Oh, I see. Someone has to locate Skky, make sure he's not near where we're going, so I don't run into him."

"You're too smart for me."

The afternoon sun washed the tree lined streets with a peaceful glow. It was what the Irish call 'a fine soft day'. Funny, Cailín thought, how you could feel that it was late summer, how you could immediately know by being surrounded by dozens of signals, many of them subtle. Funny, how some sort of – what was it? cellular memory? – reinforced that certain things were true. She wished that Logan could be here for an hour, she could hash it out with him and maybe he could explain it. In spite of all the 'knowing' that she was experiencing it would have been difficult for him at this moment to convince her that gravity existed.

The blue sky held no threat; neither did it provide any answers. A handful of people strolled across the square in no particular hurry. Three stories up on the small but stately courthouse the clock chimed twice and fell silent. Normal. Everything was perfectly normal in the small town that appeared to exist in the decade she had left earlier that day.

"They do a good job, don't they?" Rain strolled at a leisurely pace beside her, his long legs taking one stride to her two.

"Uh, yes, I suppose they do. It's odd. That everything is familiar is somehow odd." She thought about the small town she had visited a few weeks ago.

"There are a few of these around, towns I mean. Sprinkled across the map, kind of." He glanced at her, anticipating a question. "This is the only one I know of in this particular time frame, I could be wrong."

That he knew that led her to believe that he was in this more deeply than she had thought. "Why do people choose to live in the past?"

His laugh was smooth and easy. "Now there's a question for one of the shrinks."

"Smart alec." She made a quick frown for his benefit, though she found comfort in his pragmatism.

"Why do people do anything? I don't know. It's peaceful here."

"There has to be more to it than that."

"No, there doesn't. But yeah, ok, there is.

"It's a job of sorts and it pays decent. No rent, no bills. Credits given each month to exchange for necessities, and whatever."

"So? Security? They just have to act the part, like they really live 'here'."

"Something like that. They all have work of their liking to keep the town running. Pretty easy you'd say, but there's one huge ongoing requirement."

"What?"

"They can't step out of character, can't interfere, interactions are calculated."

"They're all actors then."

"In a sense, yeah, you could say that. In a sense, so are you."

She stopped so quickly that he had to turn back to face her. "Huh?"

He scratched the side of his neck. "Well, I think you get the picture. You're a tourist, vacationing here, for the time being."

For the time being. The common phrase took on new layers of meaning. "I see. I think. It would be unfair of me to do or say anything to try to prompt them to step outside of character."

"Pretty much. It's not spelled out in so many words in that mountain of paper you signed. But you're part of the cast, part of the movie in a way."

There's another hour's conversation with Logan, at least. She thought. "A lie agreed upon, all part of not freaking Skky out."

"That's about it."

* * *

"How am I going to sleep tonight?"

"Keep packing away the chicken and stuffing and that'll take care of itself." Rain laughed. "Glad you've got an appetite, good sign. And don't worry, I'll be nearby."

"Next door or something?"

"Nope. Here."

He must have spent an entire year in acting school learning that deadpan innocence. Or worse, maybe it comes naturally. "Uh. There's only this one room..." She looked around as if to verify the fact. "… just the pull out sofa."

"Plenty of room, if you don't hog."

"Are you kidding me?" Cailín sat up straight and pinned her fork to the table.

"Nope. You can't really want to be all alone. Unless, of course, you can't trust yourself. You must be a little tense, given the circumstances. I could help take the edge off…"

"It's a little late to test the purity of my motives, or anything else for that matter, don't you think?"

"Kay, we're not going to abandon you. But after you meet Skky, we'll give you plenty of space."

Knock nuh nuh knock knock… Rain was on his feet instantly.

"Looks like a present." He sat the pink bag on the table beside her. "Go ahead, open it."

"This better not be flimsy lingerie or I'll –" she tossed the layer of tissue paper to the floor and burst into laughter.

"The Boss thinks of everything."

It smacked of Smithson alright. The gray plaid flannel pajamas were the picture of tailored chic but definitely lacked allure. Fuzzy slipper socks completed the mood.

"All I need now is a black and white movie and a carton of bonbons."

"Yeah. How about some hair curlers to go with it?"

"Oh, could you find some?" she mocked gleefully.

"Uh huh. Now, what's it gonna be, young lady? Movie for real? Cards? Think there's a chess set in the closet, though I'd probably get beat."

"What? No Candy Land or Parcheesi?"

"Don't go there, it'll date you for sure."

She sighed. "Oh gosh, I do have to be careful, don't I?"

Rain quickly shuffled the cards. "I'm pretty good at this, if I do say."

"Hmm, stack the deck however you please, I'm going to shower and get into these lovely jammies."

"Alright… what if I mark the deck while you're gone?"

"That's absolutely poetic, considering." Cailín picked up her new sleepwear and ambled thoughtfully to the bathroom.

She studied the pajamas, holding them up. They looked like a perfect fit. *Gina, probably*, she thought, *Gina knows my size..* She quickly scanned the few items in the small closet and involuntarily let out an "Oh!" There, hanging behind her favorite jeans and a selection of three blouses for tomorrow, was Skky's tee shirt. It was white and bore the logo of a popular Irish pub in the Eastern United States. She had seen several pictures of him in it, and yes, it was his size, she knew. She picked it off the hanger, pressed it to her face with both hands, and drew in a slow, deep breath. A slight scent lingered in the material, earthy and masculine. Just like Spéir, just like Skky the day she'd met him at the television station. She was suddenly dizzy. She dove into the shower and let abundant tears mingle with the lukewarm water.

"I see you found your other present." Rain smiled knowingly.

"How did – did you? – Oh, never mind. Just 'thank you', whoever."

He studied her for a brief moment. "You wear it well."

She put her hand under the pajama top, and felt the material loosely circling her waist. "What if he doesn't like me?"

"You know… we don't have to go tomorrow. You've got seventy two hours."

"Seventy two hours?"

"To get, uh, acclimated."

"And if I'm not ready by then?"

"Then James Michaels, Ph.D. is your new best friend."

"Won't be necessary."

"Didn't think so."

"What if I oversleep? What if the 'trip' messes with my sleep? What –"

"Relax, you can sleep as long as you want, no matter. You'll meet him tomorrow, one time or another. I'm just that good."

"How do you feel? About manipulating people's lives that is."

"That again."

"Well, you know… what if I did all this, and he doesn't like me? At all."

"I think there's an optometrist in town."

"Stop it. You know what I mean."

"Not sure I know how to answer that."

"You mean if you should answer that."

"Anything's possible…" He studied her for a minute and leaned to one side, stretching his shoulder. "…but, Kay, you know how careful we've been. From your point of view it's been all about protecting his best interests, and that's understandable, but I don't think you've stopped to fully realize that we've always been protecting yours as well."

She looked away from him, then back. "Okay. Okay, but I'm not quite sure I understand."

"They – we – know where his head is at. We know what he's looking for, what he wants, needs, at this point in his life. Just be yourself."

"But still I wonder if it isn't wrong to manipulate… the circumstances."

"Morally? Ethically?"

"'C', all of the above."

"Alright. Call it raising the odds – to the max. And I gotta tell you – if that's wrong, then you're not the only one that's in one helluva lot of trouble.

"And by the way," he retrieved a small disc from the back pocket of his pajamas. "I'm wired."

"I'd be disappointed if you weren't, I knew you were talking out your ass."

* * *

Cailín struggled between half consciousness and sleep. The very air itself seemed to weigh down upon her, thick and oppressive, and she didn't know which way to go. She knew where she wanted to go – to him. Skky had been in her dream, far away, down a dirt road, yet she saw him clearly. He held his right hand out to her, and spoke softly, begging her to come to him. "Please," he said over and over, "Cailín, please."

She pushed herself up on one elbow, and found it necessary to use her other hand to sit upright. She attempted a deep breath and half failed. It had been Skky, not Spéir, she knew, not knowing how she knew. Spéir had often appeared in jeans and a t-shirt, so … that was it! Of course. Spéir never wore those in a dream, only when she was awake. And his hair was longer, always. Facts, details aside, she knew anyway. Just knew.

She repositioned herself to sit cross-legged, hoping to create a stability she felt lacking in her frame. She looked down at her legs, at the plaid pajamas that someone had had delivered to her last night. A realization of where she was – and why – began to slowly creep into her mind. She looked over her shoulder at the fuzzy rays of white light that intruded past the edges of the heavy drapes and laughed at the two long, rounded pillows that Rain had placed down the center of the sofa bed. Strands of his rumpled dark hair seemed to be seeking a resting place on the pillow.

They had tested her, leaving her alone with this unarguably attractive man, and she had won. He was like Brandon, irresistible yet firmly resisted. How easily Skky had held her body, mind and soul, from a distance the past nine years. Oh, it was a nice try, but they obviously didn't understand what they were up against. She laughed out loud. Maybe she didn't either.

"Always wake up in a good mood?" Rain looked at her through half closed eyes.

170

"Nuh – uh, I mean no, I'm not. Dreamed about Skky, down a road, begging me to come."

"Ah. One of those where your legs won't move."

"Now that you mention…" her hands flew to her face, and she cried.

"Hey, look," his voice had that 'I'm talking to a four year old' quality, "you *did* move, and I guarantee he *is* just down the road."

She dropped her hands and fixed a hard stare on him.

"Seriously. He is. Literally. I think maybe it's just the realization hitting you. Sleep can do that, your mind free of other stuff. Outside stimuli gone, you know, just the stuff in your head alls that's left to deal with."

"Goddam. You're related to Logan, aren't you?"

It was his turn to laugh. "Geez, that'd be all I need right there."

"I just need to see him, you know, need to know he's alright."

"I can make that happen. Gimme thirty minutes maybe."

"I thought you said lunchtime."

"We're already down the rabbit hole, anything can happen."

She stared at the blank TV screen for a full thirty seconds. "Rain? Show me the pictures again."

He let her gaze a while, with the benefit of allowing him to collect his thoughts. "That was just yesterday, Kaylin, not even twenty four hours ago. He's fine. Promise."

"Then we'll just stay with the original plan. Lunchtime. But, Rain? I can't stay cooped up in here all morning."

"Hmm. Yeah. There's three or four antique or vintage shops, whatever. We could walk around and you could explore those?"

"Sure. Just some activity that approaches normal."

"You got it. Gonna order us some breakfast. Make some coffee while I shower. Uh, please?"

* * *

Cailín looked around, memorizing everything, the small shops, the town square. It's endearing, she thought, the hand painted signs, the lack of neon. This was a day to remember, the smell of freshly cut grass, the warmth of the sun, the slight click of her boot heels on the sidewalk, because today her boots would take her where she wanted to be.

The shops were fun, and held her interest to an extent. She made mental notes of pieces to give further consideration. There was an entire corner of one shop that fascinated her. It featured a variety of wooden trunks and boxes, and she examined every one of them, remembering Speír's love of making anything and everything out of wood. In the world they shared in her dreams he had made all of their furniture, and several storage chests of different sizes. She especially loved the smaller boxes and the detail he had put into them. One box in particular reminded her of a clever piece he had made for her birthday. It was small, about four inches square, and held four tiny drawers each opening from a different side of the box. He was fond of the unusual and took great pride in the uniqueness of the pieces he made.

"Huh-mm," Rain cleared his throat.

"Oh, I'm sorry, are you bored?"

"Don't believe I've ever seen anyone fascinated by a bunch of wooden boxes for an hour."

"Oh gosh, has it been that long?"

He laughed, "Well, it's okay really, but maybe we could come back later?"

"Over here." Rain took her arm briefly and steered her diagonally across the square. The large glass panes covering the front of the pub were framed between Sam's Hardware and Velda's Vintage. Slices of sun glided through the door with them. Tables were scattered about in no particular order in Clancey's Pub.   Cloths of red, green, or blue checks beckoned to make a choice.

"Toward the back."   Rain pointed.   "Not what you expected?"

"Not sure that I expected anything, but let's sit by the window."

"Might rather be −"

"No.   Up here."   Cailín led the way up two stair steps to one of four tables that lined the built up ledge. "This is good."

Rain hoped she wasn't pulling back too much. "You sure?"

She noted that the glazed cement floor was clean enough to eat off of, then turned her gaze to the back of the long narrow room.   "I know that he… Skky, always liked to play the small pubs back home, or 'back when', whatever."

"Not the best seats in the house."   Rain muttered, wondering.

"What can I get for you?"   The waitress stood just a little too close to Rain.

"Uh, iced tea would be fine."   He waved an open palm in Cailín's direction.

"Sure."   She was quietly surveying the room and its dozen or so occupants.

"Sugar?" the girl smiled through a heavy layer of bubble gum lipstick as she sat the glasses on the table, brushing Rain's shoulder deliberately.

"No, thanks, I'm good." He glanced at her, then lowered his eyes.

"I bet you are, and sweet enough already.   I'll be back to take your orders in a jiff."   The pretty waitress sauntered off, ponytail and hips swinging.   All she needed was a poodle skirt, Cailín thought.   She already had the saddle shoes and bobby socks.

"Mmphh." Cailín's hand went to her mouth. "Good, now you have a reason to be nearly as scared as I am."

"I doubt that." Rain huffed, and pretended to have the situation under control.

"Ow, hey! Ow!" Rain tried to keep his voice down but Cailín had a death grip on his tanned forearm, nails digging in. "Take it easy, take it easy, just act normally."

"Yeah, like *this* happens everyday. Oh my – " she stopped breathing.

Skky O'Keeffe crossed the space of the room in no particular hurry, and picked up the guitar. "Heh guys, 'sup?" he said to no one in particular.

"Seriously, Kaylin." Rain tried to look like they were having a normal discussion. His acting skills were coming in handy. "Kay!" he grinned, "don't blow it now."

"Yes, of course." She relaxed her grip a bit, sitting up straighter. "Just absolutely beautiful... weather ... we're having, isn't it?"

"Uh huh, there you go. Remember after lunch we're going to go look at a real place for you to stay. And – I'm not wired, won't be anymore."

"That's, uh, that's good." *How do I stop myself from staring?* She forced herself to glance at Rain.

"This's an old song, wan me father taught me." Even his speaking voice was melodic.

"Yeah, got three places to choose from, think you'll probably like one of them."

"That's nice," she dismissed, her full attention on Skky singing an old Irish ballad.

"What did I just say?"

"Uh..."

Rain laughed silently, wondering if he needed to remind her to breathe.

There it was, the voice she adored, warm honey with a sprinkle of cinnamon.

The waitress arranged plates on the tables, sandwiches here, salads there. "Careful, it's very hot."

"What?" Cailín knew she sounded annoyed, the young woman was blocking her view, and talking while *he* was singing. *Who does that?*

"The soup. It's very hot."

"Oh. Yeah, it's unbelievably hot." She shot Rain another glance, smiling. "Of course, thanks."

Rain laughed out loud this time, and allowed himself to relax a little.

It seemed that Skky's voice simply floated through the air, spiriting her away.

"You good?"

"I'm glad we sat back a little farther, even being this close is pretty..."

"Don't look now," Rain had that sheepish trying-hard-not-to-laugh look. "but – "

Cailín glanced up, Skky was walking towards them, smiling. She was glad that she didn't have a mouthful of food or she would have choked. Skky was extending his hand to Rain. "Heh, Rain, 'sup?"

Rain half rose from his chair and extended his hand across the table. "Hey Skky, not much, how 'bout you?"

She couldn't breathe, he was gloriously himself. That's all she could think of, he was *himself*.

"Take a load off, buddy." Rain pushed the chair next to him with his foot, motioning Skky to sit down. Cailín thought she was smiling, she couldn't really tell, she felt numb. He sat with one leg extended, the other bent, as he had in the photograph.

"No idea you actually had talent, what brings you to a little dive like this?"

"Aw is nice, so it is, good people."

"Well, enjoyed it very much."

176

"Thank ye then."

"Yes, it was great!" Cailín chimed in a little too enthusiastically.

"Thank ya too, lass." She swore there was a hint of mischief in his eyes.

"Oh, sorry. Skky, this is my cousin, Kaylin Casey."

"Oh. Cousin then? Very pleased to meet ya, wee bonnie lass. Skky O'Keeffe here." He leaned forward and extended a hand.

Oh my god, he's going to touch me! His touch was warm, familiar, and it put her more at ease. He was solid, not a mirage. "Nice to meet you, too."

"So it's Kay, like K–a-y, is it?" he took his hand away too quickly to suit her.

"No, actually it's not. Its spelled C-a-i-l-i-n, and I know, well, you're Irish aren't you? You'd say 'Colleen', wouldn't you? Anyway, my mother insisted it was pronounced 'Kaylin'."

He raised his eyebrows and sat up a little straighter, "I see – 'tis lovely either way," he declared.

"A bit of a funny way to spell mine as well. Two k's, two e's, two f's."

"O, K-k, e-e, f-f, e?" of course she knew better.

"Ha ha ha!" his laugh was easy, melodic. "Noh, ah, it's S-k-k-y, an the O'Keeffe, sorta normal, 'cept for the two f's maybe."

She laughed, too, "I like the name Skky, it suits you."

"Whawt makes ya think I'm Irish?" The glint came back quickly to his eyes.

"Um, well, your accent?"

"Aye, we are colorful, aren't we?"

"In the best possible way," she smiled. She was deliberately overt, no time like to present to start. "I'm Irish, too, well, mostly," she added, "although not fortunate enough to ever have been to Ireland."

"A shame. Go someday, 'tis lovely."

Before she could answer Rain interjected. "Drink, Skky? Sandwich?"

"Ah, noh, am fine, thanks. Just stick to the water when I'm workin'." He sat up straight again, "which I should be gettin' back to."

"Alright." Rain dismissed.

"Again, well, very nice to meet ya," he said directly to Cailín, and started to walk away. "Say, uh, if you're 'round about this way tomorrow stop in for a bit?"

"I will, I really like hearing you sing." She congratulated herself, at least she wasn't screaming *don't go.* "Nice meeting you, too."

Had he lingered just a second too long before walking away? Cailín hoped.

Rain would wait until Skky had finished singing the second song, not bothering to try a conversation with Cailín, who sat, transfixed, barely picking at her food. He also noted with a smile that Skky looked directly at her several times, and made no attempt to hide it. He was singing a love song about missed opportunities.

Now Rain held his breath, hoping the song would be over before she burst into tears. It looked as though that could happen at any second. He knew he was going to have to interrupt soon.

"Alright, young lady, let's go find you a proper place to live." Rain hadn't really expected a prompt response, and wondered if he was going to have to count backwards from ten to one. "Earth to Kay…"

"Oh, I'm sorry. Um, sorry."

"No, you're not, but that's okay. We really do need to get on with this though."

He no sooner started to raise a finger into the air than the perky brunette materialized at his side. "What can I do for you, honey? Like some pie?"

"Uh, no thanks, just the check please."

"Aw, so soon?" She pouted and leaned closer. "Just sign when you're ready," she cooed. "Do take your time."

The waitress produced a device that reminded her of a cell phone. Rain touched a finger here and there on the screen and planted his thumbprint at the bottom right. "That's how you sign for what you buy here." Cailín nodded mutely, and stole another glance at Skky.

Rain held the door for her and Cailín resisted one last look back. She walked stiffly, probably holding her breath. She walked like she was in one of those dreams where you're trying to run but can't. She turned the corner quickly, placed one boot heel against the wall, leaned back, and slapped both palms on her cheeks. She stared past Rain as if she'd just seen the eighth wonder of the world. "Oh my God! He's truly, absolutely exquisite! Did that really just happen?"

"Hey, you did fine, really. Pretty normal, sorta, uh, most of the time. But fine."

"Ohh lord, he is *so* pretty."

Rain laughed, "Still not my type."

"Do you think – I mean, I didn't act like a complete idiot?"

"Nah, you didn't, not complete anyways. Don't know if you noticed –"

"What?"

"I think he was trying nearly hard as you not to stare."

"You're kidding?" she popped off the wall.

"No," Rain raised a finger, "and I was the only sober one, so to speak, at the table. He's definitely interested. Kinda cute, I felt like the prom night chaperone."

"Seriously?"

"Take my word for it? What with you being in an altered state. Guys know how guys act. And it will get easier."

"I'm coming back here tomorrow you know."

"Figured. Think it would be good if I came along, just one more time."

"Yes, it would help, if you don't mind."

"That's why they pay me the big bucks," he laughed, but it was a kind laugh. "Come on now, let's go find you a bigger place to stay." He took her arm and nudged her. "Just walk it off."

A small rose bed graced the front yard of the yellow cottage, and inside it was cheerful and cozy. The second was more tailored with a steel blue exterior; it was upscale suburbia only smaller.

"Any preference so far?"

"They're very nice."

"Alright, Goldilocks, let's go see if number three is 'just right'."

"There aren't any cars, or um… vehicles here, are there? Everyone seems to just walk."

"It's a small town after all, and vehicles are pretty much not in the picture."

"That's a bit of a throwback even for three hundred years ago, isn't it?"

"Maybe. That's kinda the way it seems to work best, well… for this."

"Oh my! Is this like that movie? The one about the guy's life, his every move on camera?"

"The Truman Show? I guess you don't remember me telling you, I'm not wired anymore."

That Rain knew the name of the movie clicked a small switch in her brain and she wondered if he had travelled the same way she did, or if he had memories of a previous life.

"Yeah, that's it. So it'd be – they can't have any cars, er, vehicles, around me, can they? What if I walked, or ran, too far past the edge of town? Would someone stop me? or something? A brick wall? An electric fence? A –"

"Kay! Wow, that mind just never stops working, does it?"

" – a wall painted like the sky?"

"We know you're not leaving here until you're sure about Skky, one way or another. And when that time comes, all you have to do is say so. You're not a prisoner here. Tell me right now you want out, and it won't take me five minutes to arrange it."

"No! No, I just, I think too much sometimes."

"Understandable, you've just made a drastic change in your life. A suggestion though, stop thinking and allow yourself to feel. It's alright, really."

They walked farther down the street, and she spotted a stone cottage and hoped that it was available. Scents from a variety of flowers mingled and reminded her of her grandmother's garden, and she breathed in the memory as Rain directed her toward the red door. The wood floor and patterned area rug provided a backdrop for a sofa that was almost too large for the room. Cailín immediately sank into a chair and sighed, "This is it."

"You sure? Don't you want to see the rest of it?"

"If it's anything like this, I'm sure it's fine."

"You want to check out the kitchen at least, then we're off to the grocery? I, uh, thought you'd at least want to see the bedroom. Surely you're not planning on spending more time in the kitchen?" he laughed.

"Funny man."

"No, just realistic."

Rain pulled his cell phone out of his pocket, punched a few keys, and said, "There. Your stuff will be delivered before we get back."

"Two pounds of bacon, ten pounds of potatoes, two dozen eggs, oh, flour, milk…"

"Whoa! You planning on feeding army or somethin'? By the way, since you didn't bother to look at the kitchen, all the staples, flour and stuff, already there."

"I just want to be sure I have enough of everything."

"So you're planning on feeding an army? Well, not like you can't come back. Here," he pulled out his cell phone again, "I'll get a list of what's there already."

"And no, just one very hungry Irishman."

"Oh, see? Knew you should have looked at the bedroom, great one for working up an appetite. I could help out with a test run, just to be sure."

"Always just right there on it, aren't you?"

"I try."

It hadn't taken long to arrange her belongings in the ample closet, and she insisted that Rain let her put things away in the kitchen. "You okay with this?" he asked.

"Oh, it's perfect! Everything I need. I can't wait to cook!"

"Then get started," he laughed, "there should be a grill and charcoal in the shed. I'll cook the steaks. How's about a vat of mashed potatoes, Miss Irish Army?"

* * *

"Wowww," Rain mumbled past a mouthful, "what did you do to these potatoes? They're awesome."

"Do you think −"

"Oh, yeah, if this is any indication he'll love your cooking. Not the only way to a man's heart, but can't hurt."

"It has to be something he misses, home cooking."

"Don't forget yourself."

"What do you mean?"

"I know, it's all about him, but don't lose yourself completely, won't come out right."

"Another eighty or ninety years and I'll be tired of his face. Then I'll start acting normally."

"I think a little reassurance is all you need, and not from me. Unless I'm completely blind you'll get that soon. Then you can relax." Rain took time out for another generous forkful. "Speaking of... you gonna be able to sleep tonight?"

"Sure. Why wouldn't I? Unless..."

Rain laughed. "What I was comin' to. Want me to stay, or no? Sofa looks comfortable enough."

"You know, I think I'll be just fine. Thanks though."

"If you need anything at all I'm just a phone call away. On the outside chance I don't answer, someone will pick it up in thirty seconds or less."

He offered to help clean up, but she refused. "It'll give me something to do, something 'normal', so I don't mind. It'll be good."

"Want to talk to Dr. Michaels about anything?"

"No. You're enough of a pain, Mr. Big Bucks, thanks."

"You remembered! That's why they − you know."

"Uh huh."

"But I should tell you, he'll want to talk to you, probably tomorrow afternoon or thereabouts."

"I know you can't tell me how, but I assume you and Logan talk?"

"Right on both counts. What I can say is that Logan seems confident."

"And of course you're in on it, too."

"Guilty. So I'll come by about eleven-thirty?"

"No. I'll meet you there, just outside the pub, at a quarter 'til."

Rain shook his head as he walked toward the door, "They grow up so fast."

* * *

It was curiously quiet. Cailín sat on a wooden bench outside the pub, either Rain was late or she was early. She leaned back, closed her eyes, and began to recall every detail of her meeting with Skky yesterday.

"Heh, lass!" Her vision was right in front of her and she tried her best not to act startled. "Can come inside, ya know." She could drown in one of those smiles.

"Skky! Hello. I'm just waiting on Rain. Now I know why it seems so quiet – no music."

"Aye well, he'll find ya, wee Cailín, clever lad that." She loved that he said her name the way it was meant to be said. He held out his hand and she took it. "Come now, am late I'm afraid. Quiet, is it then? Let's go make some noise." He made straight for a vacant table next to where he stood while singing, and pulled out a chair for her.

She reluctantly let go of his hand. "Thanks."

Two easy strides and he picked up his guitar. "Hello! How's everyone today? Good to see ya. I've had a couple requests already," he mastered pause for effect "but the guitar won't fit and I just got here, soz not time to go home yet."

She made no attempt to conceal her laughter as he offered an impish grin.

"Here's wan I wrote a while back…"

Never thought too much about it
When I was just young
Life Was Full of mysteries
And life was all for fun

Days and nights of dreamin'
The taste of whiskey on my tongue
Life Was Full of secrets
And life had just begun

185

The perky waitress from yesterday sat down next to her and leaned in to take her order. "Can I bring your cousin something? Is he joining you today?" Subtlety was not her strong suit.

"Can't miss with iced tea, let's go with that. Two, please." Cailín found herself worrying just a little on her behalf, as girls do about each other. She wondered if Rain was at all interested, or even available for that matter, or if the sweet girl was riding for a fall.

"Great! And what about your friend?"

"Um, well…" she remembered, "… he sticks with water when he's working."

"Comin' right up!"

"Thanks, Lexi." Cailín noticed her name tag for the first time.

The cell whirred in her pocket, a text message from Rain scrolled across the screen.

> yikes! srry
> meetng went long.
> u ok??? press 1 if no
> otherwse ther n 10 min

She couldn't help but wonder if he was late on purpose. She was suddenly aware that she had just walked into a pub that held twice as many people as it did yesterday – holding Skky's hand. People must be thinking that they were together! She smiled slowly, feeling like a cat caught with its face buried in a bowl of cream, and enjoyed every second of it.

Thirty minutes later, and no Rain. Cailín had finished half of a Reuben sandwich when Skky announced that he was taking a short break. He came straight to the table, pulled out a chair and sat down. "You don't eat much, never tried that one, it good, or…"

"I had a huge breakfast, and a late one. But yeah, it's good, try it?" She inched her plate in his direction.

"Air ya sure?"

"Sure.

"Oh! Forgive me, I just realized... I recognized that last song you sang. I've heard it before, several times. I didn't make the connection with your name, I guess I spend too much time at work. Your voice, though, is definitely unforgettable."

"Ah well, thanks. Hmm, sandwich not bad at all, but me granny makes it better."

"So does mine," she laughed, "but all the same, please finish it."

"Thanks, don't mind if I do. 'Twould be better with a beer, but is a bit early."

"Have a shot of caffeine then, no way you can accuse their tea of being weak." She picked up Rain's glass of iced tea and sat it closer to him.

An openly mischievous look crossed his face, "You'll spoil me."

She couldn't resist, "Yes, and you'll love every minute of it."

Rain no sooner walked through the door than Lexi made a beeline for the table.

"Hey, Skky, see you took good care of my cuz."

"Yup, 'twas rough, hadda fight our way through the mob, you see. Fought tree guys for the table, hopefully they'll be awright." He shrugged, "Dunno."

"There's nothing quite like a good pub fight. Sorry I missed it, not much else to do around here."

"Which... so what's to do around here? Nawt that I much mind the peace and quiet for a change."

"I hear ya. There's fair sized pond, hear the fishing is good. Might try it sometime. You fish?"

"Have, can't say I'm good at it."

"Eh. Just an excuse to sit and drink beer," Rain quipped.

"At dawn thirty? Dint know you were Irish," Skky said, and something clicked in her mind, she'd heard him use that expression before.

"What you been doing to entertain yourself?"

"Been nice to have time to spend with my guitars, just makin' up stuff," he laughed. "Ah. Found a right decent stretch for skate boardin' too." He looked at Cailín. "You ever do that?"

"Skate boarding? No, I can't say that I've ever tried."

"Should, is fun, so it is. I can teach you."

"Really? Is there a good doctor in town? Or a clinic for broken bones?"

"Not that hard, truly it's not. Got the whole day off tomorrow, let's give it a go it in the mornin'."

"Oh? Well, okay. I should warn you though, it may not only be me in danger of getting hurt."

"Nah. Won't let that happen. So, meet ya here in front of the pub, maybe? Say ten?"

"Sure. Yeah, why not?"

"Ya know," he leaned over and grabbed her ankle and she let out a squeal of surprise. "I really like these boots," he continued, "best not to wear them tomorrow though."

"You're crazy!" she laughed.

"Ah. You say that now. Tomorrow I'll prove it.

"So back to it for me it is."

* * *

188

He was flying down the sidewalk, arms stretched out to his sides. He looked just like an angel, Cailín thought, as the mid morning sun shone through his blonde hair like a halo.

"Sorry if I'm late." Skky swiveled the board to stop right in front of her.

"I just got here actually."

"Ah, good, 'twould be a crime to keep you waiting. Sneakers! Perfect."

"Ha ha ha, I'll need every advantage I can get."

"Not that hard really." He did a double take to her look of skepticism. "Seriously."

"Easy for you to say, you look like you were born on that thing."

"Me mum might say otherwise." He laughed.

"Bet I could get the confession out of her."

He laughed harder, to her obvious delight.

"Okay, so…"

"Hmm, well, let's walk down here a bit, less chance uh runnin' into people."

"In my case I'm sure that's literally true."

"Left handed, or right?"

"Left, why?"

"Then might be easier to put your right foot on the board to start."

"Oh."

"Like this, start easy, one foot on, push with the other a couple times."

"You make it look so easy."

"Is, really."

He motioned semi-dramatically with both hands, and she placed one foot on the board and made a small push with the other. "Eeeek!" The board shot out from under her and she had to scramble not to fall backwards.

"'S okay, just try again." He was polite enough to not let out the mirth that sparkled in his eyes.

Cailín tried two more times and failed both. "Ugh. What am I doing wrong?"

"Hmm. Try this, watch. Maybe bend your knee a little more, lower your center of gravity."

"Darn. I should have known there was science involved."

This time he did laugh out loud. "Yup, I suppose, geometry, physics. You can raise your arms before you push off if that feels better." He rubbed the side of his neck and made a face. "Lessee if I can do it slower, show ya."

He glided twenty feet or so down the sidewalk, stopped, and came back.

"I'll try that." This time she made it about three feet before she pitched forward and stumbled off.

"Progress!" he declared.

"Oh gosh, I dunno, I just can't get a feel for it," she mock pouted.

"Here, got an idea." He turned his back to her and bent his knees. "Jump on."

"What!?"

"Jump on, I'll take ya for a ride. Used to do this with me wee sis."

"Uh, well."

"Trust me," he said over his shoulder, as he wiggled his eyebrows and gave her his best evil smile.

She laughed, "It's not so much me that I'm worried about. But okay."

She put her arms around his neck and he reached back and grabbed the back of her thighs. She crossed her legs around his waist. *It was good for me, was it good for you?* She was lost in the hardness of his muscles under the softness of his t-shirt, and pressed her cheek against his neck and closed her eyes.

My God, he smells like heaven, I wonder what his skin tastes like?

190

"Uh. Your eyes are closed, I bet on it. Won't work, wakey, wakey."

She drew in a deep breath and opened her eyes. His back muscles rippled and she was being lifted up with him. For a few seconds she felt like they were flying across the universe together.

"Wahh, ohh noo!" His unintended slip was more graceful that hers, but he still had to run a few steps to regain balance.

"Sorry." He bent his knees, her signal to dismount.

"I thought you said you did this with your little sis."

"Surely I dint, wouldn't put me sis in danger like that," he said soberly.

"Very funny." She slapped his arm without thinking, and he jumped back in mock fear.

"Hope ya don't have her left hook. Sent me to the clinic more 'n once, so she has."

"Well good for her!"

She could tell by the look on his face that he was getting another idea. "How about this –"

"Oh, no, not another great idea."

"Noh, noh really, this might be easier. How 'bout I hold your hand, run alongside to steady you?"

"You've never taught anyone how to do this before, have you?"

"Noh idea why ya say that." His feigned indignation made her laugh again. "C'mon, try it!"

He took her hand and she did find it easier, so he let go and ran beside her. She made it another ten feet or so before she found herself running headlong toward the grass. He threw his arms around her waist in an attempt to right her but the forward motion was too much. He twisted so that he landed on his back with her on top of him. The laws of physics still in motion, she rolled off and onto her back. They looked at each other and simultaneously burst into peals of laughter.

"Omigosh!" tears were starting to roll down her cheeks. "*That* was attractive!"

"Never…" he was trying to catch his breath and get the words out between guffaws, "…never argue with a woman." His laughter redoubled at his own comment.

She was having the same happy problem, "You're… you're a wonderful teacher… too bad no one has ever lived to say it!"

He drew his knees toward his chest and slapped his hands over his stomach. A full minute passed before he could answer. "That'll cost ya extra."

Her hand went to her forehead, there was no regaining composure, "Save it. Save it… for the judge."

Cailín rolled onto her side, the better to see him. Still smiling, he was now still with his eyes closed. She reached out tentatively and put her hand on his arm, hungry to just be touching him again. He placed his hand on her bent knee and they both lay still on the cool grass, contented.

She could have stayed there all day, but after a few minutes he jumped to his feet and offered a hand to pull her up. "You hungry? Might be a lil early for lunch, but I'm ready if you are."

"That did make me hungry for some reason." *Just pass me a spoon and I'll eat you up. Second thought, never mind the spoon.* "I'm sure we're presentable."

"Ahh noh! Dun make me laugh anymore!"

They walked silently in the direction of the pub. It felt so natural, so right to be holding his hand.

As they drew near he broke the silence. "The food's right decent here, ya think?"

"Yeah, it's pretty good really."

"Only thing they don't have is bacon tomato sandwich. Wonderin' why? Haven't had one uh those in forever."

"That's your favorite?" She knew it was.

"Given the choice, so it is."

"You don't really want to hang out at the pub on your day off, do you?"

"Don't mind."

"I have everything we need at the cottage, I can make you one."

"A bacon tomato? You kiddin'?"

"Nope."

"Seriously?"

You'd think I'd just offered him the Taj Mahal. Am I good or what?

"Don't make *me* laugh again. Yes, seriously."

"Need anything picked up? I'd be glad to. Shouldn't be makin' you cook on your vacation. Hmm. I really want one though."

"Say no more, I love to cook and normally don't have much time to. What was it you said? 'Trust me'."

"With pleasure."

"Anything I can help with?"

"Set the table? You'll know where things are as well as I do at this point. Oh and there's potato salad in the fridge, bring that out."

"You're kiddin'?"

"No, I made it last night."

"Dear lord."

"Told you, I've missed cooking."

"So I see. Uhhh…"

"Did you just spot the chocolate cream pie by chance?"

"Heaven help me, believe I did. Em, by the way… you've turned the bacon tree or fohr times?"

"Yeah, my grandmother taught me that; cooks it more evenly."

"Hmm, well, me granny turns it seven, eight times, so she does."

"Really? My granny cures the bacon herself."

"I see. Me granny raises the pigs herself."

"Wellll, my granny makes her own pickles for the potato salad."

"Me granny grows her own potatoes."

"And mines raises chickens, so the eggs are fresh."

"Mmkay, me granny invented potatoes."

"Potatoes weren't invented."

"'Course they were. Where did ya think they came from?"

"All right. Sure she did. She had to, she's Irish."

"Yup. That's right. Glad ya understand."

"Oh, I understand. By the way, my granny invented pimentos."

"But –"

"Oh no you don't, don't go there," she waved the tongs in his direction, "same principal as 'inventing' potatoes. See?"

"Fair play it is then."

"Now some bread, and we're ready to make sandwiches."

"Eh well, me granny always toasted the bread."

"That's nice. I'll toast it then. My granny invented the toaster."

"'Tis fortunate then that me granny invented electricity, so it is."

"She probably makes the sandwich for you, too?"

"Yup."

"I can do that." She carefully stacked the bread with one too many slices of bacon, and extra thick slices of tomato. "Here you go, how's that?"

"Nice enough I suppose."

"Oh?"

"Me granny always cuts it, in triangles like."

"Fine," she sighed. "What's wrong now?"

"Noh matter. But, well, me granny cuts it twice, so fohr triangles."

"Skky?"

"Hmm?"

"Just eat the damned sandwich already."

That was the last straw, the laughter he'd been holding back broke out and she gave in as well.

Skky held both hands up, "Truce, please, before I starve."

"I haven't laughed this much in the entire past year, combined."

"Heh. I surely haven't either." His smile disappeared.

"Don't know if that should make me happy, or sad."

"Happy, I'd hope."

"Yes, happy."

"Did your granny by chance invent aspirin?"

"It's possible, likely even, I'd have to ask. Why though?"

"Because we're both gonna have terrible headaches from all the laffin'."

"I'll live with it."

"Me, too. This is all just great, really good. Mayonnaise store bought though?"

"You better not start up again. I'll find your sis and…"

"'Nuff said."

Uncharacteristic silence fell between them for a few minutes, interspersed by his compliments every two minutes, to which she'd smile and nod. Two sandwiches and three helpings of potato salad later he sat back and groaned, "Truly wonderful, thanks. Where did you learn to cook?"

"This is easy, really, but I can cook more complicated dishes, too. Oh, and from my granny, of course."

"Of course." He laughed. "My undying thanks."

Skky stood up and began to clear the dishes.

"You don't have to do that!"

"At the very least, honestly. I'll wash, you dry."

They completed the chore in a comfortable silence.

* * *

"What are you doing here?"

"Rain! Come in."

"Thought sure you'd be at the pub, it's nearly noon."

"Yeah. I slept late. Felt like baking a pie, well, this is number two actually," Cailín slid the overstuffed crust into the oven.

"I hadn't heard from you, assumed everything was good… is it?"

"We had the most fun yesterday, just the best, then I made lunch."

"Nesting, eh?"

"Maybe."

"So what's the real reason you're not at the pub today?"

"Taking a break. And yes, on purpose. Giving him the chance to make another – the next – move. Want some chocolate pie?"

"Fascinating. And yes."

"Look, it's not easy. I'd love to be there right now, I just don't want to crowd him."

"Sure you do," he laughed, "but I gotcha. Wanna do something this afternoon? Walk around, go to the lake? Open a bakery? I could take you back to the apartment, you can watch the videos there."

"Thanks, but I'm fine."

"Hmm, what am I missing?"

"I have this feeling that I should hang around here this afternoon."

"The intuition thing. You got me beat."

"You're sure you don't want to offer to sleep with me, 'sugar britches'?" she parroted Lexi's pet name for him.

"I get the impression it might get a little crowded soon?"

"Rain, I'm in for the duration. It's been maddening these last few days, now things are starting to smooth out. Spending time with Skky, finally, it's amazing. I'm grateful. I'd do it all over again, a thousand times, just to get here."

"Glad you feel that way. Happy for you."

* * *

Three steady knocks on the front door. She knew before he spoke, "Cailín?"

"It's open, come in, Skky," she said cheerfully.

"Thanks. Hahwareya, lass? How'd ya know it was me?" He laughed "I —" he took a deep breath, "— dear lord, I'd ask whawt ya been doin', but surely think I know."

"First, I'd know your voice anywhere. Second, have you hired someone to spy on me, or are you psychic?"

He laughed, "Neither."

"That's a relief. In that case, how about a piece of apple pie? Have you had lunch yet? I could —"

"Noh, noh, very late breakfast. Pie would be great though, so it would." He followed her back into the kitchen. "You were serious 'bout catchin' up on cookin', so you were."

"I've missed it, I'm really having fun. All the better when someone appreciates it."

"Yeah, nice to be appreciated sometimes." The words seemed to come out a little too seriously. "Heh, how 'bout we take this outside? 'tis nice."

"Ooh, sounds like the start of a good pub fight, 'let's take this outside'."

"Ha ha ha, nope. Unless you're mad at somebody?"

"Not at the moment. Coffee?"

"'Twould be nice, dun trouble though."

"Only takes a minute. Speaking of pubs, how did it go today?"

"Good. Well, from my perspective. People seemed to like it well enough."

"How big an audience are you used to? When you're touring?"

"Uh, well, anywhere from two to forty thousand, give or take."

"Wow! This is quite a change for you, two or three dozen people."

199

"Always liked the smaller crowds, the pubs at home an' stuff." He reached for the coffee cups. "Let me, they're hot."

A slight breeze stirred in the afternoon sun. A bird hopped across the grass, stopping now and then to chirp to its mate. The lazy drone of an airplane put the final touch on the late summer day.

Her cheek resting in her hand, she made no effort to be coy, her gaze transfixed on his profile as he unapologetically devoured the pie. She thought of the glowing praise his fans heaped on him, not only for his talent, but for his personality as well. He always had time to greet one more fan, giving autographs, throwing his arm around a succession of shoulders while the cameras snapped. He would pick up small children, much to their delight. He probably landed in more family albums than any other celebrity, she guessed. Through it all, the charm, the humor, came easily.

Skky always seemed to have a sense of wonder, an almost disbelief that he was fortunate enough to have people appreciate what he loved to do. And he never missed an opportunity to tell the press that his fans were the best in the world.

Those throngs of fans would describe him as warm, genuine, down to earth. Cailín had recognized that in him, but to her eyes he was transcendent. He was from another place and time.

She reached across the space between their chairs and touched his arm. She had to be sure he was solid. Quietly she said, "Perfect afternoon for a dream, I just wanted to be sure you were real."

A slow smile began to form. He looked down briefly, then met her eyes. "Real enough, I 'spose."

"Yes, I doubt anyone could accuse you of being anything else and get by with it.

"So what's it like? Being in front of so many people I mean? Do you ever get nervous? What do you do if you make a mistake? She took a quick breath, "Oh gosh, I'm asking too many questions, aren't I?"

"Em, well, then to answer one – if you mess up you pick up and go on best you can. Sooner you forget about it, sooner the rest will. An' yeah, it happens.

"For the rest, the energy is ahmasin, so it is. I've done it dead tired, but walk out there and can just feed on the energy. Is really kinda cool, guess you could say."

"Wow! you really love it, don't you?"

"'Tis great to do whawt ya love, to be sure."

"Yes, it would be. And after a show, then what? Is it a big letdown?"

"Noh, not really. Is a change, but then ya have the other guys who just experienced the same thing, so you're around people who understand. Still an' all, a lot of times you just want one special person to share it with.

"Damn, uh, 'scuse me, but this is great."

"Better than your granny's?"

"Let's not get carried away…" he had the mock seriousness down pat.

Cailín giggled, "Truce. My head actually does hurt from laughing so much yesterday."

"Mine, too. If ya gotta hurt from somethin', that should be it." That was the second time he'd sounded a bit down, and she was concerned.

"But you're a positive person, well, from what I know of you."

That prompted a smile. "Yup, try to be. Life should be fun, it should. Unrealistic to expect that every minute of every day, but often as possible." He stole a glance at her, "You make it easy."

"Yeah?"

"Yup."

"Skky, do you believe in second chances?"

"I do, least I hope so, lass. I do hope." He quickly broke the sober mood, "Heh, speakin' uh fun, I hear there's a wee party like tonight in the park. Barbeque and just gettin' together, games for the kiddos an such. Come with me?"

"That sounds good, yes."

"I'll dig up a blanket or somethin' to sit on."

"Should I bring some food?"

"Might be appreciated. By me, to be sure." He laughed. "Now I should probly get my lazy self up and go make some calls. Agent an such. I'll be by for ya about sex?"

"What?" She remembered to translate the accent, *wan, tew, tree, fohr, fie-ev, sex.* "Oh, yes."

"Don't worry about the dishes, go make your calls."

"Tryin' to get rid uh me, eh?"

"Not even close." She turned around and nearly bumped into him.

Skky put his hand on her waist and she looked up into his eyes. She placed her hands on his upper arms, any excuse to do that was good. He leaned in and kissed her softly on the lips. Cailín opened her eyes slowly, it was over too soon. He caressed her cheek and kissed her again, again softly, but this time longer, and she memorized every split second of his touch.

"Always kiss the cook... er, well, dependin', uh course."

"Works for me." She let her hands fall away and wondered how she could.

He stepped away somewhat reluctantly, she thought.

"Be back for ya then, tonight. Oh – and thanks." He turned and smiled and winked as he walked toward the door. "And thanks for the pie, too."

* * *

Cailín stepped out of the shower. This decision couldn't be too difficult given the limited space she'd had to pack. So far he'd only seen her in jeans and sweats, time to mix it up.

One thing was certain. Fluff. She bent over and brushed her hair forward and dried it.

If only I could call Brandon. She scooped up the cell Rain had supplied. "Jeans again? In the park, sitting on the ground, so…"

"No," Rain was decisive, "something slutty."

"Wuh… you're kidding?"

"Nope. He's male. Not kidding."

She sighed. Brandon would have been specific. The yellow skirt with tiny flower print was casual enough. She'd bought it just because she liked it and had never had occasion to wear it. Sleeveless white eyelet blouse – perfect.

She studied herself in the mirror and frowned. *Holy cow, I look frilly… and sweet.* Ten minutes and he'd be at the door. She brushed her hair into a high ponytail and quickly secured big hoop earrings. Better. *Here we go.* She plucked her red bra from the drawer. It showed through the white blouse, and the straps didn't quite stay tucked in. Good. She made a face then undid the last three buttons, then a fourth on the mid calf length skirt. Denim jacket for later… perfectly punk with her strappy sandals. It was complicated enough to keep his interest, and this was no time to play it safe.

"Hi!" she pushed the screen door open. "Help me carry the food?" she smiled over her shoulder as she turned toward the kitchen. *Yessss! He's definitely looking.*

"Sayin' a lot, maybe, that I can be trusted." He stopped and swallowed, "Er, with the food that is. Here, I'll take those."

She wondered if he was always so gallant, and decided it was likely.

"Guessin' I should leave this here?" He pushed the skateboard further to the side of the door.

She laughed out loud. "You used that for just the short trip across the street?"

"It's faster, er well, whawtever." He laughed, too. "But I must say, could be a very slow trip if you were to…"

"Hey!" she pushed into his arm with her shoulder and he broke into a 'yeah, like you could hurt me' laugh.

She noted that there was no ring on his left hand and wondered if he'd been married this time around, but she didn't ask. How anyone could ever let him go, she couldn't imagine.

"Are you going to let it grow?"

"Hm? Oh, just dint bother to shave today, sorry."

"Don't be, I like the scruff." Surely there would be some good excuse to stroke his cheek this evening, she thought. If not, she'd do it anyway. It was just too tempting.

"'S good, 'cause it seems to be growing faster lately." He looked perplexed.

He sat the food on one of two picnic tables reserved for the purpose, and took her hand. "Here's a right decent spot to camp."

She felt like a teenager, sitting on the plaid blanket he'd brought.

"There now, I'll go fetch some dinner," he rubbed his hands together and licked his lips. "Anything in particular suit your fancy?"

As a matter of fact, yes, but there are so many people around.

"Oh I'm sure anything you get will be fine," she laughed. "and I'm also sure you'll get at least two of everything." He jumped up to go fill their plates and she felt a tug. *Brain, hear this – he'll be back in a few minutes.*

204

She took a deep breath and rested her hand on the blanket where he had been sitting.

She looked up and was brought back into the present moment. Skky was down on one knee in front of a tiny girl dressed in red overalls. The child was crying and he was talking to her. He reached out tentatively and touched her shoulder. She put her hands to her eyes to wipe the tears, then looked at him and with her bottom lip still quivering, nodded up and down.

Skky stood up and took her hand. After a few steps he leaned over and said something to her and she smiled as her hands flew together with a clap. He stepped behind the child and easily lifted her over his head and onto his shoulders and steadied her with a hand on each ankle. It was a good thing because she had thrown both arms out to her sides in her excitement.

Cailín laughed out loud, the little girl must feel like she was flying. Skky's long, even strides took them toward a group of young women gathered around a table laden with quilts and other handmade items.

"Mommy! Mommy!" The girl squealed and pointed. One of the women ran toward them. Skky lifted the child from his shoulders and she dived into her mother's arms.

There was a brief exchange of words punctuated with his smiles and nods and ending with the young mother touching his arm briefly.

He returned with one plate piled high with chicken wings, and one stocked with potato salad, coleslaw, and fruit. "Couldn't figure how to divide this up. Guess we'll have to share." He handed her a plastic fork, and several napkins. "Wearin' white, not safe for barbeque. Hmm." He opened a napkin and without hesitation tucked it into the top of her blouse. A hint of a smile played at the left corner of his mouth.

I wonder if you know just how close you are to getting jumped, right here and now.

"You really like children, don't you?"

He looked up, but not at her. He took too long to answer, and when he did he spoke quietly. "I do." He shifted slightly and she regretted and wondered at his discomfort.

She had to distract him. "Oh, you must come from a large family."

He managed a brief smile, "Mm lots of cousins. Always around, so they were." He was still staring off into the distance as he spoke.

"That must be wonderful, growing up in a big family."

"You dint then?" He turned to look at her now.

"No, just one brother, and we were never close."

"Sorry to hear then."

"I've always wanted to be part of a big family, and one that was close. You know, not just getting together on holidays and stuff, barely polite."

"Kids?" he raised his eyebrows to enforce the question, he was coming back now.

"Mmm, three or four, I think. You?"

"Yeah, tree or fohr dozen." He smiled at her gasp.

I'm not letting you get by with that. "Sure, if half of them were adopted." She kept a straight face. "I mean, stranger things have happened, it's possible."

"Ha ha!" His laugh was brief. "Yeah, I 'spose it is…"

"So four then?"

"Fohr." He continued his assault on the chicken wings, a sure sign that the matter was settled.

The gathering had grown quieter, even the children were preoccupied with food.

"It always tastes so good when you're out in the fresh air, doesn't it?" Cailín figured that she was getting

206

enough exercise here that she didn't have to worry about gaining weight.

"Food tastes good anywhere," Skky said with enthusiasm. "Well, assumin' it's good in the first place, then it's better."

Long rays of sunlight snuck under tree limbs, signaling the end of the day. *The night,* she thought, *is just beginning.*

Cailín stopped, the chicken wing an inch from her mouth.

Rain was sitting at a picnic table several yards away and there was a woman she couldn't fully see at his side. The woman leaned forward, and then turned her head toward Rain to say something. She had to look twice, her hair was down and the 1950's makeup and clothing were updated, but it was definitely Lexi from the pub, and she was gorgeous.

Rain's arm was casually draped around the woman's shoulder. Her hand rested lightly just above his knee. This was not a relationship that just cropped up overnight, Cailín thought. Was he? Or she? Did they… she knew she couldn't ask. Rain glanced at her, then at Skky. He nodded and gave her a thumbs up. Maybe he would volunteer the information, but probably not. It didn't matter, she told herself, he looked happy and he deserved to be.

"Kiddos are havin' fun, our turn to play." Skky jumped up and reached for her hand.

Uh oh, here's the fourteen year old again. By reflex, she took his hand. She didn't have to ask, he was headed straight toward the swings. He guided her to one that was waist high, "Eek, I can't reach… whoaaa!" She grabbed onto the ropes as he lifted her up.

"More fun that way," he said through a mischievous grin, "'sides, you have help, hold on." He was already behind her, his hands on either side of the wooden seat. He pulled back, then pushed forward, running under the seat and sending her high into the air as she caught her breath.

He immediately jumped into the swing next to her and soon caught up. "Any wonder kiddos like it? Is like flyin'." It began to seem surreal to her, yet somehow familiar, catching glimpses of Skky as they flew past each other. She had spent years catching glimpses of him in passing, and suddenly she needed it to stop.

He leapt out of the swing with a yell, landing easily on both feet. In her mind she saw Spéir jumping down from a high stone wall just as he had in her dreams, and two worlds began to merge. A slow, knowing grin crossed her face. *His sons are going to be a handful, but who cares?*

"Your turn," he tried.

"No-oh!" she left no room for negotiation.

Skky ran toward her and grabbed the swing as it carried her backward, halting it in mid air and walking slowly backward until it was even with the ground. Her hands were already on his shoulders, and he lifted her easily and folded his arms around her, kissing her without hesitation.

"Is tough to be around you without wantin' to do that. Sorry."

She looked into his eyes and whispered seductively, "No, you're not". She stroked his cheek, pressed her body closer to his, and kissed him back.

They reluctantly released their grip on one another, and he took her hand, "C'mon lass, 'fore I forget where we are."

Jewel colored lights strung from tree branches popped on as they neared the crowd, and children squealed with delight. Cailín proclaimed, "I knew it was Christmas, I just knew it." She loved the way his smile crinkled the corners of his eyes.

They sat down on the blanket, her hand still in his. The younger children were doing a short band recital that was fraught with mistakes. "You're getting a kick out of this," she observed.

"Is great, to be sure, gotta start somewhere. Could be me twenty years ago," he mused, "or yesterday."

"I don't think yesterday."

"Feels like it sometimes, 'specially when ya forget the words."

"Does that happen often?"

"Noh, thankfully. Maybe a couple of times is all. Is quite an experience though. Heh! Time for the big stuff!"

"What?"

Several of the men were headed for the far side of the square, away from the crowd.

"You'll see in a wee bit."

She was waiting for him to get up and start jumping up and down, instead he put his arm around her shoulders and squeezed.

Boom! The sky lit up with thousands of blue sparks, "Oh!" Cailín jumped, grabbed his leg, and laughed with him. A dozen different colored balls of fire were shot into the sky amidst cheers from the crowd.

"Grand finale, I think that's our que to pack up. Good to walk it, or should I …"

"Walk! I'm good to walk."

Cailín bounced into the kitchen ahead of him. "Just set those down anywhere, I'll clean up in the morning. Some wine, or –" she turned away from the refrigerator and he was right in front of her. He took the bottle of wine, sat it on the counter, and placed his hands on her shoulders. His kisses were warm and gentle, and she returned them eagerly, her hands stroking his cheeks, his arms, and then his back as he wrapped his arms around her.

Skky laid his cheek against hers, placed his hand on her head, and held her very still as though he was trying to protect her, "Cailín," she could feel his heart pounding, "Cailín, there's somethin' I need to tell ya."

She felt own heart had stopped, "What?" she could barely manage more than a whisper, "What is it, Skky?"

He took half a step back, but his hands still held her waist, "I'm married".

"Muh –" she couldn't finish.

"Not for long," he said quickly, "is near over. Papers to sign is all."

"Oh." *They told me he would be exactly himself,* she thought, *I should have known this.*

"Dint think it was right not to tell ya, an', well ... bad timing."

"Here," a little of the shock had worn off and was instantly replaced by concern for him, "let's go sit down," she handed him two glasses and nudged him toward the living room.

"So you – you can't work it out?"

He shook his head slightly, "Noh, is over."

"What happened? You just decided it wasn't going to work?"

"Wish it was that simple. I just ... I want ... I need it to be over."

"Why..." at this point she felt it was fair, even necessary, to ask, "... did you marry her?"

"Maybe for the wrong reasons, thought it was time. We had fun, got along at first."

"What went wrong?"

"So much." He folded his hands and looked down briefly, "She has a public career, too – a model, very successful. So, like my work ... travels a lot. Worked that out well enough the first few months, sometimes she could go with me, sometimes I could follow her for a bit. Mostly scheduled time off at the same time. Then she got – I dunno, started bein' real critical, wanted me to dress to impress her friends… other stuff. So was a lotta tension. Honestly, she never woudda been interested in me if I, well, if I hadn't been pretty successful myself. She was famous on her own, but one uh those that wants even more attention, figured she'd get it by association. And she did. She married my career, not me.

"But it was done before I realized any uh this, she was clever. Shoudda been an actress, well, in fact, wanted that too. We were married though, so I tried, figured we hadda try."

"You don't think you still could?"

"I … I completely dropped outta sight this past six months. My family, couple very close friends… I told so they wouldn't worry. Kept in touch with the family, I did. Far as anyone else knew, I had disappeared."

"Where did you go?"

"Various places. Near water. But when I came here was with the intention that I'd kinda ease back into life, hopin' by the time I was ready to leave I'd try to go on with my career if there was anything left. Hopefully go on with my life either way."

"That's good." She envisioned a ray of hope, "That's good. I'm sure you still have your career if you want it. Heaven knows you have the talent and the voice."

"Well, was gettin' a bit rusty maybe. Hadn't touched my guitar for months before I came here."

"Feels good to get back to it?"

"Yeah, actually really good. So if my producer is still talkin to me…"

"Skky, it sounds like you had some major differences in values. Those don't always surface until you've been with someone for a while, and with you both being very visible, well maybe that didn't give you much chance to work it out. But relationships fail all the time and people go on with their lives. I – I guess I don't understand why you felt like you had to –"

"Cailín, I'm not really wan to run away from problems, but this… not so sure you'd wanna hear this."

"I do, if you want to talk about it," she touched his hand briefly.

"Was off on a big tour for tree months. She hadda few breaks in her schedule when we couldda met up for days at a time. But there was always some excuse. Just before I finished she took two weeks off, so I thought, well, ah tree month commitment was a long time, and I had chosen that, so ya know, was ready to take responsibility for that – and make changes in the future."

"Skky, did you love her?"

"At that point, noh. At first I thought I did. But I had made a commitment and maybe thought we could change things for the better. Was willin to try, so I was. Like I said, felt it was the thing to do. So I ended in Dublin, from there was going to New York, then flyin to our house in L.A." He looked down again, "Very good friend of mine in New York called me. Liam asked me to schedule the flights so we could have a few hours together between flights. I told him I needed to get home quick though. He insisted, said it was important – very important that he sees me. Dint see the harm, is sometimes nice to have a bit of time off the planes, 'specially get some real food and all, 'sides was a lil worried about the lad, and if he needed help wanted to be there for him. So, Liam, he's not one to grandstand or overreact, you know, not wan to push buttons 'cause he can."

His breath came at jagged intervals as he struggled to get the words out.

"So we met up in New York, Liam an me. He told me something that was difficult to – well, I dint wanna believe it, that is. My – wife – had visited a doctor in New York just days before. Paid him very well to do an

212

abortion in his office, and keep it quiet. She checked into a hotel across the street from his office so he could stop by and check on her the next three days while she, uh, recovered. A friend of hers was with her, she hired nurses at night. Was all arranged last minute, ended up having three different nurses. One of them was my friend's wife, Cheryl, the third night. Since the doctor had arranged it, Cheryl had no idea who it was until she got there. 'Course she shouldn't have, but she told Liam. She had access to the entire records of the – procedure – while she was on duty. She'd also been briefed by the doctor."

"So," Cailín swallowed hard before she could continue, "I guess the pregnancy was about three months along?"

"Noh." He covered his face with both hands, his every breath deep and desperate, and she began to feel sick. He looked at her, but then stared straight ahead while he spoke. "Maybe it would be easier – dunno really, but maybe a lil. Noh, noh. She was six and a half months. My son lived long enough to cry..."

She caught the bag of wet sand square in her midsection. *Goddamit! That's why he disappeared! That's why, and now it had happened all over again in this nearly identical lifetime.*

Grief gripped her throat with a solid fist. Her hands flew to her face as the horror of how it must feel to him suffocated her. Unimaginable. Tears streamed over her fingers as she looked at the man she loved, half expecting him to disintegrate before her eyes.

He sat with closed fists pressed to his mouth, staring at the rug for a full minute.

"Sorry, I dint mean to, uh, that is, I should..." he stood up slowly, running his fingers through his hair. He turned toward the door, "I ... I should go."

"Skky."   Cailín stood, her hands dropping helplessly to her sides as he closed the door behind him. *Fucking hell! What have I done? What have I done?"*

She reached for the wine glasses, but her hands dropped again. The night had fallen still save for the faint sound of his footsteps retreating. *What do you do at a time like this?* There had to be something…

She sank in quicksand to her knees as she pushed the curtain aside. His lone figure slowly crossed the dim street, and it was horrible to her. He normally moved quickly.

Her heart pounded in her ears, "No!" she screamed at the icy darkness that held her, "No, this can't be!"

* * *

Why'd I do that? Skky thought, *it was too much, too soon.* He felt his way to the bedroom in the dark, then switched on the small table lamp. *Dint mean to take it that far, but she asked and somehow I just let it spill.* He sat down on the edge of the bed, his head in his hands. *Probly scared her away, dunno if she really bargained for all this.*

He heard rapid footsteps, though they seemed a thousand miles away. He looked up for a few seconds. Her eyes were begging him to speak, but no words came. She was trying not to frown and not succeeding very well. Strands of hair had escaped her ponytail, her eye makeup was smeared from crying, and Skky thought she was the most beautiful thing he'd ever seen.

He looked up again, trying to find words. He watched as her eyes searched the dimly lit room and he was surprised when she grabbed his sweatshirt from the chair and disappeared into the bathroom, but he was finding it easier to breathe.

The sweatshirt hung loosely on her, halfway down her thighs, and her hands had completely disappeared in the sleeves. Any other time they'd be having a good laugh.

She walked to the other side of the bed and crawled under the covers, so he shed his shoes and jeans, switched off the light, and lay down beside her. Cailín put her hand on his arm, and he felt her trembling.

"You're cold," he said softly, his heart beginning to melt, "c'mere." He gathered her in his arms and thoughts of anything but her sweetness and softness left his mind. For the first time in months he felt like he was really going to be all right, and he fell asleep.

* * *

215

Boiling water shot through her veins. He was gone.

The aroma of fresh coffee prompted a deep sigh of relief. She dashed to the kitchen. In a pair of sweatpants and a t-shirt, he turned away from the range to greet her. "Dint wanna wake ya, out like a light, so ya ware."

"Oh." The awareness of how she must look hit her suddenly, with her eye makeup smeared. She wished she had taken the liberty of using his hair brush.

He was breathtaking, unshaven, his hair delightfully rumpled. *Is there nothing that can dumb down this man's inherent hotness?* "You sleep okay?"

"I did." He smiled. "Me granny says I pop up like toast. Mostly I do."

She laughed, "It's a good thing my granny invented the toaster, then."

He smiled and waved his finger at her, "Nooo, noh ya don't."

"Let's just say that I'm not a morning person."

"Aye, well some hot brew'll fix ya right up. Cream? Sugar?"

"Tons of both, thanks." She sat down at the table.

"Aw, you're cold again. Sorry, cool air doesn't bother me so much. Be right back." She wondered if she should see to what was on the stove, but he returned instantly.

"These won't fit at all, but whawt's new? At least ya won't freeze." He handed a pair of sweatpants to her with a grin. "Just roll 'em up, 's all good."

In a flash he sat two steaming bowls on the table. "Sorry, noh bacon."

"The eggs are great, what'd you put in them?" Cailín marveled at the fact that everything seemed so easy, so normal now.

"Same cream as in your coffee, uh splash, and some cheese here and there is all. Grab another scoop uh potatoes 'fore I eat 'em all." He was putting the food away

216

at a good clip, and she couldn't have been happier. "Nationality hazard, so it is."

She covered her mouth quickly as the unexpected laugh escaped, "Genetic memory of the potato famine?" She caught herself, and wondered if that was still cogent in an Irishman's memory. "Uh well, that was a long time ago, I guess."

"Em, well, some events are tough to forget." He reached across the table and took her hand briefly. "Thanks. For last night. Thanks for bein' here."

She couldn't find words. All she could do was look at him as she had since the first time she saw him, with wonder and longing.

"So whawt's on your plate today, lass?"

"After all that's on *this* plate, probably a four hour nap."

He laughed, and it made her smile.

"Oh, Rain offered to go antique exploring with me, you know, in some of the little shops around town. You?"

"Eh well, some errands an' stuff. Pick up some bacon."

"Of course."

"But heh, well – I was kinda hopin' for a do over."

"Oh?"

"Well yeah, another 'first date', start again, sort of."

"Yeah?"

"Yeah. Maybe do it right this time?" He rested his arm on the table, palm upturned, fingers spread, a gesture he often used when posing a question.

"Skky…" she looked at his outstretched hand. The small bump on his wrist became the center of her universe, and she was hypnotized. Slowly her hand moved towards his, and she extended her index finger and let it come to rest gently on his pulse.

"You touch my heart, like ya been sleepin' in it forever," he half whispered.

"It's my favorite song."

"Whawt, lass?"

"Your heartbeat."

He put his hand over hers for a moment before speaking again, "I hear there's one sorta fancy restaurant in town, would like to take ya there tonight. That is, if –"

"Yes, I'd like that. You don't have to though." She felt as though her voice came from half a world away.

"Aye, I don't have to, but – I truly wawnt to."

Slowly the room came back into focus, "Yes. What time?"

"Was hopin' we could figure that out over lunch. If you and Rain can take a break and come by."

"Sure. Unless I can lose him first."

He laughed, "Aw right then. Good."

"So I guess it's suit and tie for this place?"

"Well, yeah, if ya want… was kinda hopin' you'd wear a dress, but, uh," he sat up straight and gestured with both hands, "seein' as you're fond of wearin' men's clothes an' all, maybe too much to ask? By the by, those britches look better on me, the fit that is."

"No," she choked out through her laughter, "I did bring a couple dresses, I suppose I can wear one for a change, if you insist."

"Might persuade me to keep your secret."

* * *

She was happy – happier than she suspected she had a right to be. At the same time she felt a misery that she had thought would be impossible to ever duplicate. After they'd finished breakfast, she left to give Skky some time to shower and get ready for work. She went back to her cottage and allowed the tears to spill.

Twenty minutes later she picked up the cell phone and snapped it open.

"Rain! Take me to Dr. Michaels, now!"

"Yes, ma'am."

"I'm sorry – no, I'm not. Oh dammit!"

"I'll be right there."

"'Sup, Kay?" his unflappable nature could be as infuriating as it was comforting at times.

"I have a feeling you know."

"I know you didn't sleep here last night."

"Then surely you know everything else as well."

"It's possible. Or not."

"Stop it! How could you – how could *they* let me do this?"

"What? Let you have a sleep over with a man you're crazy in love with? That's rough alright."

"You know what I mean, stop acting like you don't, why the hell…" she burst into tears again.

"Okay." He put his arms around her. "Okay. Let us, them… what?"

"How could you let me do this to him? How?" she choked out between sobs.

"Whoa, whoa, wait – do what to him? Last time I knew it wasn't you that made his ex the bitch of the universe."

"No. Just stop it, you know what I mean. How could you let me make him go through this all over again? How could you, all of you, trick me into thinking that everything would be – no, how could I do this to him?"

"You?"

"Me. If not for me, he wouldn't have lived through that hell all over again."

"Now *you* stop, Kaylin. What makes you think you have that kind of power?"

"What? I – I did this, or I let it happen, I –"

"One more time. You don't have that kind of power."

"Fine!" she broke away from him, clenching her fists. "Fine! That's your pat answer. But I don't think it's to let me off the hook, I think it's to let all of you off."

"Kaylin, come and sit down. You look like hell. I'll get you some water, something, geezus."

"Geezus yourself! You act like this is an everyday thing. You act like –"

"Think for a minute. Think back to your conversations with Logan, to our conversation just a few days ago. What happened – happened. You can't go back and change that, any of it."

"To – well, to the original Skky, yes, I know. But, but this one –"

"It's no different. *This* one? You're not getting it. You got an exact Skky O'Keeffe here, better'n Xerox ever dreamed of. Remember our conversations about the soul choosing? We all believe that, including you. Remember your talks with Logan, and with me? About the reality that this *is* Skky? That he chose to come here, that somehow he chose to go through this, just to get to where he is today, to you?"

"I don't, I don't know..."

"Yes, you do. You wanted him to have a second chance. You told me yourself that you feel that *this one* is Skky. Kay? Don't you get it? He chose this, too, Kay. If he hadn't, none of this would have been possible. None of it, got that?"

She shrugged and put her hand over her mouth as Rain continued. "Yes, you chose this. Yes, we chose to help make it possible – but he had to choose, too. Had to. No matter what you did, no matter what we did, there was a fail safe – he had to agree. I'm very certain of that. You need to really, truly, get that through your head. He had a choice. He made it, here he is, and he chose to do it to get to you." Rain held his ground, his gaze steady. "There's some kind of deeper connection there that maybe none of us really understand. Kay, he did it because he wanted you, whatever it took to get to this point. *He* wanted *you*." She could only stare at him as he spoke. "I think maybe you really understand that much better than we do, so now just believe it."

* * *

"I... I dream about him sometimes." Skky clenched his hands together at his waist. "He's at the other side of a big empty room, a wee bundle, can't see his face, but I hear..."

Dr. Michaels attempted to suppress a frown, "Go on, please".

"Is – there's nothin' else in the room, just the babby basket. I'm tryin' to get to him, but I can't move, can't move at all." He took a deep, ragged breath. "And I think, if I fall forward maybe I can crawl, or somehow get there, somehow. There's not much time, I know that, time's runnin' out.

"I try to fall, I'm leaning over as hard as I can, but I can't get to the floor, nothin' works." Skky gripped his knees, and leaned forward, "Why? Why can't I move? Then the cryin' stops, quick like. I hear it, then I don't, just like that. Why can't I ... the room goes complete black, an' I wake up."

"Skky, you can't move because you feel helpless, and you know the outcome. You can't move because the damage has already been done.

"You can not blame yourself. You didn't know. You didn't have the information you needed to be able to do anything. Nothing can be changed after the fact. It wasn't your fault."

"How could she? How could she do that? I was always good to her, as good as she'd let me be. Why'd she wanna hurt me like that? An' ... just a babby..."

"Skky, I don't believe it was about you at all. If you think about it – her career always came first, didn't it?"

"I was guilty of that, too." He ran his hand through his hair, "If I hadn't left, hadn't gone on tour..."

"I don't believe that you were guilty of anything, unless you think that not being a mind reader or hiring a private detective to keep tabs qualifies."

"How could I not know? We were married, how was it I dint really know her?"

"It's not as though every husband asks every wife... what I'm saying is it's not something that normally occurs to people. It's unthinkable, why would you even ask?"

"But how could she – do that – to her own child?"

"That's a very difficult question, and not one we could likely grasp the answer to... if there is a concrete answer. Difference in backgrounds, maybe. Difference in values, definitely."

"Can ya understand why I have to be sure? I have to be sure this doesn't happen again."

"I do understand how you feel, but I also know it's next to impossible to get a guarantee. However, this process should raise the odds greatly toward a good outcome."

"I think... maybe it was too soon. Maybe I shouldn't have told Cailín so soon. I dunno, it just poured out, I just –"

"I think you were right to share it with her."

"Hope so, was a lot though. Was a lot to just be throwin' out there so soon."

"It was something she needed to know if you're to go on. She didn't run away, Skky, she ran *to* you."

"She did, I – well was somethin my family and closest friends did, caring, just be there for me. I couldn't ask for more, really. I know it wasn't easy for her."

"It's remarkable. I'm sure she didn't really know what to do, but she wanted to try. In general what do you think about Kaylin so far?"

"Ah." Michaels noted that the smile came quickly, as Skky sat upright. The grief began to dissolve from his eyes. "She's just ahmasin', so she is. So pretty, and fun to be with. Very, em, girly, feminine that is, without mistake, but doesn't mind rollin' in the grass and gettin' dirty. And she cooks somethin' great!" Skky laughed in delight, then sobered, "There'somethin else I can't really describe, somethin' about her, like she's whawt I was missin', whawt I needed all along."

"And you're comfortable with her outlook on having a family."

"Yup, well, from things she's said, yeah. She's quite a lot different than…"

"I'd agree. But you do understand that she's well on her way to having a brilliant career? In her field of expertise she has the potential to be a 'rock star'. Would it be your preference that she gives that up? Would you ask her to?"

"That'd be entirely up to her. If it makes her happy to continue, we'd work it out. I could back off on travellin' so much. I plan to do that anyway, if there are children then to be sure."

"You're falling in love with her?"

"Noh. I already have. If I had any sense I would have acted on that years ago. Can't imagine not havin' her in my life. Seems right fond of me as well."

Michaels clumsily tried to stifle a laugh by attempting to clear his throat. "An understatement – don't keep her waiting. And Skky, it's alright to trust what you feel."

* * *

Tonight there would be no worrying what to wear. Cailín retrieved the updated version of the white over black cocktail dress that she had wanted to wear to her senior prom from the closet. It was more fitted and revealing than the version she had argued with her mother over. She finished toweling off and slipped on the black thong, the only undergarment needed. She grabbed the blow dryer and round brush and decided to leave her hair loose, glad that she had layers cut into her long hair prior to leaving.

He would be on time, she was certain. Not too much makeup, but a little heavy on the eye makeup as Irish girls were fond of doing, and she'd be ready in plenty of time.

She stepped into black high heels and nearly made it to the door before he knocked.

Cailín had been calm and focused while preparing for the evening. That ended the second she opened the door. He was impeccable in a simple black suit, tie, and white shirt. Despite the fact that she had hundreds of pictures of him stored in her computer and in her memory, dressed in everything from jeans to suits, standing in front of her now he knocked every molecule of oxygen out of her body. *Does he really have any right to stand there looking like a Celtic god reborn? How is that fair?* she thought.

The suit seemed so familiar, like the one he'd worn the night she met him at the television station. She couldn't help but wonder – had they transported some of *his* clothes and presented them to this Skky, telling him they'd blend in perfectly in this staged throwback town? Suddenly she felt an overwhelming longing for the boy she'd met that night at the television station, then the sound of his voice, *that* voice, snapped her back into the moment.

"Heh." He bowed slightly, one arm behind his back. "Ye look, uh, well… ahmasin'."

"Thank you," she breathed out what she felt must surely be her last breath. "You – you're gorgeous."

"Aye well, these…" his voice trailed off in another moment of uncharacteristic shyness. He produced a bouquet. "… hope you like 'em."

"Oh, they're perfect! Where did you find daisies this time of year?"

"I have ways."

"I see. Let me find something to put them in."

"Not sure these cottages are furnished with vases and the like." He followed her to the kitchen. "Sorry, dint think about that."

"It's fine, I'm sure there's something…" she searched the cabinets and spotted a glass pitcher. She felt his eyes as she reached for it. "It isn't Waterford, but it will do fine."

He took the pitcher and placed it in the center of the table. "Here now, a bit of cheer, looks about right?" he gestured with open palms.

"Mother Nature outdid herself, that's for sure," she wondered if he caught her double meaning.

"Think our transportation is near, if you're ready." He offered his arm and she took it, half expecting her hand to pass right through him as though he were a hologram, but he was solid, and warm.

"Transportation?" *now there's a word for you… ask me what I know about 'trans-portation'.* "It's not far, we can walk. Really." She halted abruptly at the door, half jerking him back. "What?!?"

"Thought it might be a bit of a craic."

A beautiful dappled gray horse was harnessed to the small cart, its driver's hair nearly the same color as the horse's coat. "Evenin'." The farmer tipped his straw hat.

"Hello," she smiled with delight. She studied the rig trying to determine how to climb aboard.

"Here," Skky jumped up and extended both of his hands. "This might be easiest."

She found a foothold on the edge and he pulled her easily on board. "That was attractive," she laughed at herself.

"Ah, was fine," he grinned and motioned for her to take a seat. "Gettin' down will be much easier, promise."

"Easier, or tragic. These shoes aren't exactly made for climbing."

"Knew I shoudda brought the skateboard." He scratched the back of his head and made a face.

Cailín looked at him in astonishment, and they broke into laughter.

"Oh!" she grabbed the edge of the seat as the cart made a small lurch of a start.

Skky immediately threw his arm firmly around her and said softly, "Promise the rest of the evenin' will be more… civilized. Er, mostly. Well – maybe." She looked up at him, smiled, and started to speak.

"Everything all right, folks?" the farmer turned to look.

"'S all good." His eyes met hers.

"We're fine. Perfect." She snuggled just a little closer.

They rode in silence; the rhythmic beat of the horse's gait seemed to make the ride smoother. Remnants of an earlier rain shower made the pavement glisten silver under the pale street lights. Cailín closed her eyes. They could have been in a small Irish village three – no, six hundred years ago now. She could see it in vivid detail. The stones in her silver wedding band then had been a modest sapphire surrounded by small emeralds.

She had one of those funny feelings, like he was reading her mind.

"Peaceful, so it is, no cars, like a time gone by," he said thoughtfully, "like another world."

For a moment she could neither breath in nor out. *Impeccable timing, I suppose I shouldn't be surprised. If only you knew… but then on some level, maybe you do.*

"Here ya goh." Skky was on the ground in an instant, holding his arms up. Her feet touched the ground, but she made no move to take her hands from his shoulders.

"Skky, do you think sometimes it's not so bad to look back?" She immediately recognized that it must sound like a terribly incongruous question.

"Sometimes, maybe." He puckered his lower lip, "Some things need rememberin'."

He kissed her softly, briefly, much as he had the first time.

The small restaurant was surprisingly elegant, betraying its folksy exterior. The crisp white tablecloths punctuated with a single red rose and a pair of candlesticks was the very definition of 'less is more'. The aroma of fresh bread greeted them as the hostess showed them to a table.

Skky held her chair, his fingers briefly brushing her shoulder as she sat down.

"Would you like to order wine now?" the hostess queried.

"Hmm, that'll depend on whawt we order, so iced tea for now?" He looked at Cailín and she simply nodded; sparks from his touch still played on her shoulder.

"Very good, your waitress will be along shortly. Enjoy your dinner." The tall, slender woman floated towards her post near the door.

"Ooh," she barely glanced at the menu, not wanting to take her eyes from him "cedar plank salmon!"

Another young woman appeared, "Good evening folks, here's your iced tea, and shall I give you a few minutes to decide?"

"Actually, we'll both have the salmon and," he held the wine list up toward her, "this one," he laughed, "never could say it right."

"Very good, sir." The waitress smiled, "and a salad to begin?"

"Caesar, then?" he looked at Cailín, who once again nodded silently.

"Thank you," the waitress retrieved the menus and made her exit.

"Thank goodness for visual recognition," he half apologized, "the French language —"

"Is simply not compatible with Irish, I understand completely," Cailín finished the thought.

"Ha ha, noh it's nawt. Has always defeated me."

Halfway through the salad and three or four sips too many of the wine, she decided she'd best slow down, noting that Skky had barely touched his glass. The small band, oddly comprised of a drummer with only a snare, a violinist, and a guitarist, began to play. They weren't bad at all, likely they'd had a lot of experience together, and the melody of an old, popular love song was instantly recognizable.

Skky stood up, buttoned his jacket, and offered his hand. "Do me the honor?"

Cailín was temporarily mystified, was this the same young man she'd been with in the park? *Of course, he's used to being in a variety of situations, he's always been adaptable. He's still the same Skky – the same Skky he always was.*

He guided her slowly and expertly around the dance floor, holding her lightly. *This must be what heaven is like,* she thought. He began to hum along with the music, perfectly in tune. That much did not surprise her. Her thoughts came into focus as he pulled her closer and began to sing softly.

She drank in every note, hypnotized by the gentle rise and fall of his breath, imagining that she could trace its path from his diaphragm to his throat. The feel of his arm encircling her was embedded in her awareness, and his hand holding hers to his shoulder may as well have been holding her heart.

They were barely moving now, rocking back in forth almost in place. She slid her arm more snugly across his shoulders, bringing them even closer together. His erection swelled against her hip and he unapologetically shifted her slightly so that it pressed against her stomach. *My God, he's making no attempt to hide it. Hmmm I think that's good…why should he? Ohh damn!*

As the song came to an end he lowered his head so that his lips brushed her neck as he whispered, "If we were alone, you'd be gettin' kissed right now."

"Damn right," she thought out loud as she looked up into his eyes.

He smiled, and with his arm still around her, guided her back to the table. He raised her hand to his lips and kissed it before he pulled the chair out for her. "This'll hafta do for now."

They sat silently for a few moments, Skky leaning back in his chair, holding her comfortably in his gaze. It was Cailín who spoke first, "Do you miss being at home? I mean, you travel quite a lot."

He sat up straighter and scooted his chair around the table, close to her. "I do, and yeah, I miss it a lot sometimes, the family, the countryside, even the rain," his gray green eyes seemed to darken, as she had noticed they did when he was being serious. "Is always good to go back."

"My parents, well mainly speaking of my mother because my father wasn't around any more than he had to be, but they were both very pretentious." She wondered why she felt the need to spill the information, but didn't stop. "Always concerned about 'appearances' and about how much anything cost, always wanting to one-up any situation. But that's very boring, sorry."

"Nohh, lass, don't be sorry. Know the type. I'm sorry that wasn't a happier circumstance for ya."

"It's okay, I had friends, some of them very good friends, and of course, my granny." She laughed, "I spent as much time at her house as I could, needless to say. And, I had other – interests – to keep me occupied."

"Those were?" He casually leaned one arm on the table, he seemed genuinely interested, she thought.

"The usual, I guess. You know, movies, concerts," *stalking your every move, wanting to die when you married,* "playing tennis. Tennis was acceptable in my mother's idea of society, so I had no problem getting away for that."

"Really? You were good then?"

"Mm, decent I guess."

"Ha ha ha, you'd have me beat there. Heh, have seen a tennis court here, you can teach me."

"Well it's not as, um, exciting as skateboarding, that's for sure."

"Meanin' as dangerous?" he laughed.

"That too."

"And boyfriends?" his effort to make the remark seem casual failed to a large extent.

The only important and lasting one was the ghost of you, you know – from three hundred years ago. There. That should do it.

"Oh! look," she said with exaggerated enthusiasm, "saved by the salmon!"

He released a semi-audible sigh, but smiled.

"Whawt else? Tell me." He seemed more interested in what she had to say than the food, a good sign, she thought.

"I like to write. I wrote a whole book. At least I'd like to think it's a book."

"Seriously now? Bet 'tis good, did ya publish it?"

"No, oh gosh no." She realized that he was only the third other person to know about it.

"Why not?"

"Don't know, it never occurred to me. And, well, it seems kind of personal."

"I can understand, songs do, too. Is kinda like... it means somethin' to ya and whawt if nobody else likes it, or whawt if you're givin' too much away. Stuff like that. Would like to read it sometime. Promise to like it."

"Huh? Yeah... I'm not sure it's finished."

"Noh matter." He suddenly paused, fork in midair. "Heh..." his mood was definitely thoughtful. "... ever wonder where that comes from? Meanin' like the ideas, for stories and songs and such. Ever wonder?"

"No."

"Noh?"

"No. Well, meaning that a lot of it comes from life experiences I think." *Never mind* which *life.* "Or maybe just daydreams, or, like, there's a quote I really like, 'Coincidences are anonymous gifts pointing to a deeper reality.' Deepak Chopra said that, he was, I guess you'd say, part scientist, part philosopher."

"Anonymous gifts, then? And a deeper reality... I like that."

"Desert?" The pleasant young woman had reappeared and Cailín realized that their plates were now empty. "We have –"

Cailín quickly leaned close, pressed his arm and whispered, "I made a cake today."

"Noh, thank you," he needed no further prompting. "Believe we're done."

"Sorry," she apologized, "I should have mentioned that sooner." *And I hope you realize I did it for a convenient excuse to get you back inside the cottage.*

"Ah noh, not a problem, err, whawt kind is it?"

"It's strawberry, with cream cheese frosting."

"Oh? Don't believe I ever – let's go!"

She loved his open enthusiasm. He tapped the screen on the small device the waitress had handed him a few times and sealed it with his thumbprint.

The night had grown decidedly cooler, and Cailín drew her thin satin wrap more closely around her shoulders. "Here," Skky quickly removed his jacket and wrapped it around her.

"Oh, won't you be cold?"

"From Ireland, remember? This is normal."

"'Tis near too beautiful to spoil." Skky remarked, staring at the cake with its artful swirls of thick frosting.

"Thank you, but something tells me you won't let that stop you," she said, thinking how she loved anything and everything that pleased him. "How big?"

"Hmm?"

"Want to cut your own piece?"

"I'll be leavin' that to your discretion, soz if it's too big, that'll be your fault." He flashed a mischievous grin, and just as quickly sobered into practicality. "Em, was thinkin' to light the fire."

She cut a generous piece for him, a smaller one for herself, and poured two glasses of wine.

Shadows danced around the darkened room as if to some unheard rhythm.

"There now, he gestured, "like a cottage in auld Ireland." He settled back onto the sofa, loosened his tie, and freed a couple of buttons.

Instantly Cailín was choking back tears. She took a sip of the wine, hoping it would clear the lump in her throat. "I… I do want to go there, someday." She absent mindedly took a bite of the cake and the burst of flavor helped to change her focus.

"Then you will," he stated. "You will, uhh, but, well, not like that." His chin puckered his lower lip into a frown.

"What?"

"You've got –" he tapped the corner of his mouth, "just a little –" he reached over and slowly rubbed his finger over the corner of her mouth, "– icing, that is."

"Oh? Really?" Oh yes, she was going to play into this. "So, you're saying that I'm a sloppy eater? Or that I have no manners? Is that what you're saying?"

"Ya know, fact is –" he tried hard to be serious and disapproving.

"Fact is," she interrupted, "you're not exactly neat yourself."

"Surely not."

"Oh, yes, there's icing all over –"

"There isn't," he protested.

"I'll show you." She dipped her finger into the thick icing, stood up, leaned over him and drew an icing moustache across his upper lip. "There. Proof." She licked the remaining icing off her finger.

He laughed, and picked up a napkin, but she quickly grabbed his wrist. "No," she said firmly.

"Noh?" he raised his eyebrows.

"No, you'll just smear it. I'll take care of it." She placed one knee next to his thigh, braced herself with both hands on the back of the sofa behind him and drew her other knee up. She lowered herself so that she was almost sitting on his lap, but not quite. He was so still that for a second she thought he wasn't breathing, but his eyes held hers in a soft, steady focus. She leaned in and flicked the corner of his mouth with her tongue then quickly did it again as his hands went to her waist.

She drew her tongue slowly across half of his upper lip, then moved it to the other side and repeated the process. "Delicious," she let the word slip out.

She backed off slightly, his eyes were half closed, and he breathed out slowly, "Am I… presentable now?"

"Almost," she whispered. She sucked his upper lip in between hers and slowly began to tug and retreat. He was nearly free from her grasp when he suddenly sat up straight. His hands shot under her thighs and he pulled her closer. His kiss was again sweet, but this time it was also commanding. He kissed her again as her breath quickened with his. Cailín tugged at his tie and flung it away, her fingers working at the buttons on his shirt. His skin was like a magnet, one that her hands couldn't escape.

Any pretense of reserve or hesitation was absent in his next kiss.

"Put your arms around me." He stood up, lifting her with him, and kissed her shoulder as he carried her to the bedroom. He lowered her slowly, letting her body slide down his until her feet touched the floor.

"Bet you taste like strawberry cake even when there's none," he whispered against her neck as he unzipped her dress and slid it off her shoulders.

He was quick to help her shaking hands remove his trousers.

She marveled that his touch was just like Spéir's in her dreams, but how could it not be? She was finally holding her dream in her hands, and his body was so familiar, his touch almost predictable, yet wildly exciting. His fingers played across her skin as though it was a finely tuned instrument, and his mouth caressed her like a song.

She traced small circles at the base of his spine, prompting an "mmm". He was holding back, being considerate, waiting for a clear signal.

"Skky," she breathed, "I want you so much. Now. I need –" her tongue was silenced by his as his body willingly answered her plea.

A thousand feelings raced through her mind as he entered her, from the first dream of Spéir, to the first second she learned of Skky's existence, their one meeting, and back to the first instant she met him again a few days ago.

"You…" he ran his fingers through her hair, pushing it away to place a kiss behind her ear, "you feel so damned good, lass."

Cailín allowed herself to float on the effortless rhythm his body created, savoring every delicious inch of him that filled her until she could no longer hold back. She interrupted the rhythm and pushed her hips against him. His thrusts became faster and more forceful and she met every one.

"Ohh," she said out loud, "yes, Skky…"

She intended to love all of him, all that he ever had been, or ever wanted to be. She was going to be his past, present, and future, and not leave him wanting for anything it could be possible to give him.

"Cailín," though they were alone he whispered next to her ear, "Cailín".

* * *

"You awake?" his voice was husky.

"No," she whispered, "are you?"

"Noh," she felt the smile in his voice.

"I forgot to thank you for dinner last night."

"Noh ya dint."

"Listen…"

"Ever make ya mad ya can't stay awake when it's rainin'?"

"Like it makes me mad when I wake up too soon from a dream."

"Me granny says that when ya can't sleep at night, is 'cause you're awake in someone else's dream."

"Ohh… do you think that's true?"

"Maybe. Probly, I guess. Sometimes I wake up middle of the night. Dunno. Never seemed like it was bad though. Is usually very peaceful like. Maybe 'cause I like that it's not time to get up, so just relax."

"What is it about the rain?"

"Thinkin' it's the rhythm, the pitch."

"You would think that, and I think you're right."

"Reminds me of home."

"I guess it would."

"You'll see for yourself. Is great for sleep. Sometimes annoying, sometimes lonely. But it's home."

"And now?"

"Is very peaceful, bein' here with you. Like wakin' up from a dream, but still in it."

"My granny has a name for Irish people; she says we're children of the rain."

"Rain is mysterious, mystical like. Me granny says Irish people know things."

"Know things?" she repeated thoughtfully.

"Yeah, secret things. Lovely things really. The women more so, though us guys are somewhawt trainable."

"I hope so," her thought slipped out.

"Oh, there's definitely hope," he laughed.

"My granny used to tell me that thunder was just an old potato wagon rolling over a rickety bridge; nothing to be afraid of."

"She also tell ya that sometimes it threw sparks from the wheels, so be careful of that?"

"Yes!"

"Cailín…"

"Hmm?" she felt one of his quicksilver topic changes coming.

"I should have said earlier, well…" he hesitated, looking for the words. "…was never my intention this be a one time thing, somethin' that just happened. When we leave here, dun want that to mean that I may never see you again." He turned on his side to face her, his hand moved down her back and rested on her waist.

"I don't want that either, Skky." She put her hand on his cheek, "I really don't."

"I want to know ya better, although…" he was giving the words a lot of thought, she could tell, "… the first time I saw ya, is fohnny, felt like I did somehow know ya."

She searched for the right words as well. "Skky, maybe it's not so strange, really. After all, we do know things. I've never seen Ireland except in pictures, never been there, but it seems like home. I know it will feel that way." She felt the tears about to spill, "Just like the first time we met, when you touched me, you… you felt like home."

He pulled closer, "Back to sleep now?"

"Yes."

"See ya the other side of sunrise," he gathered her closer in his arms, lulling her back to sleep like Spéir did.

* * *

Cailín paced back and forth, picked up the cell phone, put it down again. She looked out the window. There was no mysterious writing in the sky to answer her question. She finally pushed the numbers and Rain was there in less than five minutes.

"Maybe I should talk to Dr. Michaels. I mean, yes, make it happen."

"Sure." He frowned. "Can be quickly arranged. You okay?"

"Really wish I could talk to Brandon, I miss him. He understood, knew me. Or Logan, Logan would be good."

"What am I? Chopped…" he trailed off, sensing it wasn't the time for levity. Rain retrieved the cell phone from his pocket. She didn't really pay any attention to what he said.

"Kaylin? Come on," he held out his hand, "Michaels can take some time in about ten minutes. Let's walk on over." They did so in silence, Rain holding her hand as though he was attending a five year old crossing the street.

The narrow five story building was wedged in between two others. 'Farmer's Co-Op' was printed in large letters across the second story of one, and 'Conyer's Insurance Exchange' was printed on the glass door of the other in bold black letters. She remembered Rain telling her that the upper floors were mostly vacant, probably used for storage. He opened the solid unmarked door as she glanced up at the second story windows from which she'd had her first view of the town. The smell of rubbing alcohol reminded her of her arrival.

To their left was the stairway that led to the apartment where she'd spent the first night. To the right there were three doors, also unmarked, in the interior. The first door must open into Michael's office.

The middle door led into the small room with tables and chairs where they'd had lunch. She remembered the farthest door, the one Rain had led her through to the open foyer from the basement. An odd combination of dread and curiosity overcame her. "Rain?" she gestured toward the last door. "Can we go take a look? I don't remember much."

"Oh. The arrival chamber? Not there. Dismantled for the time being."

"Really?"

"Yeah, really. Nothing to see but bare cement walls and floors. Pretty dull."

"But, what if –"

He was already guiding her through the first door. "Kay, there is no 'what if'."

He smiled, but she wasn't convinced.

"How are you today, Kaylin?" Michaels exhibited a mix of concern and steadiness.

She took his offered hand briefly but said nothing, and Rain guided her to the sofa and motioned for her to sit beside him.

"I'm guessing something like the snail said to the turtle, 'it all happened so fast'?" Michaels stated, without humor. "Please tell me, Kaylin."

She sighed. "Actually everything is great, perfect. But is he really sure? Is it too soon for him? Is this just a rebound?"

"Do you feel it is? Are you getting that impression from him?"

She drew another prolonged breath, "No, I'm not, not at all. But is that just how I want it to seem?"

Rain sat quietly for once, Michaels leaned forward, fingers laced. "Kaylin, for all intents his marriage ended six months ago, if not well before, I don't think you could doubt that now. That's a while to wait to 'rush' into a new relationship. And if you're wondering – I know I would – I can tell you that he hasn't pursued a relationship with anyone else the past six months."

"Really? That's funny, it never occurred to that he might have."

"So you're telling me that you get the impression from him that he wasn't motivated until now?"

"I suppose so, yes."

"Then I suggest you trust yourself and believe what you see in him. And if it helps, I'll tell you again what I know Dr. Logan and Rain both have told you. We know what he's open to, what he's looking for, and what he feels he needs. That's exactly why we brought you to this place at this time."

Rain leaned forward, "Six months ago, or even two, would have been a different story. As it turned out, over the last few weeks, relatively speaking, things evolved into a very high probability of success."

Michaels laughed in spite of himself. "That may be more Varen's area of expertise, probability. However, there's a limit of how scientific these things can be, but from my perspective there are strong indications that your relationship with Skky will continue to evolve to your mutual benefit.

"I believe there's one important thing you have to ask yourself. Do you trust him?"

"Trust him? Of course."

"Do you believe that he genuinely knows what he wants?"

She thought back to the dream in which Spéir asked if he could come back, back into her everyday reality. "I do, yes. I do."

"I believe I can offer an explanation as to why you're having concerns in spite of your belief."

"Oh? Please do."

"You've loved him from afar for six years."

It's really nine, but we'll leave it at that.

"That's more than long enough to establish a very, very solid habit. Habits aren't broken overnight. It appears that you're relating to him very well, you're tuned into him in the present. But when you're apart your mind is trying to revert to its comfort zone, to the familiar, which says that loving him from afar is normal – having him is not. The conclusion being that something must be wrong. Your brain is simply trying to catch up with reality."

"So I'm just having a separation anxiety of sorts?"

"Something like that, yes. As you spend more time with Skky that will abate."

"I like that solution."

* * *

Skky was struggling through the songs, a very odd feeling for him. Usually it came so easily. Mercifully, there were only a handful of people in the small pub and they seemed to be absorbed in conversation.

Whawt's wrong with me? His mind was filled with thoughts of her as he imagined he could feel every quiver of her body in response to his touch.

He left out a verse of the song, and placed his guitar in the case. "Sorry, folks," he said to no one in particular, "appointment to keep – thanks all for comin'. See ya soon."

He walked stiffly towards the exit, as though he was afraid that something would stop him, or worse, that everyone could read his thoughts.

He didn't knock, he simply stated her name as he walked straight to the kitchen.

She was putting the clean dishes away, wearing only a pink tank top and bikinis.

"Skky," she wrapped a smile around his name, "you're – "

He pulled her close. His kiss interrupted her, his hands on her bare hips. He couldn't remember ever feeling such a compelling need, and it was nearly frightening to him but he wasn't going to stop unless she asked him to. She didn't.

He pulled roughly at the side of her panties and the material gave away. He slid his hands to the back of her thighs and lifted her. She wrapped her legs around his waist, her nails digging into his back and shoulder.

One hand on her back, he balanced her on the countertop and quickly unzipped his jeans. She grabbed a handful of his hair and muffled her scream by biting into his shoulder. Her quickly pulsing warmth told him there was no reason to hold back.

They held tightly on to one another, trying to catch their breath.

"Cailín," he looked into her dark eyes, "I love ya. It – maybe is too soon, but I –"

"I love you, Skky," she whispered, "no amount of time can change that."

He took a deep breath and exhaled. She had relaxed, too, her hands now caressing his back. He picked her up again and carried her to the bedroom, laid her on the bed, and shed his jeans before he curled around her. For several minutes they laid in quiet contentment.

"Ah, whawt have ya done to me, lass?"

"Nothing really, not compared to what I'm going to do."

"Come to Ireland with me."

"Really?"

"Well, I dunno know. Can ya?"

"If you want, I can't say no."

"Or I could come to Chicago for a while? I needa get back on tour soon, I think, maybe the first of the year whawt with rehearsals and scheduling. I'm startin' to feel like doin' it now, but could postpone for a while."

"No, not if you're ready. I would come with you!"

"Truly? On the road, is a hassle. Dunno if you'd like –"

"All the more reason you need me."

"You'd do that?"

"Skky, you should know I'd follow you to Mars."

"Hear it's lovely this time of year."

"Stop it!"

"But, ya would?"

"I would. I do think, though, that it'd be good for you to spend some time in Ireland first. And of course I'd love to go there."

"An' I think you should, you need to see where you came from. Is in your blood, after all. I feel it."

"Then take me there."

"It's settled. Be warned, the whole family's gonna love ya, will be crawlin' all over ya."

"That's great – as long as you are, too."

"Oh, I can start right now."

"How about in the shower?"

"How 'bout that?"

* * *

"So lass, we should grab a blanket, go to the lake, an' just enjoy this wonderful day," Skky had just polished off a second bowl of homemade vegetable soup, along with several freshly baked rolls.

"How do you propose to get there?"

"Hmm? Oh, ha ha ha, well, can't help it. You're a great cook, so ya are. But, think I can still get up and walk. Unless…"

"No! walking is fine, it's great, we'll walk." His back was turned and she was allowing herself to enjoy the view as he rinsed and stacked the dishes.

"Walkin' then. I just needa run across the street and put on some shorts."

"Mm, Skky?"

"Oh ohhh, she wants somethin'…" he said with mock trepidation.

"And if I did?" she teased.

He dried his hands, turned and rested them on the counter behind him, now serious. "Then I'd get it for ya, or do it for ya, noh matter whawt."

Cailín felt her cheeks turn warm, and wondered if she was going to melt into the floor. "You're completely adorable," she said softly. "Anything?   Know what's silly?"

He was still looking at her intently, but his eyes crinkled into a smile, "Other 'n me? I give up."

"All your stuff is across the street."

"Yeah?"

"That's silly."

He took her hand, "Truly. Let's go get it."

Warm sun and cool breezes washed over them as they lay on the blanket at the edge of the lake.

"You'll get sunburned knees that way," she said, slowly surveying his body.

"Eh, who cares, this day is perfect."

Dear heaven, you're *perfect*, Cailín thought.

"You're beautiful, Cailín, in every way," he said softly, his eyes closed.

Her eyes welled up with tears, "I'm glad you think so."

"Am one lucky guy to have found ya." Without looking, he draped his arm over her body, resting his hand on her thigh, "But it works both ways, so it does."

"What does?"

"Wan day soon, soon as I can… I'll be askin' ya somethin'."

"Then you'll have it, no matter what," she smiled. "And… then it'll be my turn again to ask you for something."

"Ha ha ha, so that's how it's gonna be? Aw right, let's be havin' it."

"Don't I have to wait my turn?"

"Well, noh – I can make a score card, whawtever."

"You could do that, but you're sure? You'd want to know right now?"

"Am sure."

"I love you, Skky. I want your babies."

* * *

She rushed back from the market Tuesday evening, thrilled that they finally had corned beef. Cailín would have preferred to cook it herself, but it was getting late, and the sample the shopkeeper offered was excellent. She had a feeling that Rain and Smithson had somehow engineered its timely arrival and had to laugh at herself for wondering if it was three hundred years old.

A slight chill in the early evening air was punctuated by a moderate breeze. The streetlights would flicker on soon, and maybe they'd have dinner by candlelight. Who would feed a superstar sandwiches by candlelight? She would, with homemade potato soup, and had no doubts whatsoever that he was going to love it.

She marveled at the fact that she felt at home here, but decided she'd likely feel at home wherever he was. These happy thoughts played across her mind as she rushed toward the doorway. Through the window she saw that he had already lit a fire. Oh yeah, this was going to be perfect.

Then her heart fell. Skky was sitting on the sofa, one hand covering his mouth, staring at the floor. She stopped just short of the door and tried to slow her breathing and pounding heart. She pressed two fingers hard between her eyebrows, then started to twist a strand of hair.

No! She was going to fix this. She plunged through the door smiling, "Hey, handsome, dinner soon," and continued toward the kitchen.

"Uh." He ran his hand through his hair and squeezed the back of his neck. "Oh. Need help?"

"No, no. Just relax, I've got it." Her smile faded quickly as soon as she was out of the room. She stuffed things in the fridge, stood up and tucked her blouse in neatly. It was time to fix this or die trying.

"Skky, I thought we might put some candles on the patio, grab a jacket or blanket, and eat outside."

"Okay," his feet were up on the sofa now, but he looked anything but relaxed with his arms folded across his waist.

Cailín couldn't resist ruffling his hair as she walked around the sofa. She sat down beside him, hip to hip, and took his hand and pressed the back of it to her cheek, "I know it still hurts. I know," she said softly.

He looked at her, failed a smile, and looked away.

"Can we talk about it, please? I need to say some things."

"Sorry, uh course. Yeah." He sat up straighter and looked at her again. She hoped she was getting him back.

"I know it's hard to talk about. It's like, when she killed the baby, she killed part of you. In more ways than one, I mean."

"I, em, never thought about it quite that way, but..."

"It's like she wanted to destroy you. I don't understand why, but that's how it seems. Is that how it feels?"

"Aye, you're right. Never put words to it. Yeah. Yeah, is how it feels."

"Part of you has been gone. I don't want you to pretend to be happy at times when you're not. I want to know what you're feeling, what you need. And I want that little missing part of you back."

"Oh, Cailín, you've done a lot to bring me back, dun think ya haven't. Most of the time, I'm right here."

"Do you realize you served a purpose in all this? It was a terrible thing. It's difficult to form any understanding of what she did. So there was no way you could have even guessed. But you did serve a purpose.

"Skky, if not for you, there would have been no one to grieve for the baby. No one. No one to care, to even recognize that there was a life that mattered. I know your family must care. Now I care, too. Without you, no one would have even noticed.

249

"What are the chances that out of the hundreds or thousands of nurses in New York that your friend's wife was one of three? You were meant to know, because no life deserves to come into this world, even for a minute, uncared for. It's tempting to think it was too late, but I think it still matters.

"There's something else I believe, and I certainly don't have all the answers, but I feel it strongly."

"Whawt's that, lass?"

"If that little soul was meant to be your son, he will be someday. He's waiting in Summerland, he's safe, and he'll come back."

"'Tis a beautiful thought. Where would I be without ya, Cailín?"

"Don't try to find out. Please."

He put his arms around her and she laid her head on his chest. "I've been – I was – pretty far gone for a while. Comin' here to try to get used to doin' whawt I love to do again was the best thing I could have done. When I met you, was like all of a sudden I just woke up. Started feelin' like maybe the world could be a good place again. You give me more than I could expect or hope for."

"You're a good man, Skky, with a beautiful heart and soul, how could I not?"

"Grá liom tú freisin, a Cailín. I love you, too." They sat in silence for a moment before Skky spoke again, "Corned beef, is it?"

"Mm, I didn't cook it. I hadn't been able to find one before today." She twirled her finger through his hair, thinking his appetite was a good sign.

"I dun wanna move."

"Me either, let's just stay like this. What kind of furniture do you like best?"

"Afraid that'll be up to you," he said caressing her shoulder. "I'm hungry."

"You make the sandwiches, I'll warm up the soup."

"I need you, Cailín," he said as they walked to the kitchen.

Suddenly he took her by the arms, then put his arms around her. He backed off just a step and laid his hand against her cheek. "Promise me somethin'."

"Skky, what's wrong?" she instinctively tightened her hold on him.

"Just — promise me that nothin' will ever tear us apart. That if — may be should say when — I screw up, that you'll try to understand, that you'll give me a second chance."

She laid her head against his chest. She felt that the sound of his heartbeat was the only thing keeping her from vaporizing. "I'm all about second chances," she whispered.

"Cool night and hot potato soup, dun get any better."

"Yes, it does," she couldn't resist.

"Got me there," he winked, "but if I dun eat, then I won't have the energy."

"Oh! Can I make you another sandwich? More soup? There's dessert, too."

Skky sat back in his chair and laughed. "Oh, lord, ha ha ha, wonderin' — when I take ya to Ireland — is cool and rainy there a *lot*…"

"We won't have any trouble figuring out what to do with our time then."

They gathered up the dishes and decided to have cake and coffee inside.

"So I have to go away for a day or two …" he looked away as he sat the dishes in the sink, then back at her, "… got some business to finish."

"Oh? Then … you'll be back?" she moved closer to him.

251

"Yup, 'course I will. Leavin' Sunday mornin', will be back probly the next night. You, uh, you still be here?"

"Yes, of course."

"Cailín, am goin' to get the final divorce papers. Got a good reason to do it, get it over. Shoudda dun it a long time ago." His head to one side, he ran his hand through his hair, "But, has just been hard to face everything. Now, it needs to be behind us." He reached out and took her hands, "I want ya to be here when I get back, promise?"

"Oh, Skky, where else would I be? Unless I went with you, but I understand that's probably not a good idea. It'll be hard enough for you to get around without being seen yet." She ran her hands up and down his arms, then circled her arms around his waist. "Still, I wish I could be with you."

He hugged her closer, "Knowin' that… that'll do fine, so it will."

She looked up into his eyes, "Are you okay with this, I mean…"

"Not with whawt happened, but ending the legal stuff with – her – yeah, it's past time and now," finally, his eyes lightened a bit and a hint of a smile crossed his lips, "honestly can't wait to move forward."

She laid her head against his chest, "You have to do it for yourself, Skky, somehow, some way it all needs to be resolved."

"So I think, well, there's a reason for everything and somehow I'll understand it wan day. I do believe that."

"So do I."

He gave her a lingering kiss.

"Ready for dessert?"

"At least."

* * *

The week was going by too quickly. Cailín went to the pub with Skky every day, never tiring of his singing. Afternoons they spent at the lake swimming and soaking up the sun.

"Heh. Whawt's this?"

She was laying on her stomach, drinking in his slow and rhythmic touch as rubbed suntan lotion on her back and legs. The scent of coconut oil blended with sunshine made her think that this was better than any tropical paradise.

"What's what?" she asked lazily.

"Looks like a scar here, on the back of your foot." His finger traced the narrow line of flat, smooth skin. "Oh, and one on the other heel, too? Whawt happened?"

"Oh, that. Those were made by my shoes."

"Dear lord, why dint ya take 'em off? Musta hurt like hell."

"It wasn't an option. My car broke down one very hot summer day and I had to be somewhere, so I walked over a mile in the wrong shoes."

"Musta been important to do that."

"It was beyond important; it was like a matter of life and death to me. The sidewalk was too hot or I would have taken them off. I didn't even notice until I got home and tried to take them off. They were great shoes, killer in more ways than one. It was worth it though. I'd do it all over again. Ten times again."

"Ohh…" Skky lay down, put his arm around her, and kissed her cheek. "… am sorry, so very sorry," he said softly.

"It's not the worst thing that ever happened."

"If I'd known, I woudda carried ya."

"If you'd known –"

"Hey, people! What's up?" It was Rain.

"Don't you ever knock?" she laughed.

"Couldn't find the doorbell."

"Heh, Rain." Skky sat up. "Come to swim?"

"Yeah, thought I might. Oh, hey, how about that tennis lesson you've been threatening us with, Kaylin?"

"Sure. By the way, where's Lexi? She hasn't been at the pub the past two days." Finally a chance to give Rain some of his own medicine.

"I, uh, heard that she had to go out of town. A brief visit to relatives or something."

"Not that she can't have a couple of days off, but I just wondered."

"Heh lad, after our tennis, em, catastrophe, how 'bout we barbeque some wings? I make great sauce." Skky stole a glance at Cailín, and she nodded. "Maybe we can talk Cailín into doin' somethin' with uh couple potatoes."

"That'd be great, I'll grab some beer. Just a quick swim first." Rain headed for the water.

"I think he's lonesome with Lexi gone."

"Yeah, thinkin' they've spent some time together, hope everything's alright."

"I'm sure it is, he's a good guy."

"Have taken up all your time. Shoudda let ya have some more fun with your cuz. Feel kinda bad about that."

"No you don't." She laughed.

"Noh, I don't. But maybe we can show them around Ireland sometime. Some places I'd like to show ya first, though."

"That sounds great! Which places?"

"Tell ya later." He got up, and pulled her to her feet. "We best go change and dig up some racquets."

* * *

254

The night turned chilly and Skky lit the fire after dinner.

"This feels like our last night together." The fact that he would be leaving Sunday morning was wearing on Cailín.

"Aw now, dun think that. Will only be gone a couple days, lass."

"I know." She snuggled closer to him. "When will we leave here? What will it be like?"

"Was thinkin' the day after I get back here, I was. Go to New York a couple days, make travel plans to Ireland."

"Does your family know about me?"

"Uh course they do."

"Really?"

He smiled, "Really."

"When will you let the world know you're back?"

"Soon. News of the divorce will probly spread quick, so need to jump in fast an' make a statement."

"How will you do that?"

"Hire security, make sure the press is tipped off, show up at a fancy restaurant. With you on my arm. Ready for that?"

"Oh! I guess I need to be. Yes... I am." She felt a little chill up and down her spine, but it was a good one.

"Wear that dress? The one that you wore on our first dinner date? It's smokin'."

She laughed, "Sure, I'm comfortable with that."

"I'll have my agent arrange stuff. Gettin' from the car into the restaurant will be the truly manic part. That's where security comes in. Press won't be allowed inside. Probly have to leave by the back door, dunno yet."

"I'll just smile constantly, look very, very happy and squeeze you 'til you squeak. That's not a stretch at all."

"Not for me either. Gotta tell ya though, there will be a photographer inside. He'll take some candid shots, we'll pick the ones we like best and my agent will make those public the next day, along with a statement. Sorry, but gotta work the system – on our terms."

"I understand. I have no problem with that." She was beginning to understand what his public life was like. "It definitely has to be what's best, easiest, for you. I'm just happy to be part of it."

"Can't be any other way. And to be honest, can't wait to show ya off. Hope that dun sound, well, wrong."

"There's something you haven't thought of."

"Whawt's that?"

"I'll be showing you off, too."

"Ha ha ha, fairplay. Can definitely live with that. Next day we'll head to Ireland, things will be a bit quieter there."

"I'm just so glad that you're ready to deal with all this."

"I am, but I've been through the media frenzy before, just want it to go smooth so you're not freaked out."

"I'll be by your side, so I can handle anything. We'll make it fun."

"Think we will, yeah. New beginning, happy days."

"Skky?"

"Hmm?"

"The other day, at the lake, you started to tell me of some place in Ireland you wanted to show me."

"Yeah. So when I was ten, eleven, granny took me on a trip. Went south, just wandered through less populated areas, got to know some people, see what their life was like. Heard some interestin' stories about the auld days." She loved the way his hands were never still when he talked about things he enjoyed.

"Ran into some that spoke Irish pretty well, she thought it would be good for me, and so it was."

"Oh, how wonderful to have people to speak the language with!"

"Truly, 'course my family speaks some, too. Anyroads, we went on south to County Cork, near the sea. Came across a small village there, actually stayed the night with some nice folks. Next day we walked around a bit, just enjoyin' the peaceful countryside. On the far edge of the village there was ruins of what once must have been a fine house. The stone walls of whawt had been the main level still stood. Went inside the walls and walked around. The stone staircase was still standin'. Found out later from stories passed down that the house had had a second story built of wood. I had a kinda funny feelin'. Dunno, just seemed a magical place. Hard to explain, but I never forgot it. Just wanna show it to ya wan day soon."

"I would love that, I'll definitely go there with you. We need to do that." She fought back the tears and hugged him tight.

* * *

Morning came too quickly, but Cailín was glad that she woke up first. She propped herself up on her elbow so she could see his face better. He looked so relaxed and contented that joy washed over her. His eyes moved slightly and he smiled. *He smiled in his sleep, how cool is that?* She laid her head on his shoulder, wanting to savor the last few minutes until he needed to wake up.

"Heh," Skky responded.

"Sorry, I didn't mean to wake you."

"'S okay, imagine is about time."

"I'll make breakfast while you shower."

"Those cinnamon rolls ready to bake, maybe? Those and coffee is all."

"Sure that's all you want?"

"Mm hmm, well …" he nuzzled her neck, "not all, but probly all I have time for."

"Are you still good with this?"

"They're perfect. Oh. The trip an' all? I am."

"Good."

"Not much to do really, sign some documents. Her bank account is actually bigger than mine, and I dun want anything from her, to be sure, so …"

"The house?"

"Never was my style, so will be sold, or she can buy me out, either way – done."

"I see."

"Cailín? Am I bein' too pushy? I – I'm askin' ya to come away with me, leave your job behind, let me take care of ya. Is that too much? Is like, I'm askin' ya to live my life."

"That's not what I thought at all, I thought that you were making my dreams come true, that you were asking me to live *our* life."

"So that's how I mean it, really, if that's whawt ya want."

"I've never wanted anything more."

He was only taking one small bag, and Cailín was retrieving his toothbrush from the bathroom when there was a knock on the door.

"Who could that be? Rain usually just walks right in," she laughed.

"Ah. Would be the guy who made my trip arrangements, I'll get it."

She took advantage of the opportunity and quickly stuffed her torn pink panties in his bag. *Oh yeahhh, good job, me*, she thought.

She closed the bag and headed toward the kitchen, "Hey, I'll wrap up a couple of these rolls for you…" she stopped in her tracks.

"Oh, hello there, you must be Kaylin, allow me to introduce myself, Alexander Smithson here."

"Hello … and excuse me," she rushed out of the room. *I guess I shouldn't be surprised – but Smithson? Really?* She placed two big cinnamon rolls in a plastic container and snapped it shut.

"I think there's room," she quickly stuffed the container in Skky's bag and re-zipped it.

"So sorry, but we really must be going, Mr. O'Keeffe, pleased to meet you, Miss Casey." Smithson stepped outside.

Skky already had his arms around her, "Slán go fóill, a chuisle a chroi, gráim thú," he said after they kissed.

"Slán leat, a fear go haillan, is tú mo ghrá," she caressed his cheek as she spoke.

She leaned against the door and watched him walk away.

Rain was only five feet away before she noticed him. "Gaw! Don't sneak up on me like that."

"Distracted, are we? And is that any way to talk to the person who's brought provisions?"

"Huh? What? Are we setting up camp in the wild West or something?"

"Nope, right here. Got huge sub sandwiches, chips, beer, wine, movies – and your DVD's."

"Do make yourself at home," she huffed, realizing she was wearing Skky's t-shirt and not much else. "I'll be right back."

"We're going to the pub for dinner," he called after her.

"The pub?" she said from the bedroom.

"Spaghetti and meatballs. Best ever. Lexi makes it. Play your cards right and she'll give you the recipe."

Cailín laughed as she tucked her own t-shirt into her jeans, "I'll leave it to you to sweet talk it out of her, 'sugar britches'."

"Watch a movie? Even got a couple of chick flicks here. Or …"

"Skky's going to be gone for maybe all of thirty-six hours and you're planning to babysit me the whole time?"

"I might be. My price is high, but I can be had."

"Want a cinnamon roll? Fresh, homemade."

"Got coffee?"

"Of course." She cleared the kitchen table. "Here you go. Rain?"

"At your service."

"Skky's going to be ready to leave here soon. He wants me to come to Ireland with him, and…"

"Great! That's great. Can I have another roll, please?"

"Tsk, tsk, I guess Lexi didn't make you breakfast?" she sat down across the table from him.

"So I'll be meeting his family, and going on tour with him after the first of the year."

"Not surprised at all, but truly glad to hear it."

"Rain? Hello? When is my orientation? I can't be walking around out there not knowing – completely unfamiliar with things."

"Ah, that."

"Well, yeah – *that*!"

"He'll help you, you'll catch on quick. Can't imagine you getting lost in Ireland anyway."

"He … what? What are you saying?"

"There is no orientation, Kay."

"I – but – but that means that he has to know the whole story? How I got here … how *he* got here?"

"That's right, Kaylin. When you think about it, it really can't be any other way."

"What the hell? He'll hate me!"

"It's really very simple. The truth is the best way."

"Are you kidding me? Did I sign up for that? Someday, yes, soon maybe, but – all at once, just 'boom? Here's what happened, now let's have a nice life?' And after what he's been through…"

"The truth has to come out."

"Not – it's not that simple, you can't just…"

"He won't hate you, Kay, I promise that on my life. Think about it. Do you believe that he loves you, wants a future with you?"

"I do, but –"

"Wait, wait, hold on a sec. What if the tables were turned?"

"You mean?"

"Yeah, what if things were reversed?"

"If he had made the deal? If he had me regenerated so he could be sent to meet me?"

"Something like that. How would you feel? Would you hate him for it?"

"Of course not."

"Of course not?"

"No. If he had engineered the whole thing just to be with me, so we could have a life together, given me a second chance, how could I hate him for that? Besides, we're meant to be together, doesn't really matter how it happens, as long as it does."

"That's the bottom line?"

"That's it."

"Well then, it works both ways, believe me, we know that to a certainty. And you may or may not like this, but several of us will be there when the truth is revealed. You know how the saying goes – it will set you free. You should trust me on this, you have nothing to feel guilty about, or to worry about."

"Tennis match before lunch?" she growled.

"Whew, you'll kill me."

"That's always an option."

*　*　*

"What's happened? It's Tuesday already, he should have been back last night. Were there delays with the paperwork?" Her words were paced, deliberate, "I thought everything was set and ready, just waiting for his signature. Was there a scheduling problem?"

"Nobody's in a panic yet." Rain scratched the back of his neck, "Well, almost nobody."

"Yet? Has anyone actually heard from Skky at all?"

"No, but –" he winced.

She was calm, but unrelenting, "But what? It's been my experience that Future Connect does a stupid crazy good job of keeping tracks of their – what? – subjects? So why doesn't anyone know anything? Or you're not telling me?"

"Geez, did I hear a 'lab rat' in there?"

She crossed her arms, "If you like."

"C'mon, Kay, don't –"

"Don't what? Don't worry about the man who's the only reason I do anything?"

"Yeah, okay, okay, I don't blame you. Look, I promise that tomorrow morning I'll raise hell if he's not back, or if no one's heard from him. Make them sorry they pay me the big bucks. I will do that, and we will find out what the holdup is. Meanwhile, he's a big boy, nothin's happened to him.

"I'll even come by and take you with me and we'll stomp the brass. As if you need my help."

"Fine. Just fine. I'll watch a movie and read a book 'til I'm ready to sleep. And hope he wakes me up in the middle of the night."

"Huh? Read, *and* watch a movie?"

"If I'm lucky it might occupy half my mind."

"Hmm. A glass of wine wouldn't hurt either. But if you can't sleep, whatever, call me."

* * *

She wondered if Rain knew something and wasn't telling. No, she didn't think so. His acting style had always gone more to the genuine, true to the character, and she doubted he could have pulled if off. That thought only eased her mind for a moment, then she realized the possibility that he was being kept in the dark so he could be convincing.

"Nooo," Cailín whispered to herself, "oh, please, please, no." She covered her mouth with her hand, the other pressed the back of the sofa, and it was the only thing keeping her on her feet. *What if he knows? And no one was there to offer an explanation, I wasn't there to try and make things right.* Going to an office, signing a paper, doesn't take that long when you're expected, when you have an appointment. Sure, travel plans could have messed up, but the local weather was no threat and given that he had said he'd be back in thirty-six hours, his destination couldn't be that far away. She couldn't be certain, but felt that she was somewhere in the upper Midwestern United States. Temperatures, the weather pattern, the angle of the sun, ruled out Canada and Mexico, or even the East or West Coasts. Of course the weather could have changed some in three hundred years, she supposed that wasn't at all out of the question, still … and there was always a small chance of a mechanical failure, if anything even was 'mechanical' in this century, but it seemed unlikely. Future Connect would have arranged for private transportation. Problems with travel didn't figure into the equation.

No, something else is wrong, possibly very wrong. He knows, he knows what I've done. She staggered around the sofa, sat down, and tried to imagine how he would feel if he had somehow found out. It would be overwhelming, finding out that he existed only because he'd been 'regenerated' by mad scientists, all at the whim of someone from three hundred years ago. How could he possibly resolve that? He couldn't, she decided. How could anyone? Rain was wrong. Skky would do what any human being would probably do – run – or worse.

Had he overheard a careless whisper from one of the townspeople? Seen a stray document?

Why hadn't she thought of this before? Why hadn't *they*? Meticulous as they were, things could still go wrong. He was in touch with the world outside of this town, had an old friend run across something and figured it out? Anything could have happened.

One thing seemed certain in her mind, if he did know he felt he could no longer trust her and had run as far away as possible. If she could find him, convince him to read her book – if he would only listen she'd spill the entire story to him, including all the things she hadn't told FC, about Spéir, about the dreams, and how they'd let her believe he was dead. It probably wouldn't make any difference in how he felt about her, why should it? but maybe she could convince him that he was worthwhile, that life was worthwhile. Maybe she could convince him that his life was worth changing.

She had no other thought but for his well being as she sobbed into her hands. As for herself, there was no life unless he came out of this unscathed. She would accept her fate, maybe finding work in a strange new world and watching his career from afar through the media. Good enough, she deserved it. At least she'd know he was all right. What she could not accept was the possibility of Skky losing himself again.

There was going to be no movie to watch, no book to read. She quickly drank half a glass of wine, set the alarm clock for 4:00 a.m., and fell into a troubled sleep.

* * *

Cailín woke up five minutes before the alarm was set to go off. The room felt strange and empty without him beside her. She got up and wandered into the living room in the dark, thinking that it wasn't a good idea to turn a light on.

The realization hit her like a bullet. She wrapped her arms around her waist and doubled over. She grabbed the arm of the chair and unsteadily lowered herself onto the edge. Everything she knew of Skky in this time mirrored his life in her time. Three hundred years ago in that world, for all she knew, he'd been dead.

No, no! she told herself, he'd already lived six months longer than he had then. Unless this timeline wasn't quite the same, unless he'd been born six months earlier here. It may have been science that had gotten them here, but maybe even that science wasn't exact. Logan had even admitted that they didn't understand fully. She strained to remember every detail, every conversation she'd had with Skky, and realized that she hadn't asked his birth date, or his exact age. If this life was a parallel to his former one he could be gone soon, if he wasn't already. His time, their time, might be up.

Think, think, think, I've got to think, there's a wild card here, there has to be. She thought about Smithson, Logan, Rain. They wouldn't have allowed any of this to happen if they knew it was going to end abruptly. "There are no guarantees, of course..." she heard each of their voices, "...but we can increase the odds." *Be logical, you've got to get this right. No guarantees, fair enough. But if there are no guarantees, then it must follow that there is no predestined doom, either. The universe is not that unfair. It just isn't.*

Although she couldn't know for certain the reason his marriage ended three hundred years ago it would make sense if the circumstances mirrored each other. It would

266

explain why he'd chosen to disappear then, why he needed to take some time for himself.

That's it! The obvious jumped up and grabbed her. Three hundred years ago he hadn't met her just prior to the end of the marriage, he hadn't met her just days before he died – *That's it! I'm the wild card, and I can make the difference!*

Logan's words echoed through her memory, "Give him that second chance. Only you can, Kay."

The all too practical question of how was the next hurdle. She knew nothing of the world outside this sheltered town, let alone how to get out. She'd figure it out somehow, she knew that people still spoke English, still breathed oxygen in the atmosphere, and still acted like human beings. Maybe that's all she needed to know.

She remembered seeing a pickup truck in town when a young man was unloading fresh produce at the market. She guessed that it was roughly ten years old, in relative terms. They must have preserved, or perhaps reconstructed one for practical purposes. She had watched the young man drive it off when he was finished, it seemed to run well enough. Where would she get gas for it – assuming it even ran on gas. Maybe it was built to use another energy source. She had to find it. She remembered seeing it parked by one of the cabins near the lake. Were there even highways anymore, or did people teleport, or use jet packs, or… *One thing at a time.*

It would be light in less than two hours. She had to get moving before Rain, or anyone, could possibly miss her. She knew that they wouldn't let her leave now, there was the agreement, if she chose to leave town without consulting them, without mutual consent and their help to adjust, the pact was dissolved.

To hell with that, this is about Skky. He's the only thing that matters now. By the light of one short candle she made scrambled eggs and toast. Time to get practical. She made two sandwiches, wrapped them, took a plastic container and plopped them in it. Rethinking it she removed the sandwiches and placed several ice cubes in the bottom and the sandwiches on top. Setting the candle on the floor she searched the lower cabinet for another larger container and placed more ice and several cans of what she had assumed all along was Pepsi into it. She stuffed three paper bags together and loaded them, throwing in a couple of granola bars, apples and bananas. For good measure she threw in two sharp knives and the matches that Rain had used to light the grill. That should easily get her through the first day. Surely she would find civilization before supplies gave out.

A quick shower by candlelight and she began to dress. *It's chilly out now, that's good. Put everything you can on your back. Jeans, shirt, tank top, then sweater. Layers, that's it, and wear the boots.* Another paper bag, a few extra pieces of clothing and sneakers – dumped out on the kitchen floor to be repacked with a half a dozen bottles of water in the bottom.

Denim jacket or leather jacket? She chose the leather as it was lighter weight, waterproof, more practical. Two bags to carry, a little heavy, but doable. She'd make it to the truck. *Please, please, let it be where I think it is.*

Cailín opened the back door cautiously and looked around. The moon gave just enough light to be able to see where she was walking, but hopefully not enough to be seen easily. The pre-dawn air was cooler than she'd expected. She felt her way to the living room and retrieved the crocheted throw from the sofa and wrapped it around her shoulders. *Good grief, I must look like some sort of psycho survivalist.*

Something between gratitude and responsibility suddenly overtook her. She felt around in the dark, trying to remember where she could find the needed items.

Feeling her way around the sofa she reached the small end table and fumbled for the drawer. She pulled out a pad of paper and a pencil. She took them back to the kitchen and relit the candle. Hurriedly, she wrote, "Rain, I can't let him go." Refusing the tears that threatened, she blew out the candle and stumbled to the back door.

Whether it was Skky's voice, or Spéir's entreating her she couldn't tell, but it was the same song of despair and hope that she'd heard the night she spent in the small motel the day before she'd made the decision to come... here.

Cailín found she could half jog in spite of being encumbered with provisions. She avoided streetlights and looked over her shoulder frequently. She headed for the back of the row of shops where the pub was located to lessen her chances of being seen, and crossed the grassy area where she and Skky had laughed themselves nearly sick only a few days before and turned in the direction of the lake. Funny how a great memory can sharpen a projected sense of loss.

It was darker in the grove of trees that surrounded the lake, and she was forced to slow down. Several long minutes passed before she came to a clearing. *Where is that truck? What am I going to do if I can't find it? Hell, what will I do if I do find it? One thing, one thing, one thing at a time...*

A sliver of moonlight glinted on metal, revealing her prize.

She crept slowly toward the truck, crouching, and trying not to step on twigs or anything else that would make a sound. She stopped and straightened slowly, peering through the windows of the truck. There was no light in the nearby house. *What if they have a dog? Oh, please, don't let them have a dog.* She moved quickly now, setting her bags on the ground and carefully opening the door of the truck. The overhead light flashed on instantly. She dove inside and quickly flipped the switched. She scrambled back out and tossed her two bags onto the passenger seat, got in, and ducked down.

Keys. She felt the dashboard and found the ignition switch. No keys. She brushed the tears from her cheek with the back of her hand. She twisted around and put her hand under the driver's seat. Nothing. Stretching as far as she could, her fingertips touched what she though was metal. It was no use, if there were keys she couldn't reach them this way. Cautiously peering out the window she reached for the door handle and slid to the ground. Now she could reach farther under the seat – yes! That was definitely a key!

Now what? How much noise was the engine turning over going to make? She was going to have to be ready for a quick getaway, just in case. The engine hummed quietly, although it might as well have been a nuclear explosion in the stillness that surrounded her. There was a familiar looking bump on the steering column, and no stick shift on the floor. Automatic! That was going to help. She didn't dare switch on the lights until she was a few yards away. *Think, think, think... Park, Reverse, Neutral, Drive...* Not daring to breathe, she pulled the shift lever over one, two, three clicks. She looked quickly over her shoulder, and being satisfied that no one had gotten up to see what was going on, she began to inch her way slowly along the dirt road away from the farmhouse.

Her mind, like her body, felt lost in a wilderness of uncertainty. She sped up slowly, not wanting to have to step on the brake and activate the rear light. The road took a turn and now a row of trees sheltered her from view of the house. With a cautious sigh of relief she fumbled for a light switch. The first try yielded a quick flap of the windshield wipers. "Damn!" she whispered as though she might be overheard.

A second button wouldn't turn right or left. Nearly ready to give up she pulled on the switch and the dashboard lit up. A second pull yielded headlights.

Three miles seemed like thirty, then she saw it ahead, the dirt road came to a crossing with what looked like asphalt. Cailín relaxed a little, and felt under the seat once again, this time for the lever that would allow her to scoot it forward. She had literally been on the edge of her seat to be able to reach the pedals. Which way to turn felt like the biggest mystery yet, but she didn't hesitate to turn right. There was no way to guess and one option seemed as good as the other.

It felt good to be on the smooth pavement, and she allowed herself to hope that the first obstacle had been conquered. How many more there were to come, she didn't dare to think. Fifty miles an hour should be safe, whatever the speed limit might be. She drove for a few minutes, glad for the familiarity of something that felt normal.

Thoughts bombarded her like eighty mile wind gusts. Skky was gone! Where was he? Where was she? How was she going to find him? Her throat closed and the tears began to spill. "I can't do this, I can't fall apart now," she whispered to herself. She shoved her hand to the bottom of one of the sacks and retrieved a bottle of water. It was cold to her touch and she pressed it to her cheeks before opening it.

She glanced at the dashboard again, wondering if the radio worked, and if it did would she be able to handle it if his timing was as good as it usually was?

The radio yielded only faint static, up and down the dial. *It figures, there must be different ways of communicating now, advances...*

"Noh, not so much really." He was sitting in the same space as her bags. She could still see them right through him.

He was wearing jeans and a t-shirt, along with a denim jacket. It was odd, she suddenly wondered if heat and cold affected him at all, or if he just appeared in what would blend in appropriately.

"Noh, I don't so much feel that sorta thing."

"Good grief! Stop reading my mind. Spéir, oh – where have you been?" she choked on the words, feeling something akin to guilt, as though she'd been cheating on him.

"Well, in truth, with you mostly. But you know that."

"I guess, yes, of course." Her eyes were filling with tears again. "Where is he, uh, you? I mean…"

"Sleepin'."

"Oh, I know you can't … he is? Really? You know he's alright, and he's sleeping?"

"Sleepin'."

"I got it. It's enough, I won't ask for more. Thank you."

"'S all good, lass."

"Where I am going? Or just – where am I?"

"'S not so much a question of where." He looked sober, he was serious.

"You haven't – you, or they, didn't – he's not *gone* is he? Skky, I mean Skky. Please…" Cailín felt a wave of hysteria barreling down on her.

"You believe whawt ya wawnt tuh believe," his chin puckered his lips into a pout as he gazed ahead.

"So now you're going to answer me in riddles?" she couldn't find any anger to put in her voice.

"Not a riddle, just true is all."

"I just wish I knew where I was."

"Noh, lass, listen now. It's not so much a matter of where we are, but when." His hand passed through hers, he seemed to be trying to control the steering wheel. "Here, slow down a wee bit."

272

She saw it. A familiar green and white sign.

Chicago 35 miles
Exit 194 Right ½ mile

She took a deep breath and sobered a bit. "What? Uh, I'm coming to an actual highway that still goes all the way to Chicago?

"This should answer some questions," she said, half to herself, half to Spéir.

"Probly," he answered, "pull over a wee bit ahead. You'll see it."

It was a typical truck stop with lines of pumps stretched in front of a restaurant that segued into a convenience store. The faint hint of dawn made a scene she'd seen a hundred times surreal.

"I have to pee. Don't go away," she ordered, then softened, "please don't go away".

"Aye. Please dun forget to come back."

He says the strangest things sometimes, she thought.

Coffee! Yes! Truck stops always did it right. She rushed to the ladies room, a quick detour from what was now a mission to have a steaming cup in her hand.

She picked up a large thermal mug and filled it, adding French vanilla cream and two sugars. She inhaled and took a sip, and the consequence approximated euphoria.

The feeling dissolved quickly as she paid the disinterested teenager behind the counter. It was unmistakable – Lila Hanover, complete with her disdainful detachment, was on the cover of Vogue. *Wait – Vogue? Really? And Lila?*

Her hand shook visibly as she placed the magazine on the counter with a thunk. "This … this, too." The boy fished some coins from the drawer, looked up, then gave slight shrug. Cailín was already at the door.

Spéir approached her as he would a wild animal, one that would flee if startled. His form was more transparent now in the early light. He had become more solid when it was dark shortly before she had – had what? Left? He was in her awareness, her frame of reference, but her eyes were still fixed on the magazine cover. Lila had dissolved, disappeared, and only one thing remained:

October 2014 Edition

So much for orientation.

"In with you, wee Cailín, in the truck." He had opened the door, done it, as he did things that were absolutely necessary in the physical world.

His hand was warm, pushing on her back. She got in, and he locked the doors. He waited in silence as she stared out the window, unblinking, unseeing.

A full five minutes passed. "Okay." She reached for the coffee. "It's alright."

His voice was warm and gentle. "Lass, we all do, whawtever the reason, whawt we feel we have to do. Whawt seems right at the time. Please understand that."

The first rays of sun filtered through him. She stared at him for a while before speaking, "God, you're beautiful. I wish I could touch you, really touch you."

"You have. And I've touched you. But ya know that, so ya do." His slow smile confirmed it, but it was his eyes that convinced her.

"So, you – merge? Is that it?"

"Not really. That would mean that at some point 'we' were separate."

"Ohhh kay, what?"

"Skky, well I – he's sleepin' right now. So here I am, like I often am when he's distracted, asleep, or sometimes just in a quiet spot like. When it won't hurt to turn attention. Is like when ya come to me in whawt ya call dreams, a lot like that."

"Oh, sure, that explains it."

"Now, you're not surprised. You know that just like you know other things, so ya do."

"What things?" she sipped the still warm coffee thoughtfully.

"You've been so focused, so determined that you've ignored the obvious. Is quite flattering, honestly. We both did whawt we felt we had to do, the only way we knew how to do to make whawt we believed come true." His hand passed through hers again, she closed her eyes and let herself feel the kiss she knew he placed on her cheek.

"Your name wasn't Spéir back then, was it?"

"No more 'n yours was Cailín."

"You used it so I'd make the connection. Just one more confirmation, as if ..."

"Go home now, Cailín. Go home, you know the way."

* * *

The condo was just as she'd left it. The fridge had been cleaned out and apparently someone had dusted, otherwise things were the same. Cailín was tempted to just fall into bed and sleep until he found her. He would be coming if he was still alive, and according to Spéir, he was. She went to the closet and began to pack only what she was going to need. She left by the service entrance, and walked two blocks before hailing a taxi. The next flight left in ninety minutes and with luck there would be a seat available. Skky's sleepy gray green eyes leapt into her thoughts, but she resisted. There were things to be done before anyone could catch up with her and try to talk her out of it.

* * *

Nick Logan sat with his feet on the window ledge looking out over the New York skyline, tapping his fingers slowly on the arm of his leather chair. It had been a wild, tricky ride, that was for certain. Now, with the project near to conclusion, he was beginning to allow himself to feel some relief. He couldn't deny that he felt a large measure of happiness for the young man and woman involved, nor could he shake the idea that he should probably have his own head examined.

Smithson's proposal to conduct a controlled experiment to prove that a person would completely suspend disbelief when presented with an outrageous idea if it promised to deliver their heart's desire intrigued Logan. Admittedly, it appealed to his ego that Smithson had chosen him. He also knew only too well that he had been Smithson's first conquest.

It had looked like an almost one hundred percent certainty that there would be a great outcome, however a failure would have been catastrophic across the board. Losing his license would have been the least of it. People he'd come to care about would have been devastated. It wasn't the money, though he'd been paid a considerable amount. Overall, Smithson and his privately funded research foundation had spent a small fortune.

Smithson had put great deal on the line professionally. He was the head of the Behavioral Sciences Department of a prestigious northeastern university, and possessed a list of degrees and fellowships longer than his arm. Although his research project was not public and was not intended to ever be, a failure resulting in its unveiling would have brought a swift end to his credibility and his career.

It was the story that had hooked both of them, one of a deep, nearly unexplainable love between a young man and woman who had met only once, and an unbearable loss that had unhinged the young man who for all intents and purposes seemed to have it all.

Logan thought back to the day four months ago that Alexander Smithson had phoned him. "This is it, Nick, this is it. It's time to put the process in motion. I'd like for you to talk to a viable candidate for the project." Smithson had told him little about the dejected young man he'd come across on a nearly deserted beach just outside Gosford while vacationing in Australia, but he was insistent. " I've a feeling that we could help him out, I'm not certain what the solution is yet, but I believe there must be one. Of course I leave it to you to ask the right questions and make your recommendations. In any event, he needs your help."

Smithson arrived at his office the next day with a very subdued Skky in tow.

Logan was shocked. He'd seen Skky O'Keeffe on television several times, as had half the world. He had heard of Skky's disappearance and continuing absence as well. The man that stood before him didn't possess the energy and joy that he'd seen in his performances. The intensity, however, was still there.

"Please, come in. I'm Nick Logan."

"Heh. Skky O'Keeffe." He spoke softly, as though the very act was tiring.

Logan gestured, and hoped it seemed casual, "Take a seat if you like, and we can talk for a bit."

Skky looked around the room, "Yeah. Okay, yeah."

"Thank you, Alec," Logan gently urged him toward the door.

"Oh, yes, yes. I must be going." He leaned to look at Skky, "I'll return for you in about an hour."

"Thanks." Skky had sunk into the chair and didn't turn around.

He slowly opened up and Logan guided the conversation but didn't push. The hour hadn't seemed nearly long enough, but Logan felt that it was probably all

Skky could handle at present. When Smithson returned they agreed to hold further sessions at his Manhattan apartment. Skky wasn't ready for the world to discover his whereabouts, and it would have been a risk for him to come to Logan's office every day.

A week passed, and Logan was pleased with the progress they were making. He had encouraged Skky to stay in touch with his family and let them know that he was getting help. That part had been easy enough. Then Logan hit pay dirt with a question that provided the information that he and Smithson, for somewhat different reasons, had sought. "Skky, if you could change one thing, do one thing differently, what would that be?" Logan had seen a light return to his eyes when he talked at some length about the day he'd met a young woman named Cailín. Logan had informed Smithson of his discovery, and also insisted that they not act on it for another week or so. As intrigued as he'd been for several months now with Smithson's concept, he adhered to his first duty. He wanted to be certain that Skky was ready for their proposal, and not only in a frame of mind to follow through, but also to consider it carefully. Not the least of their concerns would be locating Cailín and ascertaining her state of mind; that would have be to done very, very carefully. Enter Brandon Sykes, the invaluable link.

Using a very discreet, resourceful, and well paid detective agency to track Cailín they had soon learned that she and Brandon were not only co-workers, but close friends, and apparently nothing more. Discovering Brandon's love of playing racquetball once or twice a week was child's play for the detectives who had also ascertained what days of the week he was most likely to play, and of course where. It had been quick, and easy enough, for Logan to infiltrate that arena. He genuinely liked Brandon and striking up a friendship had been simple enough. It wasn't long before Brandon, with the disclaimer of not wanting to take advantage of Logan's expertise in his profession, had revealed his concerns about his friend's despair over Skky's disappearance. Logan had asked him for a little time to consider the predicament, and quickly consulted with Smithson.

Logan turned around and stood up at the soft knock on the door. Skky entered slowly, index finger rubbing a circle between his eyebrows.

"Hey, boss, have a chair." Logan motioned, and sat back down. "I take it the legalities are concluded, is that bothering you?"

"All done. Noh, I'm glad, relieved. Just wish the judge's schedule hadn't tied things up two extra days, but is done now." He didn't look up. "Dint think it would have gone this far, Nick."

"Didn't think what, Skky?" Now Logan's brow furrowed, "surely –"

"Noh, divorce was gonna happen, one way or the other, to be sure," he sighed as he walked to the window. "Cailín," he turned to face Logan again. "Is Cailín I'm worried about."

"I'm not sure I understand, from what I've seen and heard everything has gone extremely well."

"It has, truly, better 'n I coudda dreamed. She's, well, just fantastically incredible."

"Good," Logan cracked his knuckles, "very good, saves me the trouble of beating you up."

"Careful, an Irishman fights dirty," Skky smiled briefly. "I'm afraid I mighta screwed up though. Whawt happens when she finds out? She might hate me forever. I can't, can't…"

"Skky, I think –"

"Never felt worse than that day when she ran out." He shook his head. "Wish it hadn't … well, that I coudda prevented it."

"It was nearly inevitable, and that's where *I* screwed up. I should have insisted on speeding things up. On the other hand, you and I both agreed that she needed time to be ready. It was a delicate balance, and I misjudged it by a few days."

"I dun blame you, really no way uh knowin'."

"You know why I agreed to this, why we all did. You needed to be sure, and you needed time away from everything, time just for her. She needed time, too. Don't overlook what you were both willing to do to get there."

"Yup, true. I just have a feelin' that somethin's wrong. Can't stay, need to get back to her."

Logan laughed, "That's because you've been apart for – what? Over seventy two hours now, no wonder."

The sharp buzz signaled Logan that he needed to pick up immediately. "What?" the color drained from his face, "yes, yes, right away.

"Got a car downstairs?"

"Uh huh, why?"

"We've got to catch the next flight to Chicago. Skky, she's gone.

* * *

The flight had gone smoothly enough, save for the fact that it gave her too much time to think about Skky. Buying a round trip ticket had been the only option; paying cash for a one-way, and having very little luggage could have triggered a security delay. Forty eight hours should be enough time. It was going to have to be.

The taxi pulled up in front of the address she had given. "Oh, wait, I'm sorry – I have an errand to do," she lied to the driver, "two blocks up the street, and I'll just walk back. I don't have the number, but I'll recognize it in plenty of time for you to stop. Thanks."

Two and a half blocks further, and Cailín spotted a decent looking hotel, and hoped it wasn't too expensive. The bonus was a drug store three doors down.

The room was not huge, but clean, and the staff was pleasant. She hung up her clothes, brushed her teeth, and left.

The lobby of the professional building was a reflection of the pricey offices it contained. She searched the long register for the right name.

"May I help you find something?" She did her best not to act startled, and turned to the doorman.

"Um, well, I might be in the wrong building," she sped up her search of the names, knowing she couldn't fake it for long. There!

Ronald S. Welch, M.D.
Obstetrics and Gynecology
Suite 510

"Is there another building of this type nearby?" The man was quiet, and somewhat disapproving, she thought. "I'm looking for a C.P.A., and I don't see the name."

"At the end of this block there's another office building, attorneys and the like, you might try there," now

282

he sounded disinterested, dismissive. *That works for me,* she thought.

"Thank you, I will." Now she had to go in the direction he'd pointed. She walked to the end of the block and crossed the street, thankful that there were quite a few people to get lost amongst. She edged her way close to the buildings so that her fellow pedestrians would form a human shield between her and what she felt might be the prying eyes of the doorman.

A stop at the drugstore and a nearby deli and she was set. She unlocked the hotel room door and nearly jumped. Spéir was lounging on the bed, propped up on both pillows, and the T.V. was on.

"'Bout time."

"Uh huh," she laughed with relief, and genuine happiness. She hadn't even had to call him.

"Oh, sorry lass, here." He scooted the pillows over, patted the bed, and leaned back at the same angle she'd found him, sans pillows.

Cailín pulled off her boots, sat back, and tore into the sandwich. "What? I missed lunch, unless you count airplane pretzels."

"Is good you have an appetite."

"Thanks. Glad you approve."

She half heartedly watched the news while she ate, then remembered there was a phone book on the shelf under the nightstand. It was five years old, people didn't so much use them anymore, but it should work.

"You have reached the medical office of Ronald S. Welch, M.D." the disembodied female voice began, "If this is an emergency, please hang up and dial 9-1-1. If you'd like to make an appointment, obtain a prescription refill, or have another matter for office personnel, please call back between the hours of 9 a.m. and 6 p.m. Thank you."

A quick call to the front desk arranged a wake up call for 7:30 a.m. Just to be sure, she set the radio alarm clock for 7:35.

It was far too early to sleep, she'd wake up in the wee hours if she drifted off now.

Spéir pointed to the remote, and she thought he meant for her to pick it up. Maybe he wanted to channel surf? Before she could pick it up the channel jumped.

"Now that's just showing off," she scolded, but laughed. "Oh, a movie. That's fine, maybe it'll take my mind off things." It might have, save for the fact that it was Heaven Can Wait. She tried to decide if that was his way of reinforcing, or if he just had a lousy sense of humor.

* * *

They went in the service entrance and took the stairs, Skky bounding up them two at a time. Logan had hoped he'd slow down before they reached the fourth floor. No such luck. The kid was either in phenomenal shape, or driven. Both, he decided. Skky called down the stairwell to him, "whawt's the number again?"

"Hold on there," Logan was seconds away. "I think I should be with you. Here," he pointed as he withdrew the key from his pocket.

"Cailín? Cailín, it's me. Cailín, ya there?" Skky knocked again, "Cailín? Please."

"I don't think she's here." Logan turned the key and pushed the door open a few inches. "Kay? It's Nick, I'm here with Skky."

Silence.

Logan stepped in and Skky pushed past him.

"Can't explain, but feels like she was here."

"Guess we should have brought Gina," Logan thought out loud.

"No need," Skky started down the hallway, "not like I'm a stranger, least I hope."

"She's not here, Nick, whawt now?" Skky looked around; the furnishings reminded him so much of her, comfortable, not pretentious, but elegant. "Dear lord, whawt have I done?"

"That's 'we'. Let's see what we can find out. He flipped his cell open. "Gina? Nick," he went into the bedroom and opened the closet. "I need help with what, if anything, is missing ... yeah, uh huh, that too." He silently thanked providence for Gina's photographic memory and continued to scoot items across the rod, "small carry on suitcase, no. What? Navy blue skirt, no. Black skirt, no. And – uh huh, thanks, Gina."

"Some things are gone?"

"Yes, she's been here," Logan glanced at Skky with a half nod as he headed back toward the living room.

"I know they were right here," he pulled the second desk drawer open. "Hmm, checkbook, passbook, gone."

"Passbook?" Skky asked.

"Yeah, her savings account book. She didn't take many clothes, but she's gone somewhere. Hopefully not for long."

Skky sank into the sofa, hugging a pillow to his chest, "Dear lord, was this how she felt when I disappeared?"

"Very similar, I'm certain. And for all she knows, you've disappeared again."

"Fook."

"I should have –" they both started at once, then shook their heads.

"I can't help but know she's not going to just walk out of your life. I suppose I should call Smithson, I'm trying to decide how far we can go to trace her."

"Wait!" Skky sat upright, "Think I know. Her granny, got to be."

"Good place to start. You want to make the call, or shall I?"

"I should. I will."

"Hey! Are you here?" Rain burst through the unlocked door.

"Lord! Do you ever knock?" Skky growled.

"Sorry, truly sorry. Take it you're waiting for her?"

"Wish. Even her granny dun know."

"I'm trying to reach Smithson, any ideas?" Logan doubted it, but it was one of those times you'll try anything.

"No, sorry," Rain said. "Why? Think he might know?"

"I don't," Logan was rubbing his forehead, "but we need to try to trace her, though I doubt she's used a credit card. I don't know how far we can go with it legally."

"Since when's that a consideration? A lil late for that." Skky put his head in his hands. "Anything happens to her ... out there alone ..."

Logan remembered the day in his office when Kaylin had figured out that he had known all along and that he and the rest would have had to known where Skky was, and so she had assumed that he was dead. He hoped she wasn't in the same state of mind now. "She's smart, Skky, and capable, she'll be alright," he said, as much to reassure himself as anything else.

"Yeah. Hey, what can I do?" Rain was quickly losing his normal devil-may-care attitude. "For some reason I'm feelin' like I fucked up."

"'Fucked up', party of three," the gravity of the situation, along with all its implications, was catching up with Logan, too, but he knew he couldn't let doubts interfere. "I'm going to find Smithson, and get Gina over here. Maybe she can help." He paused on his way out the door. "Oh, and Brandon, too. Get ahold of him, Rain."

"Am stayin' here, case she comes back. Dunno whawt else to do." Skky's words were barely audible.

"Yeah, probably the best idea. I'll stay with you," Rain offered.

"No need."

"Mm hmm, all the same." Rain planted himself in a chair and took out his cell phone. "Pizza maybe? Beer definitely."

Logan felt good about Rain being there. He was glad that Smithson had agreed with his judgment that Rain should be Kay's companion. Originally Smithson had chosen Gina, but while they got along very well, Logan had pointed out that Kay's chosen best friend and confidant had been Brandon. Rain was Brandon with an edge. Though he knew Rain had come to care for Kay and wanted to see her happy, he had an advantage in his perspective that would no doubt work well on Skky's behalf, too. Rain was

287

his barometer in a sense, if he had detected any insincerity from either of them he wouldn't have hesitated to point it out.

He had no qualms about leaving Rain with Skky. Unencumbered by professional restraints, he might actually be more effective talking to him. Besides, Rain seemed to have his laid back cool working again. Logan, not so much.

* * *

The over the counter sleeping pill had worked. It had worried her a little for the fact that she'd never tried them before, but the pharmacist had reassured her. She pulled on the navy blue skirt, white blouse, and sneakers and put her navy heels in the tote bag. That would help her blend right in, she thought, as girls in the Big Apple often did that when commuting to work through a series of subways, buses, and the inevitable walking. She rolled her hair into a French bun and secured it. Some neutral mauve/beige lipstick and the non prescription glasses she'd picked up at the drugstore made the look complete.

Spéir appeared to be sleeping, and she silently thanked him. In her dream, she had crawled into bed beside him, three hundred years ago, and slept like a rock. She guessed it was more that than the sleeping pill that accounted for the good night's sleep.

It was a cool morning, but the combination of walking fast plus all the bodies that surrounded her made it comfortable enough. She'd worn her leather jacket on the plane, but it would have seemed out of place today. Halfway there she checked her watch, the only piece of jewelry she had on. It was 8:35 a.m. and arriving too early was not a good option.

Cailín detoured into a small deli and sat down with coffee and a Danish, just realizing that she was hungry. If things worked out the way she hoped she was going to need the energy. She watched people pass and wondered what their stories were. Everyone had a story. She wondered what Skky was doing, and if he was worried. Of course he was, he would have found out by now that she'd left. Maybe Rain had told him about the note she left, surely he would have.

Twelve minutes before the hour, and it was time to go. *I can do this, I can do this,* she tried to reassure herself. She slid past the dour doorman and through the double glass doors amidst a dozen other people. She hadn't thought of it before, which was just as well, and she forced herself into the elevator. *It's no different than the one at work.* It stopped on floor three, and she was tempted to take the stairs the rest of the way, but there was no time. Next stop, four. She pulled at the collar of her blouse, although it wasn't tight. She closed her eyes for a second, but remembered that Logan had told her not to do that. It would block out everything but what she feared, he had said.

"Oh, nice boots!" Cailín said a little too loudly to the girl next to her.

"Thanks," the young woman said flatly without looking at her.

Fifth floor at last, now to find Suite 510. After a false start to the left, she turned the other way and soon found it. One deep breath, a repositioning of the tote bag, and she walked in.

"Name, please," the receptionist clipped.

She hesitated.

"Name, please," the girl sighed.

"Marie Stevens, I'm –"

"I don't see your name," annoyance had become clear cut impatience, "do you have an appointment?"

"No. Well, yes, but I'm from the temp agency. They told me I'd be archiving closed files."

"Oh. I'll get to that in a minute."

An eternity of three minutes passed during which the snippy receptionist didn't seem to be doing anything of critical importance. Cailín was amazed, the office was expensively decorated, how could they treat people this way? Sure, it was the big city and all, just the same …

The girl finally spoke into an intercom, "Yeah, Midge? There's someone here, a temp, supposed to put away the dead files or something."

Midge was a walking anachronism in her pleated black shirt, pink blouse with a large bow tied at the neck, and only slightly less than Ann Landers hairdo. "Oh my goodness! Are you the temp? I've been asking for help forever. Come with me, dear."

Cailín followed her to a catch-all room at the end of the hall. Prescription drug samples, boxes of supplies, and some instruments were strewn about in no apparent order. In the corner a four drawer filing cabinet was partially hidden by two boxes haphazardly filled with files.

"These have been accumulating for over a year. I'll be so happy to have them out of here!"

"Out of here?" Cailín repeated.

"Oh, yes, we have storage space in the basement. They just need to be filed on the shelves down there."

Basement. Elevator. It figured. The privacy would be a bonus, however.

"So just these two boxes?"

"Those, and the filing cabinet is full. Not in order though. Oh, dear, I do hope you can get this all done. Are you here tomorrow?"

"No, just today as far as I know. I should be able to do it in one day. I have a system." *How's that for professional?* "The problem I see is getting them all down to the basement. That's going to be time consuming."

"Yes, it would be." Midge frowned, "Oh! I think I have the solution. Just need to run down and see if I can borrow something from a friend." Midge ambled through the door, "I'll be back in a flash. By the way, if I were you I think I'd be putting those sneakers back on. Just sayin'."

"Thanks." She was starting to like Midge's practicality, although that and organization seemed to be two different things in this office. It was astounding that a high dollar doctor with snob appeal décor could be so lax about leaving closed files in such disarray. She congratulated herself on her guess being correct though, if not for this mess she wouldn't have a prayer of finding what she sought. It had to be in there somewhere.

An hour and two trips to the basement with the double tiered cart, and the unruly stacks of files were in the basement. It had been cold when Cailín first entered and fumbled for the light switch. The walls were concrete painted gray, which seemed unnecessarily redundant. Although the ceiling was high she felt more claustrophobic than she had in the elevator, but after three trips up and down she had some degree of desensitization.

Row after row of shelves full of boxes surrounded the long table where she would sort the files. She locked the door behind her and began.

It was noon and she hadn't felt the cold for some time, she'd been working fast and her arms were beginning to get tired and she was starving. She didn't want to stop. She'd sorted over ninety percent of the files into stacks A through Z and hadn't found the one that she sought.

"Halloo!" the voice chirped out.

Cailín dropped the file in her hands, she hadn't heard Midge use a key or open the door. "Midge, oh I guess I wasn't really expecting company," she forced a laugh.

"It's lunch time, dear, there's a cafeteria upstairs. Not a four star, but not expensive. Come along."

She didn't argue, at least she wasn't going to have to slip past the doorman a couple of more times. She followed Midge into the elevator. They stopped on three, and she exhaled and started to walk out. A middle aged woman brushed past her.

"No, silly," Midge caught the door as it started to slide shut. "This is my friend Alma, she's the one that lent us the file cart." Midge pressed the number 14.

Dammit – Cailín came close to saying it out loud – *oh, well, at this point, who cares?*

Midge and Alma carried on a lively conversation, she wondered if their gossip machine started on the first floor and worked its way up, or if the subject matter was organized in terms of the most scandalous. She decided it was random, and that anything that didn't involve her was all to the good.

"So what's your story, dear, do you live nearby? Why are you with a temp agency? In between jobs, or just like the variety?" Alma barged into the comfort zone of anonymity that Cailín was just starting to enjoy.

"Mmuh," she mumbled through a bite of the not-half-bad club sandwich and reached for a spoonful of tomato soup to wash it down with. "Sorry. I'm between jobs, yes, visiting a friend here. Well, sort of between jobs, I start a new one in Minneapolis in three weeks."

"I knew it! I knew I could place that accent," Midge smiled.

"So you came to visit your friend?" Alma wanted to know more.

"Yes, we went to high school together, I hadn't seen her at all for two years. I couldn't really afford the time off if I had much choice, so I decided to try for some fill in work. Why not? I have a place to stay, and we still have plenty of time together. It's kind of a paid – or at least not going into the red – vacation."

"How nice for you to at least sneak in a little fun." Alma beamed, "My, that's clever."

Oh, if you only knew. "It's working out well, thankfully. Pay is a lot higher here, so even if I don't get work everyday …" she trailed off, thinking that being chatty must be catching.

"Bet there's a young man just waiting on pins and needles for your return," Midge had that knowing look on her face again.

"I hope he is."

"Oh, well, you know, there's practically no such thing as being out of touch, what with cell phones and webcams and the like," Midge advised. "Say!" she turned to Alma with enthusiasm, "did you *hear* about Suzy, you know the one, she works for Dr. Berg down on two? She caught her husband – on Facebook, mind you. One day she was …" Thankfully Midge and Alma were back to being immersed in their soap opera.

Cailín thanked them for the company and excused herself. "I really want to finish the filing for you today," sounded right. She grabbed a large coffee, loaded it with cream and sugar, bought two oatmeal cookies as an afterthought, and left.

She rushed into the elevator without thinking, nearly anything was better than enduring Midge and Alma. She focused on cradling her coffee and it was only when everyone else exited on the main floor that she felt the all too familiar sense of suffocation.

Don't close your eyes, don't close your eyes. Just one more level, that's all.

She stepped out with a sigh of relief, and eyed the stack of two dozen or so files that weren't sorted yet, willing what she wanted to be among them. She picked up an arm full and began placing them on the already sorted stacks that lined the table.

Halfway through the second batch her heart stopped.

Hanover, Delilah

Of course, she wouldn't have used her married name, and it was a wonder that she hadn't made one up. Although she was alone, she looked around, then cautiously opened the file, began scanning the pages, and swallowed the lump in her throat. It felt like she was reading Skky's nightmare. The file wasn't thick, and she soon found what she needed.

No. Oh, no... the one thing I didn't think of. How was she going to make copies without trying to stealth walk past the doorman twice. Stuffing the file in her tote bag was not the best option, it would be missed eventually, and in spite of everything the idea seemed wrong.

She quickly finished the sorting and loaded the top tier of the cart. They were going to have to be filed anyway to cover her alleged reason for being here, and maybe she'd think of something brilliant as she worked.

"This is a big room, lass, ya haven't seen it all," Spéir was smiling. "C'mon."

She followed him through the stacks of files to the back corner of the room. A copy machine! It looked very old, could she dare hope? She cautiously pushed the power button. Nothing.

"Sattinger's Law."

"You are just astounding. How would you even know what that was?"

"Is all out there, floatin' around, so it is. True enough, though."

The power cord was dangling behind the machine, but no outlet was in sight.

"Here, help," Spéir was tugging it away from the wall. There was an outlet, if it even worked, and they had to turn the machine so that the short cord would reach it. Cailín plugged it in, and pushed the button with crossed fingers.

* * *

295

"Shoudda broken ev'ry rule the first time I saw her," Skky paced slowly back and forth behind the sofa, his hand caressing the fabric. "Shoudda just – "

"Talking to yourself?" Rain interrupted.

"Yeah. Evidently."

"So are you paying attention?"

"Too late."

"Nah, don't think so. No sense looking back, you know. What's done is done."

"Yeah. Twenty-twenty hindsight an' all."

"No sense. We all got a bad case of that right about now. You know her, smart girl, knows what she wants. So – there's apparently something she feels like she has to do."

"Glad you know that. Dun know where she is, if she's…"

"Skky. Skky! She's been here. We know she's been here. She's fine. Took only a couple things, she's coming back. She knows that you know you can find her here. Meanwhile she's on some kind of mission. Don't know what, but willing to bet it'll make sense when you find out."

"Any word from Alec?"

"Nope. Got any sense, he's more stressed than you."

* * *

"Marie, ohhh Muhh-reee," Midge sang out. Cailín grabbed the filing cabinet to steady herself, and drew in the deepest breath she could manage.

"Midge?" she hoped her voice wasn't too shaky, "I'm back here, nearly finished."

"That's wonderful!" Midge yelled as she headed toward the sound of Cailín's voice.

"Oh! I never would have imagined," Midge's ample figure rounded the corner. "What a relief to have that mess cleared up."

I only hope I feel the same way by this time tomorrow. She sent a genuine smile in Midge's direction.

"Your must be tired. Your efforts are appreciated, and I'll give you just the best report to the agency."

Oh crap, I'll need to make up a phony bill or something. No, Midge is scattered, she'll forget all about it.

"Now, you're sure they're all filed in the right place…"

"Yes. Yes, of course. Otherwise why bother?"

"Of course, dear. I didn't mean…"

"It's alright, I understand, it's very important. And I wouldn't do that to you, Midge, since you're the supervisor."

"You're a good girl, know how these things work. Now, I really hate to bring this up, but being a professional, I know you'll understand. "I need to check your bag. Meds and so on lying around. You know."

The floor dropped out from under her, and her hand flew to her stomach before she could stop it.

"What's the matter, dear? You seem distressed."

She blew out a sigh as she remembered that Spéir had insisted on taking the copies. "Oh. No, I'm just very tired. Not used to all this mostly physical work I guess. Thank goodness you allowed me to wear my sneakers. Even so, I'll be having a good soak tonight."

She took her shoes out of the tote bag, and emptied the contents on the table. "That's about it, I travel light," she smiled. *Thank you, Spéir, thank you, thank you.*

"I wish I were so organized. My husband says one day the kitchen sink *will* turn up in my bag."

Cailín laughed, not with her, but from relief. "Well, when you travel – the airlines – you learn to keep it to a minimum."

"I suppose so. I'm overdue for a vacation." Midge frowned, "Um, is that a zippered pocket? Would you mind?"

"Not at all." Cailín unzipped it and turned the lining inside out. "I know, not very practical. I really should put my wallet in there, shouldn't I?"

"Yes, dear, can't be too careful in the big city."

* * *

298

"Where is it? Where is it?"

"Easy, lass." Speír was lounging on the bed, and pointed to the small dresser.

She retrieved the two copies, put one in her tote bag, and the other in her carry on. "Thanks. Thank you. I couldn't have done it without you."

"'S all good. Tired then?"

"I'm exhausted, I just want to eat and sleep."

"Come sit, eat, then I'll take ya away."

* * *

This is going to be the fun part, Cailín thought, *well, sort of.*   Pink sweater, two sizes too small, black skirt rolled up short, big hair, and stiletto heels.   It was an ensemble that begged for another layer of eye makeup and bright pink lipstick to be applied.

She blew a kiss toward Speír, who appeared to be sleeping. She looked up and down the hallway, took off the shoes, and ran to the back stairway of the hotel. Outside, and with the shoes back in place, she practiced her flashy girl saunter on the half block walk to the bus stop. A couple of wolf whistles told her she was doing it right.

Though it was tempting to avoid walking, she got off the bus a block short of her destination. She retrieved a piece of bubble gum from the tote bag that was now embellished with bright daisy stickers she'd found at the drug store.

A "Yeahhh baby!" from a disembodied male voice offered the opportunity to practice the attitude.

"Hey! Whaw chew lookin' at? Get lost," she turned and said to no one in particular.

The lab had a private entrance from the street. Inside there were four partitioned cubicles that offered what passed for privacy. She started toward the cubicles but was stopped by a female voice, "No, no, over here, please".

The receptionist waved her over, "Just give me your name and an assistant will call you."

"Oh, um, Janie. Janie Smith."

"Okay, Ms. Smith, just a sec and someone will call you. Won't be a minute, you're here very early." The girl, who couldn't have been more than eighteen, smiled meekly and typed something into a computer.

"Oh?" she hoped that wasn't a strategy error and sighed impatiently for effect, "Yeah, well, got lots to do today."

"Janie," she turned toward the male voice, "cubicle four, please."

She minced toward the farthest cubicle, and was greeted by a middle aged man wearing an argyle sweater vest. "Ms. Smith, I'm Mr. Rogers." *Of course you are*, she thought. "Please be seated."

"Oh, hi, um, how are you?" her voice quavered. *That's okay, 'Janie' would be nervous.*

"How may we assist you today, Ms. – Smith?"

"Uh, well, I – my friend Audrey said you could do it." She looked down and flicked at the corner of a red lacquered nail with her thumb. "A paternity test? Is that what you call it?"

"You wish to verify the father of a child?"

"Well, yeah," she chewed the bubble gum furiously, blew a bubble, and popped it. "Yeah, I need to check if my boyfriend – my fiancé I mean – yeah, you don't wanna hear all about that, do you?" her smile was shaky.

"It's not really necessary," he sighed, as he tapped first the point, then the eraser of a pencil on the form in front of him. "What we do need is a DNA sample from all three of you."

"Three?"

"Yes," he sighed again, still working the pencil, "DNA from you, I take it you're the mother?"

"Yeah, definitely. It's my kid for shoo-ah. Hurt like a bitch, know what I mean?"

"Very well. DNA from you, which is not a problem, as you're here."

Cailín raised her eyebrows and made an "O" with her lips. She crossed her legs and started swinging one furiously. Oddly enough it calmed her nerves.

"No need for concern, it's quick, and painless." His monotone was supposed to come off as 'professional', she guessed. "But we also need DNA from the child, and from the – your fiancé – as well."

"Oh," she made a small frown, and popped another bubble, "I think I have whatcha need, well, if what Audrey said …"

"Why don't you just show me what you have?"

"Okay, yeah, well I have these paypuhs, see? From the hospital, I mean. There's one from me, my stuff, and one from the kid." She pulled two sheets of paper from her tote bag. "It's supposed to tell what the genetic – something – I don't know all that stuff, any way it's supposed to say what you need to tell, ya know?"

"Yes, of course, the genetic markers," he responded flatly.

"Yeah!" she sat bolt upright and forced a huge smile, "yeah, that's what they called 'em."

"The names have been marked out," he glared over the top of his glasses.

"Oh, yeah, I know, you can't be too careful, carryin' this stuff around, ya know what I mean? What? It's my kid, else why would I have the paypuhs? I paid good money –"

"Very well, we still need a DNA sample from the – from your fiancé." The pencil continued to twirl.

"Yeah, shoo-ah." Cailín reached into her tote bag and pulled out a clear plastic bag containing several strands of blond hair, "yeah, soz, anyway Audrey said this would work."

"This is a sample of your fiancé's hair?"

"Yeah, it is. Pretty, ain't it?" she sighed and blinked her eyes. "He has the softest, prettiest hair. See all the different shades of blond? We should all be so lucky. But, um, well, just to be shoo-uh, might wanna test the brown part on the end. Sun bleached, know what I'm sayin'?"

"This will take a little longer, analyze this sample, then compare," said the bald man behind the desk.

"Shoo-ah, I figured. Okay, so, how long?"

302

"If you could come back about three o'clock…"

"Three! Oh crap – no! I mean, I got stuff to do, ya know? Audrey said – so okay, tell me, what does this test cost?"

"The test fee is three hundred fifty dollars."

"Geez, yeah okay, so I gotta know. So what takes so long? I mean, I thought it was fast? You got computers and stuff. According to Audrey, what she said, you know, it's fast."

"The test itself is less than two hours."

"There we go! Two owwuz then?"

"Technically, but there are others from yesterday to be completed first."

"Oh, I see. Yeah. Okay, people in line in front of me," she reached into her tote bag again, "so this could maybe put me to the front of the line? She spread seven one hundred dollar bills out on the desk.

"Please come back in two hours, Ms. Smith," He didn't look up. "Your test results will be complete."

"Two owwuz," she glanced at her wrist, "damn it! I left my watch at home. Oh, well. Yeah, two owwuz. Cool. Big load off my mind. Either way, I mean, I gotta know and stuff, know what I mean?" She checked the clock behind the receptionist's desk, blew another bubble and popped it as she walked out.

* * *

"Any word yet?" Skky was pacing again, and Rain doubted he'd slept much.

"Well, no," Rain said regretfully.

"Why not? How many guys on the case?"

"Hmm, two."

"Whawt the hell? Double that, noh – triple it, dun care whawt it costs."

"I'll have to square it with Smithson," Rain flipped open his cell.

"Screw that, just do it," Skky was definite.

"Yes, never mind that, contact them directly," Logan affirmed.

Rain made the call to the detective agency, then placed a call to Smithson.

"He's on the way here," Rain turned toward Skky and Logan.

"Mmm," was Logan's only response.

"Why?" Skky asked.

"He says he's certain that she'll come back here."

"Glad he knows," Skky mumbled.

"I think so, too," Logan affirmed.

"Maybe," Skky shrugged. He looked at Logan, then Rain, "Did tell her that I'd been delayed, dint ya?"

"No?" Rain glanced at Logan.

"We were instructed not to. Rain wasn't told." Logan owned it.

"Damn. Whawt?" Skky was incredulous.

"Son of a ..." Rain began, then just shook his head.

"That was all part of it, Skky, and I'm sorry. Smithson was afraid if Rain knew, he wouldn't have been able to pull it off," Logan spoke genuinely. "I should have intervened. I should have drawn the line."

"Yeah. And suppose I shoudda guessed at that point. But where'd she go, and why? 'Less she just wants to get away from me."

"I'm sure there was a good reason, and I'm sure that wasn't it," Logan offered. "Try to sleep a bit, Skky, you need it. We'll wake you the minute we hear anything."

Skky laid down on the bed. It had been hours before he'd been able to fall asleep the previous night. He felt close to her here, the faint scent of lilac reminded him of her. He put his hand under the pillow to scrunch it up and get comfortable when he felt something. He sat up and pulled out a piece of paper folded into a triangle. He opened it up and began to read. Running one hand through his hair he whispered, "whawt?"

* * *

Two hours sat on the top of her head like a cement block. A newsstand across the street caught her eye. If Skky had been spotted, it could have already hit the papers. Cailín took her time, stopping to look in shop windows as she walked to the corner, then crossed the street. *This is crazy*, she thought, *I feel like I'm in a spy movie. They have no reason to believe I'm in New York, even if they're looking for me.* Still, she kept up the act.

There was nothing about him, if there had been, it would have been on a cover. She couldn't decide if she was relieved or worried.

It was too early for lunch, but she'd missed breakfast. She kept up the window shopping guise until she came to a diner. A television set on the wall behind the counter caught her eye, so she positioned herself in the closest booth, facing the screen.

"Good morning, had a chance to look at the menu yet, or can I get you some coffee?" The boy couldn't have been more than nineteen, and she couldn't help but wish that he was in a college classroom somewhere. He was nice looking, maybe he was trying to break into acting.

"That'd be nice, yes. I don't really feel like breakfast, but I guess I'm too early for lunch?" He was looking at her curiously, she'd forgotten to keep the smack in her speech.

She stared at the morning talk show just starting.

"Here you are."

"Thanks. Is there anything besides breakfast?"

"Well," the young man offered "I think I could manage a chicken salad sandwich, maybe some soup?"

"That would be great." She smiled, but her eyes didn't leave the screen.

* * *

306

The DNA test results were as she suspected, there was less than a one percent chance that 'Janie's fiancé' was the father of the infant in question. Janie had asked a rather aloof Mr. Robinson no less than three times if he was 'shoo-uh'. He finally told her to think of the one percent as the equivalent of zero, there were just too many differences.

She rushed back to the hotel, brushed Janie out of her hair and washed the makeup off her face. A quick shower and a double check of the room, and she grabbed a cab to the airport.

This truth would not exactly set him free, she knew, because Skky was a kind and sensitive man. Still, it was an important truth that he needed to know. It obviously wouldn't change his feelings about his by now ex-wife, and there would still be grief, a sense of loss regarding the child.

Although she had promised herself she wouldn't, she pulled the copy of Lila's medical chart from her now daisy free tote. She flipped over the first page, and read the last entry:

```
Efforts to resuscitate
premature male infant
failed.
```

Way to cover your ass, 'doctor', she thought, *burn in hell right next to Lila Hanover*.

She knew Skky was a strong man, and though he wouldn't forget, he would move forward and she was determined to be beside him.

Now to find him.

* * *

Cailín leaned back in the airplane seat next to the window, grateful that the flight wasn't full and the seat next to her was vacant.

She closed her eyes and smiled in anticipation as the plane started to move down the runway. Takeoff reminded her of making love with Skky, the steady acceleration that lifted her free from the earth until she was floating in a cloud where nothing existed but him.

"Coffee?" the flight attendant startled her out of her reverie. "Oh, I'm sorry, were you sleeping?"

"Its fine," Cailín said sheepishly, realizing that they must have been airborne for several minutes. "Water, please."

She reached into the pockets of her jacket, fishing around for one of the granola bars that she had a habit of stashing. Instead she pulled out two small pieces of paper, and unfolded them. There was the receipt from Maybelle's diner, and a hand scrawled note. *The potato soup recipe! I forgot...* She was astounded as she read:

> Darlin girl, anyone can learn to
> make good potato soup. Only
> you know how to love your man.
> He's waitin for you, go git him.
> Aunt Maybelle knows.

Who could argue with Aunt Maybelle's wisdom? The timing was as perfect now as it had been the day she wrote it. *That's right, Aunt Maybelle*, she thought, *I do know how*.

She thought back through all her conversations with Smithson and wondered when, or how, she could have realized what was really going on. That he was behind it all, she felt certain. Why he did it she could only guess. Given his apparently close association with Logan it had to be some kind of psychological experiment. But it was

Smithson who had used them all, appealing to each in a way that would ensure their participation. He had used Skky's grief and fragile state of mind, and hers, to draw them in to an extraordinary set of circumstances that promised both a guarantee, when the simple and logical solution would have been merely to arrange for her and Skky to meet and have some time together.

She couldn't bring herself to fault Skky, especially knowing what had caused him to withdraw from the world. Now, he would be having the same misgivings about going along with Smithson as she had had along the way and the sooner she found him, the better.

The joke was on Smithson, she decided. He would never know the missing piece of the puzzle, the noteworthy anomaly in the equation. He would never know about Speír.

She tried the other jacket pocket for the elusive granola bar and this time retrieved the letter, Speír's letter, folded into a triangle. The other copy was where she always kept it, at home under her pillow. Though she knew it by heart, she felt compelled to read it again. Cailín smiled, and fell asleep.

* * *

Skky read the letter carefully, then re-read it. The words were somehow not unfamiliar to him. He fell asleep with the first sense of peace he'd felt since the last time he held her.

* * *

Cailín took the stairs up to her condo, not in the mood to cope with the elevator. Half a flight of stairs left, and she paused on the landing.

What do I do now? I know. One call to Brandon should produce Smithson and Logan, at least, in record time.

She turned the key and started to step inside. She stopped and stared for a few seconds before entering, then quickly closed the door behind her. Brandon and Gina sat closely side by side on the sofa, his arm around her. Logan sat at the other end of the sofa, head back and eyes closed. Rain was lounging at the table with a cup of coffee, Smithson paced in front of the balcony door.

"Kay," Rain began, as he sat up straight.

"Where is he? Where is Skky?" she said firmly, looking around the room.

"Kaylin," Rain tried again.

"No!" she screamed, "where is he? Where. Is. Skky?"

Apparently everyone had lost their ability to speak.

"What is this? Some kind of goddamned intervention?" she glared directly at Smithson. "One simple question – answer me *now* or I swear –"

"Cailín," Skky said softly as he came into the room, blinking slowly, his hair slightly rumpled.

She spun around to look at him.

"Need all ye to be leavin' now," he made a sweeping motion with his arm and pointed to the door.

"Kay, we –" it was Brandon.

She turned her head briefly toward him, "You heard him, get out. I don't blame any of you at all," she focused on Smithson again, "save for one. But get out."

Skky nodded slightly, "Later, please."

"Out, people," Logan ordered in a tone that left no room for interpretation.

311

Cailín and Skky held each other in a steady gaze until the click of the door shutting signaled the exit of the last one. Skky pulled two items out of his back pocket. One was a pale blue envelope with her handwriting on it. The other was a sheet of white paper folded several times into a triangle.

"Cailín, I understand," his voice was still soft, his eyes pleading as he walked toward her.

She brushed a tear from her cheek. "So do I."

Spéir materialized behind Skky, walking toward him. He walked right into Skky, disappearing as Skky dropped to one knee.

Skky took Cailín's left hand and placed a small sapphire surrounded by emeralds set on a silver band on her finger.

It was a perfect fit.

* * *

Attribution:

Lyrics: *Life Was Full*, lyrics © 2015 by Eve Shannon. Partial lyrics only, used in context by permission.

ABOUT THE AUTHOR

Since childhood Eve Shannon has been an avid reader, and lover of stories and dreams. Her skills were sharpened by her enjoyment of writing reviews of favorite television series on network forums. She received favorable comments on her entertaining and often biting insights, and after two years decided that she should be telling her own stories.

Eve's philosophy is that every good story starts with the question "What if?" and when strong characters graciously inhabit your dreams and daydreams, allow them to tell their stories and do your best to interpret and preserve the integrity of ideas and emotions.

She is currently writing two more novels, and *Bright Son Dark Death* is anticipated to be published in 2016.

www.ingramcontent.com/pod-product-compliance
Lightning Source LLC
Chambersburg PA
CBHW070649180626
46817CB00006B/2295